# SCONES AND SCANDAL

## THE PERIDALE CAFE SERIES - BOOK 22

## AGATHA FROST

## About This Book

**Released:** *May 25th 2021*
**Words:** *60,000*
**Series:** *Book 22 - Peridale Cozy Café Mystery Series*
**Standalone:** *Yes*
**Cliff-hanger:** *No*

With Julia South-Brown enjoying her newborn daughter's every milestone safe in her cosy cottage, and with maternity leave cutting her off from the rumour mill of her café, she doesn't realise just how much local news and gossip she's missed. Between a wave of break-ins and thefts, Peridale isn't quite the safe little village she remembers.

But when the leader of Peridale's Eyes, the local neighbourhood watch group, meets her end on the same day Julia's neighbour Leah's house is broken into and robbed, Julia finds herself pulled back into the familiar world of clues, suspects, and motives – not to mention her gran's rival neighbourhood watch group.

Dot South knows this is her moment to shine. For years, she's been dreaming of starting a neighbourhood watch group of her own. Now, with a murder on her doorstep and a bunch of hapless amateurs bungling every attempt at solving it, who better to form and lead a newer, better version of Peridale's Eyes?

Or should she say … *Dot's Detectives*?

WANT TO BE KEPT UP TO DATE WITH AGATHA FROST RELEASES? *SIGN UP THE FREE NEWSLETTER!*

**www.AgathaFrost.com**

You can also follow **Agatha Frost** across social media. Search 'Agatha Frost' on:

**Facebook**
**Twitter**
**Goodreads**
**Instagram**

# ALSO BY AGATHA FROST

## Other

# 1

*S*ilence in Peridale.

Pulling back the curtain as she watered the potted devil's ivy on the window ledge, Julia South-Brown scanned the street below. No car engine or child's laughter broke the calm, and even the birds seemed to be resting their vocal cords for a change. If not for the fluttering curtains in an open window across the green, she could have been convinced she was looking at a painting.

*The Perfect Peridale Spring Day*, by Mother Nature.

The bedroom in which those curtains fluttered belonged to Julia's gran. In this peaceful moment, the light breeze was the source of the twitching and not Dot keeping herself abreast of the day's goings-on.

Julia's was the only set of eyes witnessing the

beauty below. High above St. Peter's Church, the sun shone bright and warm from its cloudless blanket, lighting up the delicate petals of the flowers on the village green like stained glass.

Mother Nature had borrowed a day from the summer ahead.

It was about time.

Rain had plagued them for far too much of the spring, and only a week ago, an unseasonal sprinkling of snow had welcomed in the month of May. Perhaps people had grown too used to the recent gloom to trust the forecast of a nice day, leaving their picnics unprepared and their footballs buried in the shed.

Julia appreciated the silence regardless of the reason behind it.

True quiet had been scarce lately.

The last drop of water left the can, sending Julia to the small flat's kitchen for further instruction. Running her finger along the illustrated guide taped to the cupboard next to the sink, she found the next plant.

The monstera in the bedroom.

The only plant that filled Julia with dread.

Over the months Jessie had lived in the flat above the post office, Julia had noticed her daughter's plant collection growing. She hadn't realised how seriously Jessie had taken it. The pristine, precise guide written in Jessie's neatest handwriting made her daughter's parting request of 'don't kill my plants' feel more like a challenge – or a threat.

So far, the indoor garden was hanging on.

All except the monstera in the bedroom.

After filling the can with a little more water than specified, Julia crept into the bedroom with a held breath.

"Oh, don't you look sad."

Most of the stems were sagging, only two leaves pointed upwards . . . and that wasn't the worst of it. While the two proud leaves remained brilliant green beneath a waxy shine, the rest looked like month-old banana peels. The browning appeared in small spots first, until patches took over entire leaves. Praying for a miracle, Julia plucked another browned leaf and dumped the water into the soil.

On her way to the door, she tugged at the corner of the perfectly made bed to smooth out a phantom crease. Not that it mattered; it had been five months since anyone slept beneath those sheets.

The plants had been experiencing their own extended silence lately.

Maybe the monstera knew Jessie was absent and was proclaiming its displeasure the only way it knew how.

Determined to make the most of the unexpected

calm, Julia returned to the kitchen and binned the leaf. After pouring a fresh cup of peppermint and liquorice tea, she sat in one of the hard metal seats at the small dining table positioned on the cusp of where the kitchen met the living room.

Last week's issue of *The Peridale Post* lay abandoned, open to a full-page advertisement for a summer funfair. Dried droplets of Olivia's repeated morning feedings had bled the ink in places, though Julia's coat had taken the brunt of it. At least the endless rain had her in an easy-to-wipe raincoat, so the gloom had its benefits.

Uninterested by the sports pages, Julia flicked backwards until she found the picture of Hugo Scott, a local Member of Parliament recently at the centre of a scandal concerning leaked sleazy pictures. Thankfully for Mr Scott, MP, a local private investigator had proved the pictures were fakes.

Julia's friend, Johnny Watson, edited the newspaper. However, she imagined the decision to bury the 'apology' story on page twelve next to a story about a cat who took a bus hadn't been his. In their censored forms, the fake pictures had dominated the front pages of most local papers lately.

The headline, however, had Johnny written all over it:

## INNOCENT! POLITICIAN'S PRIVATE PICS
## PHOTOSHOPPED PHONIES!

The actual apology for the newspaper's part in spreading the misinformation didn't appear until the final line. A few lines before that, they gave credit to 'retired detective inspector, bestselling author, and private investigator, Barker Brown.' Meagre as the column's inches were, they'd made their way into said private investigator's scrapbook with a fervent declaration that he was done with 'big profile' cases for a while.

A loud engine broke the silence as Julia came to the end of the cat story. The ginger feline, photographed in the grip of a young girl, not only went to Riverswick on the bus but also caught the correct return and was home before anyone noticed he'd gone.

Julia finished her tea and closed the paper.

Back to reality.

Leaving the rinsed cup on the draining board for next week, she peeled back the curtains as a large white van pulled up in front of the café next door. Maternity leave or not, Julia couldn't bring herself to stay hidden in Jessie's empty flat while Katie dealt with the delivery.

Besides, she'd left her holding Olivia.

Jessie's flat door locked behind Julia as she walked past the two cars parked in the street below it. Despite what Penelope Newton said, there was more than enough room to walk past Katie's powder pink Fiat 500 and Julia's vintage aqua blue Ford Anglia.

The two familiar delivery men who rarely said anything to Julia were already there. The older chatted to Katie on the doorstep while the younger whipped in and out with armfuls of stacked boxes.

Julia peered through the café's window and past the beaded curtain, where the steel island in the kitchen seemed more than full. Why, then, was the well-muscled lad unloading yet another round of boxes off the back of the van?

While Katie's pink acrylic nail scribbled on a digital screen, Julia slipped unseen into her café. Kenny, according to his name badge, darted around her and added more to the pile before rushing out again. She hurried in and pulled back a sheet of bubble wrap. Punnets of strawberries filled the plastic tray, which would have been fine if at least a dozen *more* trays weren't also filled with punnets.

Other boxes held more tubs of butter than Julia had seen at any one time, and then she discovered flour in an even greater quantity than the butter. If not for Katie's high-pitched and piercing girlish giggle, Julia might have wondered if this was some bizarre, Wonderland-inspired dream full of multiplying food. She went to the door before Kenny could run in with another stack.

"I don't know what it feels like," Katie said, still on the doorstep but now rubbing the edge of the older man's shirt. "It's not quite cotton. A poly-blend?"

"It's boyfriend material," he said, his jaw working chewing gum as one brow arched. "Or maybe a drink tonight material?"

Robbie, according to his name badge, winked at Katie as he leaned against the doorframe and his eyes focused distinctly south of her face.

"Married with a baby," she said, giggling again, "but I'm flattered."

Robbie's brows darted higher as his leer grew.

"*Married* and *baby*," she repeated without the accompanying giggle.

"So, that's a no?"

"Yes, a *no*." Katie flipped her blonde hair over her shoulder and spun around. "Oh, Julia. When did you sneak in?"

"I think there's been a mix-up." Julia blocked Kenny and his endless boxes. "There's enough strawberries, butter, and flour in there for the next two series of *The Great British Bake Off*."

"Come again?" Robbie's gaze hovered on Katie's ample chest. When Julia cleared her throat, he blinked and added, "Oh, yeah, it did seem a lot more than usual."

"But I only ordered the *usual* stuff," said Katie, craning to investigate the kitchen. "Oh, my. I double-checked." She stared desperately at Julia. "I double-checked, Julia, I swear."

Resting a hand on Katie's arm, Julia forced the delivery man to look her way with a few clicks of her fingers. She brewed her best smile in an attempt to appeal to his better nature, but his wandering gaze almost immediately returned to its prior engagement.

"Sir, her eyes are here," said Julia, pointing at Katie's face. "Could you at least check if this is a mistake? There's probably someone out there expecting to feed a small army with this stuff."

The leer vanished, taking his last desperate shred of charm with it. His gum flew over his shoulder, and he hawked and spit before resettling himself with his thumbs hooked in his beltless trouser loops.

"Sorry, love, not my problem." He shrugged as he stepped back into the road. "We just deliver what you order."

Robbie nodded at Kenny, prompting the younger

man to ditch the rest of the order on the pavement. Kenny slammed the back doors and climbed into the passenger seat.

"We're a small village café," Julia said, taken aback by their nonchalance. "What could we possibly want with all this stock?"

Robbie looked up at the sign and offered another open-armed shrug. After slapping the sides of his legs, he turned and hopped into the van.

"What a pig!" Katie pulled her phone from within a pocket in her pink, bedazzled apron and zoomed in on the licence plate as the van drove away. "That company is getting a strongly worded email."

"And while you do that, I have a call to make."

Julia dug past the baby bottle and toys in her handbag. Ripping back a bib revealed a finger-smudged screen. She scrolled to the number for her suppliers and put the phone to her ear, staring down into the contents of the bag.

"Katie, where's my baby?" Julia whipped around, going straight to the empty pram next to the counter. "Where's Olivia?"

"Oh." Katie chuckled. "She's downstairs with Barker. He came as the van pulled up and took her."

Julia's heart rested; a major panic averted.

"It wasn't that I *forgot* she existed," Julia said in a

quiet voice. "I just got caught up in the moment and slipped into that café-owner role a little too easily."

"You don't have to explain." Katie stacked plates at a table and, after looking around the empty café, said, "One time, I took Vinnie shopping, and I forgot he existed for a whole twenty minutes. I left him by the shoes. I felt so much like my old self again, I made it all the way to handbags before realising I wasn't pushing a pram around. Thankfully, he was fast asleep right where I left him." She laughed and added, "Don't tell your father."

"It's best not to play the 'what if' game," Julia said, putting the phone back to her ear. "We'd never get anything done if we spent all day worrying about all the times something bad *almost* happened. What fathers don't know won't—"

An automated electronic voice chirped through the phone, sending Julia into the kitchen. While the robot read her the options, she peered up at the boxes stacked as high as skyscrapers. She opened the back door and perched on the doorstep facing into the alley behind the café as she pressed five for 'Existing Orders'.

Olivia's laughter floated up from Barker's office below the café, followed by what sounded like a monkey, or maybe an elephant?

Julia's arm hairs rose as a smile pushed up her

cheeks. It was impossible not to smile when a child was laughing, but hearing her own child's laughter stirred a feeling so intense it was hard to remain on the doorstep and listen to the robot when Olivia cuddles were only steps away.

Unfortunately for Julia, there were no cuddles on the menu. Only twenty-five minutes of hair-pulling customer service frustration while they palmed her around like a gift in pass the parcel.

"Can I put you on hold?"

"Do I have any choice?"

A click was followed by a bubbly pop song distorted by thick static fuzz. Why did it have to be the same song every time? Against her will, she'd learned every word.

The yard gate creaked open, and as if the hold music weren't bad enough, the bird-like, pinched face of Penelope Newton poked through the gap.

"Katie said you were round the back," Penelope said in her ever-nasal voice; she always sounded like she was recovering from a cold. "I need to talk to you about the parking situation."

Julia didn't hold in the sharp exhale through her nostrils; it had become automatic whenever 'the parking situation' came up.

"I'm a little busy," she said, pointing at the phone. "Stock issue."

Anyone else might have left it there, but not Penelope. When the leader of Peridale's Eyes had a bee in her bonnet, nothing stood in her way. She pushed further into the yard, clutching the gate like a shield.

"I thought you should know I intend to escalate this matter to the council," Penelope stated with her usual expressionlessness. "Since you've proved this can't be resolved, I feel it's the only recourse I have left."

Another sigh.

Until Penelope Newton had decided the alley between the café and post office would be the primary objective of her neighbourhood watch group, nobody had ever complained about Julia parking there.

"I moved Jessie's car to my cottage," Julia said, resting her hand on the phone even though the horrid hold music still blared in her ear. "There's more than enough room for people to get through now."

"That's not the point," Penelope drawled. "The alley is a public right of way, not your personal parking space. The people of Peridale deserve to be able to—"

"Mrs Brown-South?" a human voice called into her palm.

"It's South-Brown," she corrected, taking the opportunity to slip back into the café before Penelope launched into her usual diatribe. "Please tell me you've figured it out."

"I've spoken to my manager, and there's nothing we can do."

"That can't be right," she insisted. "I've been using your company since I opened, and I've never had an issue like—"

The beads parted, and Katie sheepishly walked in, clutching the laptop with its screen facing outwards. Julia squinted; getting her long-distance vision checked was still on her to-do list. She beckoned Katie closer until the invoice came into focus. Amongst the usual order, three items stood out:

201 x 1 kg butter.

132 x 1 kg flour.

123 x 500 g strawberries.

"Can I put you on hold?" Julia said, tapping the 'hold' button on the screen. "Katie, I thought you double-checked?"

"I should have *triple*-checked." She bit into her lip. "I'm so sorry, Julia. I left him with the laptop. It was only for a second, but he must have changed things."

"Who?"

"Vinnie," she said. "We've been teaching him numbers on the laptop. I didn't think he was paying that much attention. He must have bashed some keys. I only nipped to the loo."

Julia hung up without explaining, payback for the thirty-six-minute phone call from customer service hell. Foot tapping, she stared blankly at the stacks of boxes and let the cogs turn.

"At least it's all things we can use," she thought aloud, "but we likely won't get through it all before it expires."

"We could freeze the strawberries," Katie suggested. "Strawberry milkshakes and lemonade for summer?"

"Good idea." Julia dug out one of each over-ordered item. "Make up some labels with the cost price of each and put them on the counter. Let people buy as many as they want."

Katie jumped right into the task, though she couldn't seem to look at Julia. Before Julia could dwell on the right thing to say to stop Katie from blaming herself, the back door opened, and Julia's two favourite people walked in.

"Oh, come to Mummy," she cooed, immediately scooping Olivia out of Barker's arms. "Have you been having fun in Daddy's office? Have you? Have you?"

Olivia thrashed her arms, blowing a raspberry, her new favourite trick.

"She was *so* close to saying it," said Barker after kissing Julia on the cheek. "Da-Da. Say it, Olivia. *Da-Da*."

"All the books say at least six months." Julia tugged a fistful of her hair from Olivia's tiny clenched fist; letting go wasn't a skill she'd managed to learn yet. "And that's just for sounds."

"But *our* baby is *obviously* a genius."

"I think everyone thinks that, Barker."

"But ours *is*."

They entered the café, which had acquired a few more people during Julia's tedious phone call. Katie arranged the three items neatly atop the glass display cabinet, but Evelyn and Shilpa didn't appear to notice. Their faces lit up the moment they saw Olivia.

"Oh, look at her!" Shilpa clenched her hands. "She's so sweet. It almost knocks you sick."

"I felt her energy moving closer," Evelyn declared. "Such a pure aura."

Outside, Julia's gran, Dot, danced around the abandoned boxes on the pavement. She went to push on the door, eyes homing in on the 'NO DOGS' sign. With a huff, she handed her lead to her husband, Percy.

"Happy, now?" Dot called as she barged in, letting the door slam shut behind her. "My family out in the cold since they aren't welcome in your café?"

On the edge of the green, Percy settled onto a bench. Their white-haired Maltese, Lady, curled up on one side of his feet, and their French bulldog, Bruce, sprang into Percy's lap.

"It's a lovely spring day," Julia pointed out, settling Olivia against her shoulder. "Nice to see you, Gran."

"I can even take them on the bus." Dot corrected the angle of her brooch. "Why do you hate them, Julia?"

"How could I hate them? They're adorable." Julia lowered into a seat at the table closest to the counter as Barker took the other side. "People aren't usually eating their lunches on the bus. Besides, you never know who has allergies."

"Are either of you allergic to dogs?" Dot asked.

"Well, actually—"

"Alright, Evelyn," Dot cut her off with a wave of her hand. "I don't have all day, and for once, I definitely cannot stop for tea. Not after what I've just heard."

Going by how Dot was biting her lip to conceal her evident excitement, the gossip had to be juicy. Her gran was probably itching to rush home and camp next to the phone to call every person lucky enough to be in her phonebook.

"Go on," Julia urged, nodding at a chair.

"It's about the neighbourhood watch," she said, perching on the edge of the seat as though she didn't even have time to sit. "I just overheard something from their meeting in the village hall."

"I've had it up to *here* with them," Shilpa announced, hand at her forehead. "Have they been harassing you about the alley too, Julia?"

"As recently as ten minutes ago," Julia said, pinching her nose. "Penelope stopped by to tell me she was taking it to the council. She must have been on her way to the meeting."

"The council?" Shilpa shook her hands up at the ceiling. "That woman has her priorities all wrong. When I tried to tell her about all the shoplifting from the post office recently, she ignored me. Obviously, she only cares about this silly parking dispute."

Dot cleared her throat.

"As *I* was saying," she continued, "Percy and I were taking an early afternoon stroll around the graveyard with Lady and Bruce as we usually do at this time. Lady picked up a scent, so I let her follow it. Some so-and-so had thrown chicken bones into the flowerbeds at the back of the village hall. They can kill animals, you know." She pushed up her curls and glanced back at the dogs. "I was in the flowers prying the bone from Lady's mouth when I heard Peridale's Eyes in the biggest argument I've ever heard."

"What were they arguing about?" Evelyn asked, gasping.

"Everyone was going at it at once, and their voices echoed all around the hall. I couldn't make heads or tails of it." She paused, and her eyes lit up. "But it *ended* with Penelope Newton declaring, 'Peridale's Eyes are over, and everyone should get back to their own lives,' before she stormed out!"

"I felt the tension in the air." Evelyn looked around. "It's been far too quiet today."

"Hmmm." Dot glanced at Evelyn; Julia's gran had never been one for the B&B owner's mystic ways. "Regardless, now is our chance."

"Our chance for what?" asked Julia.

"To start our very own neighbourhood watch." Dot beamed from ear to ear. "There's never been a better time."

Katie placed a cup of peppermint and liquorice tea in front of Julia and a coffee in front of Barker. Sipping the sweet and minty tea, Julia searched through her memory for any time she'd ever expressed a desire to start a neighbourhood watch group.

"Wait," Evelyn said, "you started one a few years ago. I remember because you wouldn't let me join."

"We were full," Dot replied flatly. "And that was different. I made the mistake of bringing together too many people in my age group. I assumed everyone was like me – as sharp as a pencil – but I quickly learned that wasn't the case."

"Well, I'd join," said Shilpa after a sip of her latte. "Like I said, someone's been shoplifting from the post office, and Penelope has no interest in helping."

"Our *first* case!" Dot's smile grew. "Julia?"

Julia glanced at Barker, who had his 'I'm staying out of this' smile firmly fixed in place. As Olivia's lids fluttered shut, Julia lowered her into the pram beside the table for a nap.

"I really don't think I'll have time," Julia said, gently rocking the pram while Olivia settled. "I have my hands pretty full lately."

"I'm not asking you to join the Special Air Service, dear." Dot's lips thinned into a tight line. "And besides, it's not like you're a single parent. I thought Barker was taking some time off after helping that politician who got caught with his trousers around his ankles?"

"*Falsely* accused," Barker reminded them.

"I saw the pictures."

"They were fakes." Barker looked as though he might opt for a more extended argument but, in the end, settled for: "Never mind."

"I think Evelyn's keen to join," Julia said.

Evelyn looked expectantly at Dot.

"I would, as it happens." She leaned in.

"Someone's been sleeping in my shed, and I'd quite like to figure out who."

"Can't you ask the tea leaves?"

Julia arched a brow at her gran. Dot stared at Evelyn as though trying to cook up a reason other than 'we're full' to avoid spending more time than necessary with the mystic, but she eventually conceded with a smile and a nod. Evelyn seemed pleased.

"You know what it's like around here, Julia," Dot said as she rose from her chair. "Today it's Peridale's Eyes with parking complaints, and tomorrow it's a new group knocking down your café."

"I don't think any neighbourhood watch group comes with that much power," she replied, ending the rocking as Olivia's soft snores silenced the café for a moment. "Or any power, for that matter. I thought it was just about keeping an eye out for trouble?"

"It can be so much *more* than that!" Dot backed to the door with an irrepressible spring in her every step. "Think about it, Julia. I know you won't be able to resist. First meeting at my cottage in two days. Must dash. I have many phone calls to make. We need the *best* minds in Peridale on this."

Dot hurried to the bench, disturbing Percy and the dogs from a collective midday snooze. Dot took Lady's lead, and soon, they were scurrying across the green to their cottage.

"What do you think?" Barker asked, blowing on his hot coffee.

"I really don't have time," she said, eyes on Olivia. "She'll be bored of the idea by next week, anyway."

The postman stopped by and handed a stack of mail to Shilpa as she left, who passed it to Evelyn, who turned it the correct way before giving it to Julia. The postcard depicted a field of tulips gorgeous enough to put the village green to shame. Julia already knew Jessie and Alfie were in Amsterdam, but postcards arrived at random intervals she couldn't anticipate.

Passing the rest of the café's mail to Katie, Julia turned and read aloud to Barker:

*Hi Mum, Dad, Olivia, and Everyone Else.*

*Amsterdam is great. Weather nice. Nicer than there, by the looks of it. Snow in May? No, thanks. We went to a flower show the other day, and we've seen a lot of windmills. They really are everywhere. It's been fun. We're moving on to Berlin next. Staying with one of Alfie's friends there. Give Olivia a kiss from me.*

*PS: Writing this on a boat going down a canal at night, and it's bloody gorgeous. Jealous?*

*PPS (or is it PSS?): Can you send me a scone or some fish and chips, or something? Food's been decent, but missing British nosh :(*

*PS3: Miss you all too, obviously.*

"She's right," Barker admitted. "I am jealous."

Smiling as she read over it again, Julia crossed to the string of postcards on the café wall under a handmade 'Jessie's Travels' sign. An idea formed as she attached it to one of the empty pegs.

"Katie?" she called, already heading for the beaded curtain. "I think I know how we can get rid of all of this extra food, and you can thank Jessie for it."

## 2

The orange sunset bled into the kitchen of Julia's cottage, signalling the end of a day that had somehow turned into one she hadn't wanted to see end. Baking hundreds of scones and making nearly as many jars of jam should have been an arduous task, but with good company, it had turned into the most fun Julia had experienced in a while.

"Another perfect batch, Katie," Julia said over Katie's shoulder as another tray of chocolate orange scones emerged from the oven. "Good idea on the flavour combo. Smells delicious."

From there, Julia turned her attention to her father, Brian, at the camping stove on the breakfast bar. He sprinkled more sugar into the pot as he frantically stirred with the whisk.

"Don't let it boil," she instructed. "Simmer and stir."

"Aye-aye, Captain." Brian saluted. "Your mother's recipe?"

Smiling, she nodded at the handwritten recipe book opened on the stand. "The scones too. Turns out Jessie's not the only one helping without actually being here."

"It's a genius idea," Brian said, stirring the red gloop. "Who doesn't love jam, and who doesn't love scones? It's why they go so well together. It's a shame Vinnie didn't add on some vats of cream while he was hitting the keyboard because you're going to sell all this and more."

Julia stared at the stacks of finished scone boxes in the hallway containing every flavour from the traditional plain to Katie's chocolate orange to Julia's personal favourite recipe, cherry and almond. The bigger the pile grew, the more it scared her, and they'd hardly made a dent in their overstock yet.

"We're going to need to really *push* them," Julia said, transferring the last cooled batch to cardboard packages of two, four, and six. "And we're going to have to keep making them every time we sell out until the levels are back down to—"

The egg timer on the edge of the counter rattled,

signalling the end of another fifteen minutes. Brian slid off his stool and twisted it back to the start.

"My turn with the kids," he said. "Barker's probably been counting down the seconds in there."

When they were alone, Katie pulled one last ball from the large pile of dough, shaped it, and moved towards Julia with her doughy fingers extended in the other direction.

"I really am sorry about all this," she whispered. "I thought I was finally getting on top of things."

"You *are* on top of things," Julia reminded her, continuing the boxes. "This is just one little mistake, Katie. I've had fun tonight, haven't you?"

"I have, actually."

"And even priced low to sell as many as possible, we'll still make a great profit once that dent in the bank account is filled in." She hoped. "This might turn into the best May we've ever had."

Katie thanked her with a smile and had a sip of her wine before continuing to shape. Being upset at Katie for something that could have happened to anyone wouldn't fix anything, but maybe near one thousand scones would. Besides, Julia had missed the thrill of a task that didn't revolve around feeding, nappies, and sleep schedules.

"Easiest audience I've ever had," said Barker as he

sat at the jam station and grinned. "All I have to do is pull a funny face and Olivia's in stitches."

"If Jessie were here, she'd make a joke about your normal face being funny-looking," Julia said, diving in to stir the jam as a bubble popped the glossy red surface. "Simmer and stir."

Barker took the whisk and continued where Brian had left off. Katie stopped shaping her dough and, this time, wiped her hands clean.

"Now that you're here," Katie whispered, nodding at Barker before jerking her head towards the sitting room, "and *he* isn't, I wanted to ask a huge favour of you."

"Anything."

"You might regret saying that."

Katie reached into the back pocket of her tight jeans and pulled out a folded sheet of paper. She clutched it in both hands as she steadied herself.

"We've had an offer on the manor."

A similar relieved breath escaped Julia and Barker's lips at the same moment.

"That's amazing news," Julia whispered. "It's about time."

"Does all this whispering mean Brian doesn't know?"

"Oh, he knows," she said, unfolding the paper with trembling fingers. "He wants to bite the guy's hand off. You know what your father is like. Rush, rush, *rush*!"

Just hearing Katie's hesitation knotted Julia's stomach. Wellington Manor, Katie's ancestral home, had been on the market for over a year now, and they'd had no serious offers despite dropping the price several times. With every month, Katie seemed to grow more anxious about letting go of the debt-riddled money pit. Still, Julia had hoped an offer would chase away those reservations at once.

"James Jacobson." Katie slapped the paper, a printed screen capture of a social media profile, onto the counter. "Sounded like a made-up name to me, but he's on Facebook, so he must be real."

"Don't believe everything you see online." Barker squinted at the picture of the man. "Profiles can be faked."

"See!" Katie tossed a hand in Brian's direction. "Your father thinks I'm going around the bend. I don't trust this guy. He gives me a bad feeling."

"Want me to look into him?" asked Barker.

"Would you?" Katie deflated. "I can't afford much—"

"I'm not taking your money, Katie." Barker folded the paper and slotted it into his pocket before quickly returning his lapsed attention to the jam. "You're family, and it shouldn't be too difficult to verify the identity of someone with that much money to spend. Unless he's a mastermind, he would have left a paper trail somewhere. How's his offer?"

"A little under, but—"

Frantic knocking at the door cut Katie off. They immediately walked into the hall. Brian, with Olivia wriggling against his shoulder, appeared from behind the sofa. Julia reached out, but the door opened from the outside.

Leah Burns, who lived in the cottage across the lane and was, consequently, Julia's closest neighbour burst in. Panicked eyes scanned the hallway as if to confirm it was safe before she shut the door behind herself.

"Sorry," she said, tucking her sandy blonde hair behind her ears with shaking hands as the keys hooked on her thumb jangled. "I didn't mean to barge in. It's just . . . I-I think there's someone in my house."

Summoned by the same call to action, Barker and Brian rushed to the front door. Julia took Olivia from her father as he left before guiding Leah into the sitting room. Her neighbour crept to the window and pulled back the curtain.

"I've been up north all day," she said, glancing back at Julia before returning her attention to the cottage across the lane. "Final planning meetings for that huge Yorkshire wedding I told you about last time

I saw you. Usually, I-I've been home for hours by now."

Julia joined Leah at the window and pulled the curtain back further. Though hampered by the red rose bushes in Leah's garden, Julia saw Barker search an empty, brightly lit living room. Bouncing Olivia as she fussed, Julia hoped Barker wouldn't regret wading in so quickly.

"What happened?" Julia asked, peeling Leah away from the window.

"I opened the door and heard something," she started, moving Vinnie's toys from the corner of the sofa so she could sit. "Something smashed upstairs, and then I heard running footsteps. I didn't stick around to see the rest."

"Are you sure it wasn't Johnny?" Julia asked, stepping over Vinnie, who scribbled in a colouring book on the hearth rug, oblivious to the drama unfolding around him, and the lines of the sheep on the page.

"He's still on crutches."

The hit and run.

"Of course."

Katie returned with a steaming cup of tea in one hand and her chilled glass of wine in the other. She began to offer Leah the tea, but she took the wine and finished half in seconds.

"It's getting worse," she said, clutching the wine glass with shaking fingers. "The crime, I mean. With Johnny's hit and run and all the break-ins, is it my turn?"

"Break-ins?"

"I heard something about that in the café the other day," Katie said, staring into her unwanted tea as she settled next to Vinnie. "Couple of houses, isn't it?"

"I heard it was way more than a couple."

"That gossip must have passed me by," Julia said, trying to contain Olivia as she wriggled like she had somewhere to be. The clock confirmed she was five minutes late on her next feed. "It's amazing what I miss when I'm not in the café every day."

The front door opened, and Julia was relieved to see her father's face, albeit redder than it had been when he'd left.

"There was someone." He flattened a palm on the wall and leaned against it to catch his breath. "Little beggar bolted through your back door. I tried to chase him, but he was about a third my age and skinny as a rake."

Leah put back a hefty slug of wine.

"Did you get a good look at him?" Julia asked.

"Only saw him from behind," he said, looking back at the front door. "Here he is. Barker found something."

"Unless this is yours?" Barker held up a shoe; he clutched it through his shirt sleeve. "It was on the stairs, and I couldn't find the match. I know Johnny still has his cast on, but I can't see him in a pair of white trainers."

"Brogues only," Leah said, shaking her head at the dirty shoe. "I've never seen it before."

"Gotcha!"

With the shoe and his phone, Barker shut himself in the dining room. Katie picked up Vinnie and took him into the kitchen with Brian trailing after them.

"I can't believe someone broke into my house," Leah whispered, shuddering as she glanced towards the window. "I don't care what they took. It's the intrusion."

"You can stay here tonight," Julia offered. "The guest bedroom is now a nursery, but the sofa is quite comfy."

"I don't want to intrude." Leah smiled at Olivia as her frustration turned into grumbling. "You've got your hands full. I'll stay with Johnny. Maybe for a few days. If anyone breaks in, he can whack them with a crutch."

Barker returned minus the shoe, tapping his phone up and down in his palm as he stared into the middle distance.

"The police will send someone up," he said after a

focusing blink. "Might be a little while, though. Something has—"

The phone in the kitchen cut him off. It rang twice before someone picked it up.

"It's your grandmother," Brian called from the kitchen. "She's asking for you."

Julia passed Olivia to Barker before heading into the kitchen. She turned off the spitting strawberry jam; the batch had burnt past the point of no return. Accepting the phone from her father, Julia resisted rushing straight to Olivia's hungry cries.

"*Julia*!" Dot cried at the exact moment the egg timer signalled another completed fifteen minutes with its insistent rattle. "You'll *never* guess who's been found dead in the graveyard, and I'm not talking about the people six feet under. Let's just say, I don't think Penelope will be bothering you about your parking spaces anymore!"

**3**

———

"*S*he looks more like you every time I see her." Evelyn wiggled a finger into the pram as they settled in the armchairs by the bay window. "They look like angels when they sleep. How are you finding it?"

This question was the one most often repeated since Olivia's arrival, and it had a vastly different answer depending on the day, or even the hour, it was asked. Julia stifled a yawn and followed a butterfly's dance across the B&B's wild garden as another beautiful spring teatime showed its colours outside.

"Let's just say I'm glad she's finally asleep," Julia opted for. "She's usually full of energy at this time, but I couldn't seem to appease her last night. I don't think I had a single uninterrupted hour."

"I remember those days." Evelyn smiled fondly, taking a moment to glance at one of the many photographs of her late daughter arranged around the B&B's sitting room. "Astrid always slept like she had the anxieties of the world on her tiny shoulders. Poor Olivia likely picked up on the terrible energies in the air after the unfortunate incident at the graveyard last night." Snapping her fingers, she jumped up. "I have *just* the thing."

Julia opened her mouth to ask Evelyn not to bring out one of her 'healing' teas, the effects of which varied as much as Julia's answers about Olivia depending on the person asked. The only consensus was that after one of Evelyn's special brews, nobody left in the same mood they'd entered. Thankfully, Evelyn merely headed to a glass cabinet and retrieved one of her many velvet satchels of crystals. The hand went in, and a shimmering rock came out.

"Golden pyrite," she said, twirling it like stardust in the golden hour sun before tucking it into the bottom of Olivia's blanket. "A protection stone. Put this beside her cot. After all the strange occurrences lately, you can never be too careful."

Julia smiled her appreciation. Thanks to Evelyn dishing out her stones like Werther's Originals, Julia was amassing quite the collection. How many other villagers had accumulated such extensive crystal collections over the years?

"When tragedy strikes so close, it's hard not to absorb the energy." Evelyn pulled together her kaftan as she sunk in the armchair. "Gives a new meaning to the word *head*stone. I don't think Penelope's moved on yet. I can feel her in the air."

Julia wasn't sure if she was feeling Penelope Newton in the air, but something was off. She'd noticed it even before leaving her cottage that morning. This new silence was a far cry from the peaceful kind she'd experienced yesterday.

"Detective Inspector Christie suspects foul play, naturally," Julia said, revealing a snippet of their brief conversation after he'd finally ventured up to deal with the break-in at Leah's cottage last night. "In his words, how often does someone slip and fall so hard into a headstone that they immediately need one of their own?"

"It hardly bears thinking about."

More than once in the intervening hours, Julia's mind had forced her to imagine what her last moments having her skull crushed against a slab of marble might feel like. It was enough to induce a headache.

"I can't wait to tuck into some of the jam," Evelyn announced brightly, changing up the mood. "It smells amazing. And scones with little pots of cream! Such a pretty presentation."

Julia glanced at the stack of boxes she'd sold at cost; Evelyn planned to give them to her current guests as gifts. Julia had spruced them up with mini cream pots from the cash and carry and some ribbon from the craft shop.

"Might be a little on the runny side, but it'll firm up."

"Only means it's fresh." Evelyn chuckled as her gaze drifted to the grandfather clock in the corner of the room. She leapt up again at once. "Goodness me, would you look at the time? I've let the whole day slip away. I need to get to your grandmother's for the meeting."

Who, Julia wondered, had been the first person her grandmother called with the news that she'd brought her meeting forwards a day? Dot had called Julia at barely a few minutes past eight.

"Is it that time already?" Julia casually glanced at the clock. "I'll let you get off."

"I really hope discovering the identity of my shed visitor is a priority," she said as she swept to the door in a flurry of fabric. "They were back last night. It was a pleasant evening, so I stayed out until I couldn't keep my eyes open. They took the provisions I left for them, but they were gone by sunrise."

"Have you considered putting up cameras?"

"I'm not looking to catch them out." Evelyn rushed around Julia in the hall and opened the front door. "They're doing me no harm; I simply want to know who they are so I can offer my help. Even with all my rambling regulars at this time of year, I have empty beds enough that nobody should be sleeping in a shed with the spiders."

"That's like how I first met Jessie," Julia said as Evelyn helped lift the pram over the doorstep. "I think she's driving into Berlin today."

"Oh, I'd love to get back there." Evelyn thrust her arms out to the open air. "To see the world again. I paused my travels for one winter, and I've barely left the country since." She looked at the clock above the door to the police station and jogged to the bottom of the garden path. "Are you coming to the meeting? You can tell me more about Jessie's adventures."

"I wasn't going to go." Julia pushed through the open gate, and after Evelyn shut it behind her, they set off. "I didn't want to give my gran false hope that I'd be joining."

"Then I shall have to love you and leave you." Evelyn embraced Julia before giving Olivia's cheek a rub with the back of a finger. "I doubt your gran's the type of woman who appreciates lateness. In fact, I can feel her foot tapping from here."

As Evelyn, wrapped in her black mourning outfit – she had a kaftan for every occasion – hurried through the village, Julia followed at a more leisurely pace. She passed The Plough pub, which she rarely ventured into these days, though it was suitably packed in the nice weather.

Across the green, the impressive structure of St. Peter's Church almost obscured the investigation unfolding behind it. If it weren't for the official-looking cars and vans parked along the road, it would be easy to believe this was a day like any other, even with the strange feeling in the air.

Perhaps the unsettled feeling stemmed from her interaction with Penelope within the same hour she died. Julia had barely said two words to her, walking off when Penelope was mid-sentence. If she hadn't been so stressed with the suppliers, perhaps she wouldn't have felt so guilty for her abruptness – not that her memories of the woman were fond. One look at the alley reminded Julia just how difficult Penelope had made her life recently.

In the pram, Olivia's lashes flickered and blinked open. She had Barker's eyes, and she never looked more like him than when she was cranky.

"Welcome back," Julia whispered softly, hoping the nap had improved the footing on which they'd left things before venturing to Evelyn's. "It smells like someone needs a change."

The lane to her cottage was close.

The café was closer.

She set off to her gran's cottage.

She didn't have the café keys on her. Probably.

"I *knew* it!" Dot snapped her fingers as she opened the door. "You *cannot* resist a mystery, Julia. Baby or not. I couldn't have planned this better if I tried."

"Careful, Gran." Julia pushed Olivia over the threshold. "You're going to make yourself a suspect with words like that."

"Don't be ludicrous." Dot clutched her collar. "Why on Earth would *I* want to kill Penelope Newton of *all* people? I hardly knew her. She never gave me the chance. When I tried to join her stupid group, she said they were . . ."

Dot's sentence fell off a cliff as she turned all her attention to fluffing up the curls at the nape of her neck.

"Full?"

"Something to that effect." Dot peered into the sitting room, where it sounded like Evelyn was already giving someone a palm reading. "Hardly a motive, dear."

"And holding a meeting to immediately form a group

to take over from the victim's?" Julia closed the front door behind her. "Less than twenty-four hours after Penelope was found dead a stone's throw from your cottage?"

"You couldn't possibly think I—"

"No, *I* couldn't," Julia cut in with a wink. "I'm kidding, Gran. Unless you have something to confess?"

"I confess I must be the one to tell my granddaughter she isn't as funny as she thinks she is."

Dot flicked Julia's ear through her hair.

"I assume you were here with Percy all night?"

"Lady and Bruce *too*," Dot said through pursed lips. "Honestly, Julia, I might forget to mention Olivia to see how you like it." She took a calming inhale, and in a lower tone, said, "But, yes. Percy and I were here all night. We were enjoying our after-dinner sweets when we heard the commotion outside. Some dog walker found her. I *knew* we should have taken them out earlier, but Percy was adamant about watching the news, as always."

Dot wafted her hand, hinting at some conflict she didn't care to share. Knowing Dot and Percy as she did, Julia imagined their arguments would be cause for more amusement than concern.

"Yes, Gran, it's a shame you didn't discover a dead body," Julia said flatly. She checked that the dining room was empty. "Do you mind if I go in here to change Olivia?"

"You don't need to ask."

After pulling the door nearly shut, Julia unpacked the changing gear from the bottom of the pram and set to work putting Olivia into a fresh nappy.

"I thought there'd be more people here," Dot whispered through the crack in the door. "I've got Shilpa, Percy, and Evelyn rocking back and forth clutching Amy Clark's hands. Hardly the dream team, is it?"

"Don't forget Lady and Bruce."

"Very funny." Dot cracked a smile. "After something like this, aren't people bound to flock in wanting to help? I spread the word far and wide. Called everyone in my phonebook. I'll give them another ten minutes."

Dot left Julia to finish changing Olivia, who, more interested in grabbing at her toes, wriggled and kicked around on the mat.

Julia had been surprised to see so few people in the sitting room. Like her gran, she'd expected a decent turnout in a village where gossip ruled – and no gossip ranked higher than that of a suspicious death.

For her gran's sake, she hoped more people arrived.

Maybe she should stay?

Ten minutes to show moral support and keep the numbers up?

"Who am I kidding?" Julia whispered to Olivia as she clasped the buttons of a fresh lilac babygrow over the new nappy. "We both know I can't leave now."

After abandoning the pram in the dining room, Julia and Olivia sandwiched themselves between Amy and Shilpa on the sofa. Dot smiled vaguely at her, clearly preoccupied with staring at the small clock on the mantlepiece. Julia helped herself to a plain digestive, recognising the basic white and red packet as the cheapest you could buy at the local supermarket.

"Where *are* they?" Dot hissed, transferring to the window, and picking up the binoculars now hanging from a dedicated hook. "They should *be* here. "

"Who exactly are we waiting for?" Amy Clark asked, happily sacrificing her fingers to Olivia's clutch-and-not-let-go game.

"Everyone," Dot muttered, lenses pushed up against the glass. "I should be turning people away."

"*We* are here, Dot." Shilpa stiffened, shaking her head. "The village is only so big, and I'm beginning to suspect that you don't think we're up to your standards."

Shilpa rose, and, though their conflict was

apparent, it only took a stern look for Amy and Evelyn to rise with her.

"That's not what you meant, is it, my Dorothy?" Percy dabbed at his forehead with a handkerchief as he desperately looked between the women. "She meant no offence."

"You're right, Shilpa." Dot let the curtain fall and pulled away. "Ladies, I'm sorry. Should we get this show on the road?"

Shilpa lowered back into her seat, Amy and Evelyn going with her. Julia was impressed. More formidable people had tried putting Dot in her place with a song and dance and failed.

"I never thought she'd say sorry," Shilpa whispered to Julia.

"They're in short supply, so savour it."

Dot assumed her position in front of the fireplace and cleared her throat as the room quietened. Olivia moved on from Amy's fingers on one side to Shilpa's bangles on the other.

"Well, I suppose we should get—"

Dot's eyes lit up as the doorbell rang. She hurried off and returned with two of the last people Julia would have expected to see.

"Sorry we're late," Leah said, shrugging out of her coat as she walked in. "Blame Johnny."

"I could hardly come with one crutch, could I?" He

followed her, although at a much slower pace. "How was I to know it had rolled under the bed?"

"*Twenty* minutes!" Leah huffed as she balanced on the edge of Evelyn's armrest. "I spent twenty minutes turning his cottage upside down, and it was mere *inches* away from the other crutch."

"Which, when you think about it," Johnny said, collapsing into a chair Percy ferried in from the dining room, "is the only place it could have been. I couldn't have gone anywhere on one crutch to lose the other."

"Any luck finding the person behind the wheel?" Percy asked. "I still can't believe they drove off and left you for dead."

"Thankfully, only a broken ankle," Johnny knocked the blue cast on his left foot.

"They weren't to know that."

"That's what keeps me up at night," Leah said, "and now we have another likely to be unsolved mystery. When do the police ever find these people?"

"Which answers your question, Percy," Johnny said, resting the crutches against the picture rail behind his chair. "Two months in, I doubt I'll ever get closure, but at least it was only an ankle."

While everyone was looking at Johnny, Julia kept her eyes on her gran. Dot waited at the mantle with clasped hands, doing a terrible job of keeping her pleased grin in check. Evidently, she didn't need the whole village . . . just enough people to make the cottage feel as full as it only ever did on Christmas Day.

"Peridale's Eyes never had a newspaper editor," Dot said, rubbing her hands together, before quickly adding, "Not that we didn't have a fine calibre of people before, but it's nice to have a finger in every pie."

"Speaking of Peridale's Eyes," Evelyn announced, turning inwards. "If we're to be a group, won't we need a name?"

"*Oh!*" Amy Clark sat up. "I've been thinking about this. How about Eyes on Peridale?"

"That is essentially identical to the group we're hoping to replace." Dot's tone rose, forcing her to push forward a nose-crinkling smile. "But it's one to consider, I suppose."

"How about Peridale's Third Eye?" Evelyn's enthusiastic smile faded when Dot's nostrils released a sharp blast of breath at the suggestion. "Or . . . something else?"

"I like it," Shilpa agreed. "It has layers."

"Again, it's *virtually* the same." Dot's widening gaze let on that she couldn't believe she had to deal with such suggestions. "Let's get away from the eye thing. In fact, a name isn't important right now."

"To business, I say." Percy winked at Dot. "Listen up, everyone."

Dot thanked him with a smile before clapping her hands and throwing her arms wide like a circus ringleader about to perform a trick.

"Picture the scene," she began, scanning the room. "You're in the graveyard alone and it's dark. But you're not really alone, are you? Because *bam*!" Her hand slapped down on the mantlepiece. "Ladies and gentlemen, I'm afraid the break-ins and shoplifting will have to wait. We already have our first case, and it's a *murder* investigation."

Julia cradled Olivia, startled to tears by the bang. Dot seemed more frustrated by the noise than apologetic that her theatrics had caused it.

"I didn't realise I was signing up for a murder investigation," Johnny said, scratching at his ankle cast with a pencil. "I'm more concerned about finding whoever broke into Leah's cottage last night."

"Think of the stories for your paper, Mr Watson," Dot said in an excited whisper. "Time and again, Julia has proved that the local constabulary doesn't always have both eyes – or even one of them – on the ball."

"On the Ball would be a good name," Amy pointed out.

"Oh, I quite like that one actually," Leah said, leaning across Julia. "Snappy."

"It makes us sound like a bunch of seals performing tricks at the zoo for kippers." Dot sighed, rubbing at her temples. "Can we get away from the naming for a moment? Here's our chance to put our own stamp on what a neighbourhood watch team *could* be. We don't have to spend our days harassing people over parked cars when our homes are being broken into and you can't stroll in your local graveyard of an evening without having your skull caved in."

Dot paused as though to assess if she'd gone too far, but everyone appeared to hang off her every word.

"Peridale's Eyes needs their prescription checked," she rallied, pacing with her hands behind her back. "They've let this village – *our* village – down too often. And what have we done about it?"

She paused, and the group looked amongst themselves.

"Exactly." Dot wagged a finger. "Maybe *we're* the ones letting this village down because we've let these so-called 'Eyes' run rampant, harassing small business owners while local crime skyrocketed! But my friends, there's good news." The pacing stopped, and her face softened. "Look at us. We spread far and wide across this village. The editor, the organist, the post office . . . person, the B&B owner, the dog walkers – regretfully

47

not the ones to discover poor Penelope's body – and . . ."

Dot paused on Leah.

"And Julia's friend," she said with a pinch too much gusto. "Not to mention Julia herself. Café owner, mother, super sleuth, and most importantly, my granddaughter. If she applied to the station, they'd put her in the top job right away, you know."

"I don't think they would, Gran," she said. "I think you need qualifications and years of training for that."

"Qualifications?" Dot arched a brow. "*Training*? Why, when we have *results*? There's probably more than a few prison cells with pictures of your face on their dartboards, Julia."

Julia could hardly believe her ears, and she couldn't believe that everyone was eating up every word. It was impressive; she'd give her gran that.

"But now to the task at hand," Dot said, centring herself with a slow blink. "We can solve this, and when we do, people will be banging the door down to join. And you know what I'll say? We're full. Here and now, we have everything we need . . . in *Dot's Detectives*!"

"No," Shilpa said, shaking her head.

"Absolutely not," Johnny added.

"Oh, I don't like that one." Amy shuddered. "I still think Eyes on Peridale is the best one."

"Forget the name." Dot lifted a clenched fist in the air. "Who's with me?"

Clearly, her gran was waiting for everyone to bounce up and raise their fists with the same enthusiasm, but in the blink of an eye – or the uttering of a 'Dot's Detectives' – the spell had broken.

"I guess I'm in," said Leah. "Anything to feel safer."

"I'll give it a go," Shilpa added, checking her watch, "but I think Julia should lead us. Like you said, she's the most qualified."

"Oh, I'm flattered." Julia leaned in and whispered, "I'm not actually joining."

"Then why are you here?" Dot demanded, and this time all eyes shifted to put Julia in the hot seat. "You're as intrigued as I am. As we all are. It's human nature."

Julia considered her options as she stroked Olivia's back.

Could she really say no?

Did she want to?

"At least come to the meetings so we can pick your brain," Dot said. "A halfway point."

"Fine," Julia said. "That seems fair."

"Then we are a team!" Dot bit into her lip and announced, "Percy, fetch the board."

After setting Bruce on the carpet next to where Lady had curled up by Dot's feet, he scurried into the hallway. Dot exchanged the packet of plain digestives with a tin of luxury selections as he dug around under the stairs. Percy rushed back and set up a large presentation board.

"The stationery shop had a sale on," explained Dot.

"Oh, which one?" asked Evelyn. "The B&B's printer is in desperate need of an upgrade."

"I bought it a while ago," Dot said as she wrote 'SUSPECTS' at the top of the board in big letters. "You never know when you're going to need a large notepad."

"Where do we start?" Shilpa asked. "Anyone could have done it."

"Anyone, yes," Dot said as she continued writing. "Anyone in Peridale's Eyes, that is. Yesterday afternoon, Percy and I heard a vicious row in the village hall between them all, mere hours before Penelope was found a few paces away in the graveyard. Dead."

Dot pulled away and underlined the first of five names she'd written down.

"Ethel White," she announced. "A busybody in her seventies who I've heard can't keep her nose out of anything. I only know her from around the village, but she strikes me as a woman I could never get on with."

"I'm in her bridge club," Amy revealed. "I could interview her?"

"A great start!" Dot wrote 'Amy' next to Ethel's name. "Anyone else know anyone on here?"

Julia waited for someone else to chip in before reluctantly deciding to share her connection to one of the names.

"I kind of know Victoria Grant," she said, repositioning a drowsy Olivia. "She goes by Vicky. She owns that new coffee van on Mulberry Lane outside Dad's antique shop. She seems nice enough. I only popped by to introduce myself so it wouldn't be awkward, considering she's now technically my competition."

Julia had also saved her from sending out flyers by spotting a typo before she'd spread them far and wide around the village, but she kept that detail to herself; she didn't want to embarrass the woman.

"Oh, it's foul coffee," Shilpa said with a gag. "Not a patch on yours."

"And I don't think any of her cakes are fresh," Amy whispered. "Last week, I had the driest angel slice I've ever tasted."

A glance at the display case in the small van had told Julia they weren't fresh; she recognised their technical perfection from her supplier's website. But that wasn't her secret to divulge, either.

"Then Julia shall interview Vicky," Dot said after writing her name on the board. "Makes the most sense."

Julia couldn't argue with that.

She could stretch to one interview.

Meetings, and *one* interview.

"Don't forget I know Gus Morris, Penelope's widower, dear," Percy pointed out between biscuits. "Although considering Gus's wife just had a surprise meeting with a headstone, I doubt I'll be seeing him at this week's choir rehearsal."

"Rehearsing for anything exciting?" Shilpa asked.

"Just the summer fetes," Dot answered for him as she added Percy's name to the board. "Let's not get off track. Any other names? We're doing great. Only Desmond Newton left. Anyone know him?"

"Newton?" Leah spoke up. "He must be a relation of Penelope's, no?"

"Maybe." Dot scribbled down the detail. "Anyone know where to find him?"

Nobody stepped forward.

"Are we nearly finished here?" Shilpa asked, already pushing herself up. "I'll never get dinner sorted if I don't get home within the hour."

"And I need to start the evening duties at the B&B," said Evelyn.

"Then I guess that's our first official meeting over."

Dot popped the cap onto the pen. "Great work, team. Let's reconvene here in two days, same place and time. Keep your eyes open and your ears to the ground. We *can* do this."

Rather than stay for an extended session, Julia left with the group, and they all went their separate ways. Overtaking a woman being dragged along by a huskie, Julia headed for the church. She'd thought about going straight home, but a familiar chalky cloud had pulled her in.

"Evening." Detective Inspector John Christie exhaled cherry-scented smoke he'd pulled in from an electronic cigarette device. "Look at the little thing. She's flat out. If only I could curl up and have a nap like that."

"Tough day?"

"Like you wouldn't believe." He forced a laugh, pocketing his device after a few short blasts. "I imagine your husband has had an easier time of it?"

"He's looking into a potential buyer for the manor." Julia's gaze drifted over his shoulder to the small group of white-outfitted crime scene investigators currently sipping coffee from cups sporting Vicky's Van's logo. "Any leads?"

"If only we were that lucky." His hand brushed over his rough stubble. "It's not like a graveyard on the edge of a forest is a prime location for camera coverage. How's your neighbour holding up after last night?"

"She's still a few handheld electronics short."

"Nothing the insurance won't cover."

"A feeling of safety in her own home?" Julia followed Christie to his car on the edge of the green. "I hear there's been an uptick in break-ins lately. Should I be worried, Detective Inspector?"

"A few more than usual, but we're on top of it." He checked his watch. "I have a meeting with the serious crime unit in five. I need to go."

"No problem," she said, looking back at her gran's cottage. "As a friend, I thought you should know that my gran has set up a new neighbourhood watch team. I imagine you'll be hearing from her."

"Oh, bloody fantastic." His eyes rolled around in a perfect circle. "That's *all* I need. And to think, I'd just got rid of one. That Penelope was in the station reporting the strangest of things every five minutes. You'd think she had better things to do." He smirked. "She must have really hated you. Tried to have you in over where you parked your car."

"Never knew the woman."

"Isn't that always the way?" Christie climbed into his car and slid down the window. "Tell Barker to get his backside down to the pub one night if he can tear himself away from happily ever after. We need a good catch up. Hardly seen him this year, but I won't hold that against either of you, considering."

With a wink and a smile, he rolled the window up and sped off, leaving Julia to set off home with Olivia fast asleep in her pram. The gentle winding incline to her cottage, the last home before Peridale Farm, always felt steeper on the way back. According to her sister, Sue, walking with the pram was good post-baby exercise. Every time Julia felt like she was getting used to it, Olivia grew bigger, and heavier.

Back at the cottage and slightly out of breath, Julia changed Olivia again before settling her in the cot next to their bed. After squeezing the golden pyrite in her palm, she placed it on her bedside table and hoped for a peaceful, safe night. Then she checked the locks on the bedroom windows, bolted the front door, and went in search of Barker.

She found him in the garden, wrapped in a blanket with his laptop on his knee, reading glasses perched on the end of his nose, and a bottle of beer in his hand. He opened his arm to her, and she slid under the blanket and against his warm side.

"Manor stuff?" she asked.

"The starts of."

"Was Katie onto something?"

"Maybe." He shut the laptop. "Maybe not. There's a pattern emerging with this guy's property portfolio that I want to take a closer look at, but it can wait. Where's Olivia? It's been the kind of strange day that only a snuggle will fix. The air hasn't felt quite right."

"Not just me then."

"Did you hear about the new break-in?" he asked, pulling his phone from his pocket. "It was all over the Peridale Chat group this afternoon. A cottage near the Fern Moore end of the village." He scrolled through his phone. "Strange. It was here earlier. Seems to have been deleted."

"Odd," she said, yawning again. "I think I joined my gran's group."

"Quelle surprise." Barker kissed the top of her head. "Christie will have the murder wrapped up in no time, and you'll be able to focus on stolen plants and late buses . . . or whatever it is neighbourhood watches do."

Julia laughed, though she didn't think that's quite what her gran had in mind. Another yawn interrupted her mid-laugh, and she found herself more than ready to crawl into bed, if only to escape the nagging, unsettled feeling hanging over the village.

# 4

It wasn't that Dot had forgotten that a photograph of her father hung in the entrance of St. Peter's Church, but it had been a while since she'd stood still in the right spot for long enough to actually look and not just glance at it.

They were close when he was alive, but it wasn't until years after her father's death that Dot realised she hadn't asked him enough questions about his life when she'd had the chance. Every year since, Dot forgot more of his stories. She'd loved her father deeply. Unlike her cold and callous mother, whose life's work involved controlling Dot's every decision, her father had been more laid back.

"Everyone is the hero of their own story," he'd say scratchily, lifting her onto his lap and washing her in his hot cigarette breath, "and nobody tries to be the hero more than you, Dorothy."

She'd never quite grasped his meaning, but she did miss him. He died far too young. Though, when her mother died at the same age, Dot had felt it was right on time.

The photograph painted new details over the blurry blank face her memories had been working with since the last time she'd seen an image of him.

It couldn't have been that long, could it?

A few years, at least.

She still thought about him occasionally, but she might not have sought out the picture in the church if memories of him hadn't pushed to the forefront of her mind as she gave the rousing speech required to unite her new team.

*Be your own hero, Dorothy.*

"*They* turned *me* away," she said to Lady and Bruce, curled at her feet and lulled to sleep by the rehearsing choir. "We'll show them what Dot's Detectives can do."

A fine name too. Percy agreed. She had been mortified when they laughed at her suggestion like theirs were better. Eye this and eye that; she'd rather have no name at all than have Peridale's Eyes think she took any inspiration from them. Their downfall was all the inspiration Dot needed.

"Anywhere nice?"

Dot turned away from the picture. Father David was walking towards her in his black robes, smiling.

"Come again?"

"In your mind," he said, tapping his temple and joining Dot at the picture. "You were in a world of your own. I hope I didn't startle you." Linking his hands behind his back, he leaned in to examine the photograph. "Ah, yes! The infamous 1956 choir committee bowls finale in Riverswick. That's your father on the end, isn't it?"

Despite being younger than Dot, Father David had always made it his business to know his congregation. Dot appreciated it, even if she confined her church visits to events, holidays, and the odd times she joined Percy for choir rehearsals.

"They suffered a horrific defeat," Father David said, rocking back on his feet with a chuckle. "Riverswick showed them up, and they never played again. We haven't had a bowls team at the church since."

"To the day he died, he swore that they cheated," she remembered tenderly. "How, we could never quite figure out."

"And now it's just a picture on a wall and a story we keep repeating." He stepped back. "Funny how that works, isn't it? It almost shows how pointless those resentments can be."

"Tell that to whomever killed Penelope," she said in a quieter voice, sensing an opportunity. "Especially so close to the church." She sat, and after adjusting the hem of her skirt, said, "I bet the police are keeping you up to date?"

"Aside from calling this morning to let me know they'd be allowing public access to the graveyard again, they have told me very little."

"Oh."

"Gus and Penelope were regulars here. Unfortunately, negativity always plagued my interactions with Penelope. She always had something to complain about. Their grandson, however, I do know. He—"

"Will you excuse me, Father?" Dot interrupted, her eyes darting into the church as the choir finished rehearsing. "I'd quite like to talk to my husband. Am I okay to take the dogs in?"

Dot walked in while Father David said something vaguely biblical-sounding about all creatures being welcome in God's house. She'd have to remind Julia of that. She swore she'd never seen that 'NO DOGS' sign at the café until Lady and Bruce came along.

Bruce tried to bound ahead when he noticed Percy, though the French bulldog's tiny frame meant

Dot's shoulder remained firmly in its socket. Thank goodness they'd done their research on dogs for the 'elderly'. Aside from some issues with accidents on the carpet when the rescue dogs first moved in, she'd had no complaints.

In fact, she'd fallen completely in love with them.

"He's over there," Percy whispered as he kissed Dot. "He hasn't said much since he arrived. I think he wanted to take his mind off things with some singing."

Dot would have spotted the recently widowed person even without Percy's instruction. A slender man with thinly combed-over grey hair dabbed at his eyes with a tissue while the rest of the choir closed in around him.

"They're like grief leeches," she said. "At least I have a reason to talk to him."

"Should I go over?"

"It's better if I do it," she said, handing over Lady's lead.

"Oh, really, my Dorothy?" Percy scratched at his bald head. "It's just . . . I know the chap rather well."

"Don't worry," she said, straightening her brooch. "I know what I'm doing."

Lingering by the end pew, she flicked through a songbook keeping her eyes on Gus. Finally, the sight of a suspect. *Did he do it*? He was crying real tears; his shredded tissues proved that. A choir meeting was the last place Dot would have gone if she'd just killed her husband.

Dot approached Gus as the group trailed off and left him at the back. He squinted at her as though trying to place her face.

"I'm sorry for your loss," she said softly. "It's simply awful what happened."

Gus offered the generic 'thanks for caring' smile Dot had perfected in the days after her first husband's death. How well she remembered the exhausting mix of people feeling obliged to say something and the horror when no one brought it up because it was the only thing she could possibly think or talk about. The familiarity of the look shifted towards confusion with a downturn of his eyebrows.

"Thank you," he said with some hesitation. "Sorry, you'll have to forgive me. I'm afraid I don't quite know who you are."

"Dot," she said. "Percy's wife? I was briefly part of your little choir thing the Christmas before last. I was stood just next to you, I think."

"Ah, yes," he said uncertainly, looking her over. "I remember."

His suspicious gaze shifted to the songbook in Dot's hands, and the frown deepened. It was upside down. She quickly corrected it, even as her mind shouted at her to get it together. She'd get nowhere acting like an amateur, especially interviewing one of Peridale's Eyes.

What if he was already on to her?

Gus nodded a puzzled goodbye before continuing down the aisle. The rest of the choir lingered by the door – no doubt ready to marinate in the man's sorrow once again.

*Be bold, Dorothy.*

*Be your own hero.*

"I've started a new neighbourhood watch group," she called after him. "I thought you should know we're looking into what happened with your wife."

Gus turned, his frown even more pronounced.

"What is it with *you* people today?" He let out a throaty laugh. "You're as bad as Ethel. She was on the phone this morning trying to arrange another Peridale's Eyes meeting. I . . ."

Gus flicked his hand and left without bothering to finish his sentence. Clutching her brooch, Dot watched him go. As Percy hurried towards her with worried eyes, Dot spun to a tap on her shoulder.

"Have some respect," a woman said, drying her hands with a blue paper towel as the bathroom door swung shut behind her. "The poor man always has enough going on this time of year, what with Shawn's anniversary. And adding Penelope's death? Last thing he needs is someone like *you* sticking your nose in."

"Sorry, do I know you?"

"Really, Dorothy?" The woman tutted. "I was stood right behind you when you were in the choir."

Dot looked the woman over, though she could have sworn she'd never seen her before. She attempted an 'oh yes, I remember' smile, but the woman hurried off after the rest of the leeches.

"I think he did it," she declared when she and Percy were alone. "Did you see how he just overreacted? Maybe I went in too hot."

"What did you ask, my dear?"

"It's all a blur." She tugged at her collar; why did she insist on wearing it so tight? "I got some intel for the board, though. Ethel White, to whom he crudely and incorrectly compared me, is brazenly trying to carry on the group without Penelope."

"Sounds like a motive to me."

"My thoughts exactly." Dot tapped her chin. "We need to talk to Ethel. Even if she didn't do it, she might know something."

"Right you are," he said, his lips tightening. "It's just, I thought you were leaving Ethel to Amy?"

Dot glanced over at the organist, dressed in pale pink and baby blue. She closed the lid of the instrument, trapping her finger in the process.

"I don't think she's up to it, do you?"

But that didn't mean they couldn't use her.

Ignoring the lead Percy held out, Dot hurried over to Amy with a wave and a smile, already cooking up a reason to invite her round for tea.

"These scones are divine," Amy Clark said after another cream and jam filled bite. "Your granddaughter has gifted hands. I can never get mine like this."

Dot bit her tongue and smiled as she topped up Amy's tea to the brim. She was sure Katie had made most of the scones, though at least to Julia or Pearl's recipe. She was getting good at biting her tongue. She hadn't said anything when Amy put the jam on before the cream.

*Cream before jam, always.*

At least she agreed with her mother about one thing.

"Is that a new cardigan?" Dot asked suddenly. "It's very . . . pink."

"This?" Amy looked down and shook her head. "I got this old thing from the charity shop years ago. It's held up well, but – Oh, would you look at that. I've slopped some jam."

"Here." With a sickly smile, Dot plucked a tissue from the box. "Three ply. Only the best."

Amy accepted the offering and rubbed at the stain while Dot bit her tongue yet again.

*Dab don't rub.*

Perhaps she agreed with her mother on two things.

"We've always been friends, haven't we, Amy?" Dot smiled, pushing the tray closer. "Have another scone. I have more than I could ever eat."

"Oh, thank you." Amy dabbed her lips with the scrunched tissue. "I probably shouldn't. We usually go to The Comfy Corner after bridge."

"That's today?"

"Soon, actually." Amy checked her watch. "I can only stay for a little longer."

Dot swallowed her sigh. Why hadn't the woman just said so? She'd wasted two delicious scones and a good tissue to get to that information. At least Amy's admission presented an opportunity for Dot to redeem herself after the friction with Gus.

"Why don't we set off now?" Dot stood, pulling Amy off the sofa before she could pick up her scone. "New members are welcomed, I assume?"

"Oh, I think so, I'm not sure if—"

"You can vouch for me."

Dot pushed Amy in the direction of the front door before calling into the dining room that she was popping out and wouldn't be long.

Bridge club, as it turned out, was held in the perfect location for Dot to continue her investigation: Ethel's home. Ethel lived a short walk across the village in a detached cottage with a scruffy garden. The surrounding area was quiet save for the noise pouring through the open window. Dot heard cackling women from the gate.

"Laughter right after her leader's death?" Dot whispered to Amy as they walked up the garden path. "From now on, we're Dot's De—" She stopped herself and corrected with: "We're on our as-yet-unnamed neighbourhood watch team's time."

"I've been thinking about that—"

"If it's another eye-related or eye-adjacent idea, I don't want to hear it."

"Never mind then."

Amy knocked on the door three times before letting herself in. The laughter stopped, and all eyes zoomed towards the newcomer. Dot presented her best smile, but few returned it. Some faces were familiar, but only because she recognised them as living in the village. Everybody was at least a decade younger than her, not that they looked it.

"This is my friend," Amy said, breaking the awkward silence that had grown after the women's laughter had so abruptly ceased. "Everyone, Dot. Dot, everyone."

"Yes." Ethel's gaze was as scrutinising as Gus's had been. "I know you from here and there. Are you to join our group?"

"If you'll let me."

Ethel, a short, slender woman with violet-hued silver curls, homed in on Dot with laser focus, and the women followed where she led. After staring at her for an uncomfortable amount of time, the women looked amongst themselves as if having a telepathic conversation. Dot bit back the urge to tell them where to stick their stuffy silence and shifty looks, but she refrained. She'd bitten her tongue a record number of times in the last hour.

"We were all new once," Ethel said with a nod, holding out a hand. "Let's see if you melt into our pot."

Dot smiled her appreciation, though she sensed she was on trial from here on out. Suited her perfectly fine, thank you. She was there for information and information only. She'd ditch them long before they rumbled her; if she worked hard, she could be in and out within the hour. Bridge's complicated rules always bored her to sleep.

"Make some room for our newcomer, girls," Ethel ordered from her slightly elevated armchair in the corner. "How's your game, Dot?"

"I play decent bridge."

"Oh, you didn't think we *actually* played bridge, did you?" Ethel cackled, and the women squealed like piggies with her. She reached into a drawer and pulled out a gold-engraved metal tin. Flipping the lid revealed a deck of cards. "I hope you brought your purse."

They settled quickly into a low-stakes poker game with penny bets. Dot could hardly believe there was a secret poker group in the middle of the village. How had she never heard of it? She'd had her own organised poker nights over the years, but nothing had stuck. That wasn't to say she was out of practice, though. Percy had gone from an ear-tugging bluffer to a semi-decent opponent under her tutelage.

Meanwhile, she'd become even better.

Not that she could show it.

Not yet at least.

She had to blend in with the women and the furniture, though Dot struggled to tell the difference with some. Except for Ethel, it was a room full of Amy Clarks. She held court like no other, leading and dominating most conversations. Dot had to admit Ethel was good at spinning a tale, though she never paused for anyone else to get a word in.

Thankfully, Ethel's bullet train sped through every conversation station until it finally arrived at the one Dot had been hoping for.

"I don't know what she was doing in that graveyard," Ethel said, dealing out the cards for another game, "but I can't say I was surprised when I heard it was Penelope who had died."

"That's a wicked thing to say," said Martha, evidently the woman designated to volley questions when Ethel did pause to sip tea, deal cards, or play her hand.

"I said I wasn't *surprised*," she replied with a matching wicked smile. "I didn't say I was *glad*. I will admit it makes things a little simpler for me. I was going to wait to announce this until later . . ."

Ethel paused and the tension mounted. At first, Dot thought she'd lost her train of thought, but Ethel gave herself away with a quick scan to check people were waiting with appropriately bated breath.

"What the heck!" she cried. "I might as well tell you girls now that I *will* be taking over Peridale's Eyes."

Ethel paused for gasps, and gasp they did, though Dot did not join them; it was old news.

"Now that Penelope isn't in charge," Martha said, "who's to say who can and can't join?"

"Of course, we'll still have *standards*," Ethel said with some firmness. "But if enough of you meet the measure, who's to say we can't have combined 'bridge' and neighbourhood watch meetings?"

While the personality-deprived women chattered about Ethel's proposal, Dot did everything she could to avoid rolling her eyes. *This* group of women running the neighbourhood watch? Perhaps Dot's team comprised only what she had on hand, but this lot left more than a little to be desired.

Dot had intentionally thrown all her good hands, but just from quick glances at the women she'd been sandwiched between, neither had a brain between them. They were throwing as many winning hands as Dot.

Unless they were doing it on purpose.

Ethel did seem to win most of the games.

"Listen to this," Martha said as they started a new game. "Someone is going around trying to rally troops to start a new group."

"What?" Ethel took a brutish slurp of tea. "Who?"

Dot sank behind her cards, wanting more than ever to become one with the furniture. None of the women immediately looked at her, though it wouldn't be long until someone figured it out; she'd called everyone in her phonebook.

"I got a call about that the other night," one woman said. "You know, I have no idea who she was."

"Can't be anyone important," Martha said quickly as Ethel silently seethed in the corner. "Nothing to worry about, I'd say."

Dot physically bit her tongue this time. She tried to disguise her little yelp behind a cough as she shifted in her seat. She felt Amy's eyes on her, but she couldn't bring herself to look up.

Since they weren't onto her, she could afford one question; she'd just have to make it a good one.

"I heard Penelope was a terrible leader," Dot said, tossing in a pound coin before taking another card. "She was borderline harassing my granddaughter."

A few suspicious eyes turned her way, though Dot suspected it was because she'd finally chosen to vocalise something other than 'stick' and 'I'm out'.

"You heard right," Ethel said. "Penelope always had an agenda, and she made that agenda very clear before she died. She's had us all keeping her secrets without knowing why. But now, it's . . ."

Ethel's voice trailed off to nothing, and Dot caught the unmistakable internal struggle of someone trying to hide their wide-eyed panic after saying too much. Dot had worn the very same look moments ago, but thankfully, nobody had witnessed hers.

Dot had Ethel right where she wanted her.

"Secrets about what?" Martha, apparently the only one brave enough to speak, pushed.

"It doesn't matter now," she said. A betraying tremor tainted Ethel's casual laugh. "Silly neighbourhood watch politics. She took her role as a leader too seriously and, like I said, she had an agenda. She carefully policed what things we could and couldn't look into, and always went out of her way to make sure her orders were being followed."

Ethel inhaled deeply and smiled around the room, skimming over Dot as if she were no longer there.

"Don't worry, ladies," Ethel said, topping up some teacups and once again skipping Dot's. "If you join, I'll make sure everyone gets a voice. It's about time this village had some real eyes watching it."

*And they're not yours.*

"An agenda?" Dot risked another question, and the probing looks followed. "What agenda was she pushing?"

"Like I said," Ethel replied, still avoiding Dot's gaze, "it doesn't matter now. She's not here to push it."

"But you said her agenda wasn't obvious until recently," Dot said, feeling braver despite the stuffier silence. "So, you must have discovered something as a group that cast Penelope in a different light."

"I said no such thing." Ethel dismissively waved her hand as she pushed all her coins into the pile in the middle of the table. "All in. Who's with me?"

A couple threw in their coins, but most folded. Dot looked down at the hand only one king away from a royal flush.

"Yes, you did," Dot insisted, adding all her coins to the bet. "You can't deny it. We all heard you."

Dot searched the room for someone with some sense. None braved her eye, not even Amy Clark.

"I don't think that's what I heard," Martha said, picking up another card. "It doesn't sound like something Ethel would say."

"None of this matters," Ethel said, laying out her cards. "What matters is that we have an opportunity to move forward on a better foot. Four of a kind. I take it I've won this round as well, ladies?"

"Royal flush." Dot laid her cards on the table and scraped the coins towards her. "And for your information, *I* am the woman who started another group. I'm somebody, and I have a respectable team, including a newspaper editor. Amy's in it, too, so you can count her out of your half-baked revival."

Dot scooped her winnings into her handbag, counting at least twenty individual shiny pound coins amongst the more minor change.

"Amy, are you coming?"

Amy hesitated, but she folded and followed Dot to the door.

"Thanks for all you said." Dot was barely able to conceal her grin. "You've given us a lot to investigate."

"What on Earth are you talking about?" Ethel demanded, meeting her eye again.

"Penelope's murder," she said, pushing up her curls. "Our as-yet-unnamed group is looking into the murder."

"Neighbourhood watch groups don't solve *murders!*" Ethel laughed. "You *silly* woman."

The rest followed like nervous hyenas.

"Mine does." Dot ripped open the front door. "And you've just put yourself at the top of my list of suspects."

The gaggle of women went on cackling, but Dot could barely hear them over the theory boiling in her mind. Julia's joke about Dot being behind the murder to start a rival group. Still, the theory wasn't so preposterous when attached to Ethel.

"That woman is power-mad," Dot said as they hurriedly walked away from Ethel's cottage. "Did you see how they ignored their ears and bent around her delusion just to please her? It was insane! Why didn't you back me up?"

"Oh, I, erm . . ." Amy scratched at her hair. "I'm sorry, Dot. I panicked. Ethel scares me."

"Scares you?" Dot cried. "Grow a backbone, woman. She's a charlatan *and* a mediocre poker player. But no matter. That went much better."

"Better than what?"

"No need to dwell on the failings of the investigation," Dot said. "A successful interview has just been conducted, and we have some important details to add to our board."

"Right then." Amy stopped, and Dot realised they'd reached the corner of her street. "You'll be wanting to get back to that. I'll see you at the meeting tomorrow?"

"Yes." Dot clutched the strap of her bag in both fists. "Unless you wanted to come back for another scone?"

Amy's face lit up, and they continued together. Though Dot hadn't previously given Amy much of her time, and Amy had lost her ability to speak when Dot needed back up, at least she'd been loyal enough to follow.

"I'm sorry about that," Dot said as they walked through the village. "You might need to find a new bridge club."

"It's alright. I was going to quit anyway. I always lost money."

"We'll show them, Amy," Dot said, looping her arm through the organist's, scratchy pink cardigan. "Just you watch. We need to discover what this secret agenda is. It's the key to all of this, I know it."

## 5

_T_he pleasant spring weather continued into the next day, prompting Julia to stow a picnic basket in the bottom of Olivia's pram before leaving the cottage. The graveyard hadn't been her intended location to eat scones, but it was as good a place as any.

"I should have brought flowers," Julia said aloud, pulling back the plastic of the now-crinkled bouquet she'd left on Mother's Day.

Barker licked cream and jam from his lips as he set his scone on his plate. Dot and Percy had replaced Katie and Brian for the previous night's scone production factory line at the cottage. Under Julia's guidance, most of the new batch had turned out just as well as the first when forgetting the burnt tray that had gone straight into the bin.

"Someone's been here recently," he said, turning over the card attached to the fresh-ish red roses leaning against the stone. Setting his reading glasses on the end of his nose, his lips pricked into a smile as he traced the words. "'Still thinking of you, Pearlie.' They didn't leave a name, but I recognise the handwriting."

Julia didn't need to hear a name or ask who the handwriting belonged to. Only her father had ever referred to her mother, Pearl, as 'Pearlie'.

"If I die, will you still come to visit my grave decades later?" Julia asked, pulling Olivia back from belly-crawling off the edge of the blanket.

"You're not allowed to die before me," he said through a mouthful of jam and cream. "And thanks. I was starting to forget how morbid this place was until you said that."

Julia scanned the graveyard as she finished assembling her scone, but she didn't pick up on any morbid energy. The cemetery had well-tended grass; shade from the early afternoon sun thanks to Howarth Forest; and a soundtrack of bright, bubbly birdsong. In the dead of winter, perhaps she'd understand. On such a lovely day, the place was as alive as the green or Mulberry Lane, and they weren't the only picnickers, either.

While most seemed to be visiting relatives they'd come to terms with having lost, across the graveyard, nearer the imposing shadow of the church, fresh grief and raw pain hung in the air.

Julia couldn't see the skinny lad's face under the shadow of his black peaked cap, but his shuddering shoulders betrayed his stifled sobs. When she wondered if her mere observation might be an intrusion, the young man crouched. His black outfit blended into the shadows, and the staggered rows of stone hid him well.

For the best.

Julia found it challenging to look away from such pain. Not to stare. She could easily recall similar pain from her life, and it triggered her instinct to help, stranger or not.

"Wasn't Penelope found over there?" Julia asked before biting into her scone.

Barker smiled wryly as he dabbed at the corners of his mouth. Craning his neck, he followed Julia's gaze to the rows nearest the back of the church. He nodded.

The boy reappeared, kissed his fingers, and pressed them against the stone before walking off with his chin tucked into his chest. Rather than heading to the exit as most people would have done after a visit, he went towards the village hall.

"I had a feeling that's why you wanted to come here."

"Olivia and I come here all the time," Julia protested, even as an arched brow joined Barker's smile. "Okay, so *perhaps* I was curious."

"Perhaps?" Aided by the stone, Barker pulled himself upright and scooped up Olivia before she could attempt another great wriggle for freedom. "Knowing this village, I'm surprised people aren't forming an orderly queue to see the place where Penelope Newton died."

After finishing the chocolate orange scone, which wasn't quite as tasty as the ones Katie made, Julia packed up the pram. She touched the cold stone and promised she'd bring flowers the next time.

"Gerald Martin," Barker stated when Julia caught up to him and Olivia with the empty pram. "1912–1952."

Despite the length of time since Gerald's death, a fresh sea of flowers lay at his headstone. Julia wondered if any had been laid for the plot's original tenant. With one hand on the pram's handle for balance, she pulled back the tag of the top bouquet, one of the simpler bunches, comprising of pink and white carnations.

"'You were right'," she read aloud, showing Barker the sloppy handwriting. "That's all it says. No name. What do you think that means?"

"Maybe she had a bet with a friend over who would die first?" Barker suggested, glancing in the direction the lad had gone. "Do you think they're from that guy?"

"I couldn't see if he had any in his hands."

Julia put the tag back and ran her fingers along the engraved dates. Gerald Martin was only forty when he died, the same age Julia was now. She felt nowhere near ready to die, but she doubted Penelope, though thirty years her senior, had either.

"Mining accident," Barker explained as he placed Olivia in her pram. "Christie dug into the guy's background looking for connections to Penelope or anyone else in her group, but he seems to be unrelated. He was an only child who never had children."

As she passed Olivia her favourite rattle, Julia couldn't look away from the headstone. Decades of rain had darkened it, and moss had crept up through the grass as though trying to reclaim the material. No cracks or blood remained behind to attest to Penelope's fate, but she hadn't expected any. The crime scene cleaners were always meticulous. If not for the flowers and the grass being more trampled here than anywhere else, she might have walked past without knowing this was the spot where the horrific event had happened only nights earlier.

"If this headstone doesn't mean anything," she mused, eyes darting from picnicker to picnicker dotted amongst the neat stone rows, "why kill someone here? It's so open."

"According to Christie, her phone records show that a withheld number called approximately half an hour before the estimated time of death." He paused, acknowledging a woman with a nod as a giant husky bounding forward on a short rope lead dragged her past. "They're trying to trace it. From the camera footage they've stitched together, it looks like Penelope came straight here. I think it's safe to assume the phone call is what brought her here."

"But by who, and why?" Julia stepped back and looked around the graveyard. "Presumably someone she knew if she came here voluntarily?"

"Very good."

"I'm just thinking about where we are." She stepped back and tilted her head to look up at the church. "Why do people come to graveyards?"

"To mourn the dead," he replied when she paused. "Go on; I'm intrigued."

Julia gathered her thoughts as Olivia's rattle-shaking gave way to a nap, right on schedule.

"People come to mourn during the day," she said, tucking a blanket around her sleeping daughter. "At night, it's still a big, empty, open space with no camera coverage. Aside from dog walkers and maybe kids hanging around, I can't imagine many other reasons to come here."

"So, you're suggesting Penelope might have met someone here because she was scared of them and wanted to feel safe while still having some privacy?"

"Maybe." Julia shrugged. It had made more sense in the shower, with a brain still muddled by early morning sleepiness. "Or the killer chose this place knowing it would be empty." She shook her head. "Although, there's something about smashing the head on the stone." She acted out a simplified version of what she imagined the move would have entailed. "This doesn't strike me as a particularly premeditated method of killing someone, which lends some credit to my gran's theory that one of Peridale's Eyes did it. Penelope stormed out of their final meeting. Maybe she thought she was meeting someone here to resolve whatever caused the bust-up?"

"I'd say it was resolved, alright."

"We still don't know what that argument was about."

"The way Christie was talking on the phone this morning, you might not have to wait much longer for an answer," he said, lowering his voice despite the nearest person being several rows away. "Your gran isn't the only one sniffing around Peridale's Eyes. Christie swears he's on the brink of getting a confession out of one of them. Wouldn't say who. Sounds like they're all co-operating, and he wants to keep it that way." He cleared his throat and, louder, said, "But you've made a good point. It could go some way as to explaining *why* the graveyard."

"And the forest," she said, nodding to the edge of the treeline. "An easy getaway, whether or not it was a premeditated murder."

Barker smiled from ear to ear. When he didn't speak, she looked around to see what she'd missed.

"What?"

"Nothing." He shook his head. "It's just nice to see this side of you again. It's been a while." He hitched up his sleeve to check his watch. "I should get going. I said I'd meet Christie at the café for a catch up, amongst other things."

Julia opened her handbag to hunt for her phone; she was surprised her gran hadn't yet called to remind her of their meeting today.

"Other things?"

"Your father and Katie's buyer," he said. "I wanted to verify a few details, and it's been a while since he gave me any divorce updates. Lost something?"

"My phone." She patted down her pockets. "Did I leave it at the cottage?"

"You took a picture of Olivia when we first sat down," he reminded her. "I can go and get it for you."

"No, it's okay." Shielding her eyes from the sun, Julia looked back to her mother's grave. "It's not far."

While Barker pushed the pram around the side of the church to wait by the gates, Julia weaved through the headstones to the familiar location of her mother's headstone. The sun's reflection beamed off the glossy glass screen of her phone, half-tucked under the crinkled flowers.

The phone reacted to her touch, lighting up to show the picture she'd snapped. Olivia's gummy grin beamed at the camera, still toothless. According to the midwife during her last weigh-in appointment, the first tooth could come in any time now. Julia hadn't expected to be the mother who took pictures of her child several times a day, but Olivia did cute things far too often not to capture them. She forwarded the picture to Jessie, who immediately replied with a yellow face with hearts for eyes.

"*King!*" a woman's voice cried from within the forest. "Get over here right now! Don't make me chase after you!"

Four headstones down, the husky that had passed them earlier bounded out of his owner's grasp with a stretched grin and a full mouth. He circled several graves, and he was big enough that his salt and pepper fur grazed the tops of the headstones. He dropped his prize and flattened himself to the ground.

"King . . ." The woman's warning caused him to bounce up and down as she emerged from the trees, her knitted rainbow hat making her hard to miss. "This isn't a game."

King obviously disagreed. He nuzzled his treasure, and despite seeming almost as tall as Julia's vintage car, his steps were light. His owner waved half a frayed lead at him; the other half trailed from his collar.

Julia almost left then, armed with the story of a dog being adorable that she could tell her gran to stop Dot thinking she hated the species, but King's prize grabbed her attention. Both owner and dog looked up at her with very different eyes. She couldn't quite make out the woman's, but King's were brilliant white lined in black, with tiny pupils.

Nothing like Lady and Bruce's eyes.

Everything like the colouring of the dampened shoe between his paws.

"Second one this month," the woman said, brandishing the piece of rope. "They're supposed to be for horses. I love the big teddy bear to pieces, but I'm starting to think I may have overcommitted to—"

"Maybe don't touch that shoe," Julia interrupted as the woman reached out. "Unless it's yours?"

"I think he found it in Howarth House," she said, frowning at Julia as she changed direction and curled her fingers into King's thick leather collar.

While the woman attempted to connect the two halves of the lead with a knot, King flopped onto his side and let out a soft howl. As cute as he was, Julia's gaze turned towards the forest. The fresh spring leaves on the dense trees limited visibility beyond the very edge.

A twig snapped under Julia's foot.

She hadn't realised she'd stepped forward.

Whether from memory or the house being so big, Julia could just about make out the house's outline, and it was drawing her in.

"Did you find it?"

Barker's voice pierced through the spell, breaking it, and she retreated from the forest as he approached with the pram. The woman had her rope tied together. However, she was staring at Julia with all the suspiciousness she likely deserved at that moment. She tugged on King's lead, and he dragged her back into the forest.

"Is that what I think it is?"

"The elusive other shoe."

Barker stared up at the unbroken blue above.

"It didn't fall from the sky," she said, nodding towards the trees. "According to King's owner, it was in Howarth House. Could it be a coincidence?"

Though the white trainer with black piping was generic, it matched the scruffiness of the one Barker had found on the night of Leah's break-in; the only difference was a coating of mud.

"Probably isn't. Let's be real." Barker let go of the pram, squinting towards the treeline. He stepped forward, looking down as he snapped the two halves of Julia's twig into quarters. "I'll have a look. Wait here."

By the time Barker got to the edge of the forest, Julia was already trundling along behind with the pram. Not only were there walking trails and plenty of people using them, but it was broad daylight in a busy graveyard.

If Barker noticed the sound of the pram's wheels crunching through the twigs and undergrowth, he didn't look back to confirm it. He only stared at the house as it came into focus, like it was pulling at him the way she'd felt only moments before.

The forest floor gave way to an actual stone path, where a group of kids were playing house in a hollow tree stump. She passed two stone posts for a gate belonging to a wall that had long since gone.

When Julia was a little girl, people teased of a

witch who roamed the woods, with many saying the abandoned house was her evil lair. The late Victorian-era house wasn't as old as Wellington Manor, and nowhere near as grand, but disrepair had aged its gothic frontage by centuries. It looked like a light breeze might make it crumble.

"I can't believe someone just left this place to the elements," Barker said, his first acknowledgement of Julia's presence since entering the forest. "How long has it been like this?"

"As long as I can remember."

"Then I imagine the structure is barely holding up." He stopped caressing the window frame and climbed through the hole where glass would have once been. "Stay here. And actually stay this time."

Julia was more than happy to oblige, though she'd prefer if Barker's delivery didn't sound so much like Dot's when commanding the dogs. As much as she appreciated the architecture, she preferred her homes with windows and without vines and weeds growing from every crevice.

As unsettled as the possibility of the shoe coming from the house left her, she wasn't scared of the building or the surrounding forest. It had been years since she believed in witches, and it was hard to be frightened when she kept catching the rainbow hat of King's owner out of the corner of her eye.

"It's clear up here," Barker called through a smashed hole in a window above Julia. "There's still some furniture in here. I'm shocked your dad hasn't scoured the place. I'll check the other side."

Julia pushed past the blocked-off front door and circled the house, checking the windows that weren't boarded. The rooms were near bare, the ceilings exposed, and the plaster walls crumbling. If any furniture remained downstairs, it had long since been abandoned.

At the back, a low wall had survived to fence in a small patch of the woods, though it wasn't difficult to imagine the wild greenery once belonging to a garden or vegetable patch. She reached for the gate, which, though nearly rotten, had also survived, but froze when something shiny in the undergrowth caught her eye.

A needle attached to a syringe.

"Bingo!" Barker called through another smashed window at the back, lifting a crinkled plastic bag for her to see. "Call Christie and tell him I've found Leah's Blu-Ray player."

**6**
_____

The drive to the nearby village of Tetbury took at least thirty minutes. And only in low traffic, when the lights played along, and no tractors or lost lorries kept movement to a crawl.

Twenty-two minutes after hanging up the phone, Leah burst into the café, despite having just been in Tetbury for her bride's dress fitting. After a shared glance, she and Julia retreated to the kitchen to speak far from the café's always-listening ears.

"They've found him?" Leah asked, breathless.

"I said we found his other shoe."

"But in his hideout?" Leah chomped on her fingernails. "You said he's been hiding in Howarth House."

"I said he *might* have been."

Julia guided Leah around the stainless-steel island and settled her on a stool. The stock boxes now took up the counter against the wall. Even with everything they'd already used for the scone marathon, many boxes remained. As though on cue, Katie appeared with a latte and set it in front of Leah, who looked as though she wished it were another chilled glass of wine.

"I can't sleep," she whispered when Olivia was their only audience. "Even if Johnny's ankle cast wasn't whacking me in that tiny bed of his, I still wouldn't be able to shake the thought of someone in my house . . . It's too close to everything that happened when I first came back."

Julia had to admire Leah's ability to refer to the ordeal of being taken from her home by old enemies and tied up in a basement for several days as 'everything that happened', but whatever helped her cope.

"I understand why it reminds you of that," Julia said, resting her hand on Leah's trembling fingers, "but this is different."

"And if I'd been home?" Leah slurped the latte. "I *should* have been home."

"Then the light would have scared them off, and it would have been someone else. There's already been another, according to Peridale Chat."

"But now that they know where he's lying low, they'll catch him, won't they?"

"I hope so," Julia said as positively as she could. "Let's just wait to see what the police find."

Leah stared hopefully at Julia, the creasing concealer under her eyes barely enough to lighten the dark shadows. Julia wouldn't have noticed, but Leah always looked so bright-eyed and bushy-tailed; she really must not have been sleeping well.

"I tried to call your gran this afternoon," Leah said after a calming breath, clearly ready to steer the conversation in other direction. "When I told her who it was, she asked 'Leah who?'"

"Unbelievable. She's known you since you were a kid." Julia glanced at Olivia, sound asleep in her pram, though the twitching brow and puckering lips warned she wouldn't remain that way for much longer. "I'm guessing it wasn't a social call?"

"I wanted to see if she had anything for me to do before the meeting tonight." Julia smiled at this reminder of Leah's teacher's pet days at school. "Probably for the best that she fobbed me off. I'll need to give my bride the biggest bunch of flowers I can fit in my car. I've never left somewhere quicker. Just the thought that this might be knocked on the head almost sent me to sleep . . ." Frowning, she sipped her latte and added, "Bad choice of words, considering."

"How's the dress look?"

"It's all neck, sleeves, and ruffles," she said with a shudder, holding her hands out wide around her hips, "but I smile and pretend I don't hate it because they have more money than sense. I can only do so much. When I plan *my* wedding, it'll be—"

Leah's brief levity vanished in a wobble of her lips. As she stared up at the ceiling lights with glassy eyes, it was clear she was choking back tears.

"Oh, no." Julia retrieved the kitchen roll and ripped off a sheet for Leah. "That can't be good."

"It's just—"

"*Julia!*" Katie pushed through the beads, red-faced and wide-eyed. "You'll never guess what I *just* overheard about your gran. She—" Katie stopped with a squeak when she noticed Leah. "Oh, I'm sorry. This is a bad time."

"No, no." Leah buried the threat of tears behind a smile. "I'm just overwhelmed. What did you hear?"

Leah pulled a compact from her bag – much emptier than Julia's as of late – and attempted to pat out her undereye with some powder. Sighing, she snapped it shut and tossed it back, ready for Katie's attention to divert back to them after she watched some customers leave.

"Okay, they've gone," she said as the bell above the door jingled behind her. "Two women from some bridge club? They didn't mention your gran by name, but . . . Well, I'll let you decide. Apparently, some friend of Amy Clark's gate-crashed their last meeting, started an argument with Ethel, cheated her out of her winnings, threw a cup of tea in her face, and said she had started a rival group to *frame* Ethel for Penelope's murder."

"Some of that sounds like my gran," Julia said, unsure if she should laugh or cry. "*Most* sounds like the overactive imaginations in the gossip network."

"That's not the weirdest part," Katie said, folding her arms and popping one hip. "I know they're useful, but who'd want to join a club for bridges?"

In the ensuing silence, Julia and Leah shared a glance, but Katie's laughter at her joke didn't come.

"Not brid*ges*," Julia said, biting into her lip to stop a reactionary chuckle. "Bridge. It's a card game."

Katie's tanned face turned a shade so red it almost looked purple. Clenching her eyes, she winced. The bell above the door rang again and she spun into the café with a rattle of beads.

"Saved by the bell," said Leah, holding back a laugh. "Bless her. You forget she's our age."

"And my step-mother."

"Now *that* I can't wrap my head around."

"And Olivia's step-grandmother."

"Okay, now I'm just dizzy."

"I've found it's best not to try. I take Katie as she comes."

"Honestly? When I first moved back, I never imagined I'd like her." Leah glanced through the beads. "But she's alright, isn't she? She puts it all out there, and she still has an innocence about her." Leah shook her head. "I thought Amy was supposed to be interviewing Ethel?"

"You know my gran," Julia said with a sigh. "She can't help getting involved. Either way, it sounds like she's working her way through the suspects. Shilpa overheard that something similar happened with Penelope's husband after a choir rehearsal."

"Maybe we should say something to her?"

"How do you think that will go?"

"Good point." Leah's fingers drummed the countertop. "I'm starting to think this group wasn't such a good idea."

"Starting?" Julia winked. "We're not going to solve anything by harassing suspects when we still know so little about who Penelope *was*. Other than the busybody obsessed with where I parked my car."

"Speaking of Penelope," Leah said, clicking her fingers together. "When I couldn't sleep last night, I was thinking around in circles, and she came to mind. Is there any chance she's related to Melinda Newton?"

"Now there's a name I haven't heard in a while."

Julia blew her lips as the years melted away in her mind. "Do you remember the time she burnt down half the girls' bathrooms because she was smoking in there?"

"Mrs Benson caught her, so she stuck it in the toilet roll holder."

They both laughed. Nobody had resented Melinda for her mistake. The school had given everybody the rest of the day off, and in the corridors, Melinda was a legend that lingered at least until Sue's turn at the school a few years later.

"I wonder where she is now."

Leah's face dropped, and Julia knew the answer. A few years ago, such a face would have shocked her, but Gerald Martin wasn't the only forty-year-old in the graveyard. She'd seen more classmates in the newspaper's obituaries over the last two years than ever before, though she hadn't caught Melinda Newton's name.

"How did it happen?"

"No idea," she said. "I didn't know either until this morning. I mentioned that I'd thought about her, and Johnny told me. Said it happened a while ago. Do you think there's a connection to Penelope? Or Desmond, whoever he is?"

"It could be a coincidence," Julia said for the second time that day. "If it's not, it could help us get to know Penelope better. A daughter? Or a sister? I think you've just given yourself a mission to get on with after you deliver those flowers. Something to take your mind off . . ."

Julia's words fell away as Barker strolled in through the back door. She looked around him into the yard behind the café, but he was alone.

"Right," he began, rubbing his hands together, "there's good news and bad news."

"Just tell us, Barker," Leah urged, hand on stomach. "I feel sick."

"It looks like he was there." He closed the door behind him and leaned against the island. "And I found a bag of stuff that we think might be yours. No laptop, but he's probably already sold it. There's been reports of someone trying to flog electronics at Fern Moore."

"I don't care about the laptop," she said. "Please tell me that isn't *all* the good news?"

"He wasn't there." Barker offered an apologetic smile. "And only *your* things seemed to be present. The lack of any other items reported stolen makes us think it was only a temporary hiding place for that night. Looking at a map, if he hit the angle right, there's a good chance he ran directly there through the fields."

"Explains the mud," said Julia. "I imagine his sock was worse. If he was even wearing socks."

"He's probably used that place before, and he left stuff there, so he might come back," he said, leaning in closer. "The police will keep an eye on it. They swept the forest at first light the morning after Penelope's murder, so that might have scared him off for good, though."

"So, he's still out there? And could be anywhere?" Julia asked. "What more do we have now that we know where he ran to?"

"A second shoe?"

"I shouldn't have got my hopes up." Leah finished her latte. "I don't think I'll rest until he's caught."

"The police are doing everything they can."

"When does that mean anything?" Leah jumped off the stool and flung her handbag over her shoulder. "Thanks for doing something at least, Barker."

Leah kissed Julia on the cheek and left through the back door. Julia had been hoping to discover what had nearly driven Leah to tears. She had a feeling that was no small part of why Leah's exit had been so hasty. Julia sighed. There was always the meeting later.

"What an afternoon," Barker said, running his hand across his stubbly jaw. "For a second there, I thought we had him. I was sure he'd be hiding in one of the rooms. That place is huge. It's gorgeous. I can't believe it's been left there to fall to pieces like that."

"Sums up how this investigation is going," Julia said. "Well, not gorgeous, but I wouldn't use that word for the house, either. Are you still meeting Christie?"

"Maybe later."

"Can you have Olivia for fifteen minutes?" Julia sniffed into the pram. "Smells like she'll need changing when she wakes up."

"You know you don't even need to ask." He kissed her, his thumb rubbing her shoulder. "Fifty-fifty, remember. I meant what I said earlier. It's nice to see this side of you again."

"One interview," she affirmed, stroking Olivia's soft cheek. "It's about time to gather some useful information. Won't be too long."

After packing up a box with one of each flavour scone and enough cream and jam, she tied her fanciest ribbon yet and left the quiet café. She'd intended to walk straight to Mulberry Lane, but Shilpa waved her over as she passed the post office next door.

"Your gran is no different than Penelope," she said, lifting a bucket filled with familiar pink and white flowers. "I just told her someone had stolen a bunch of these, and she didn't even stop to talk about what we could do. What's the point in a neighbourhood watch if it's not watching the neighbourhood?"

After promising to talk to her gran about her priorities, Julia left Shilpa to the business of carrying the flowers back inside. Lingering on the corner, Julia looked at the church. She'd seen identical pink and white flowers on Gerald Martin's grave with that sloppily written message on the tag.

'You were right.'

When he'd crouched down, had the young man been leaving stolen flowers? Had he been reading a tag as Julia had done after him? Or had he been writing one? She supposed those flowers could have been left at any time, but they were fresh, and the messy handwriting had the look of youth to it. If that boy had stolen and left them, what had Penelope been right about?

More importantly, would discovering the answer to any of these questions get her any closer to a concrete answer about what happened to Penelope?

Rounding the corner onto Mulberry Lane, she felt as though she were clutching at straws. Hopefully after this outing, she'd have something more useful to report at the meeting.

She passed the burnt-out shell of Trotter's Books, still unsold after Julia's eventful turn in a book club in the lead up to Christmas. Heavily pregnant, she'd found herself sucked into the middle of a mess so big that she'd spent the following months certain she'd never follow another trail again.

The colour of coffee beans, Vicky's Van blended into the shadow of one of the large trees at the bottom of the winding street ahead of Julia's father's antique's barn. Not that it was easy to miss. The queue of eight made sure of that.

Tacking onto the back, Julia made it nine.

While she waited, she wondered if this new offering was impacting her café. She'd never been able to gauge how many shoppers fell within her target demographic. Vicky's Van was undoubtedly busy, but Julia didn't recognise many of the people waiting their turn. Tourists and out-of-village shoppers, no doubt. Plenty of those made their way to her café. Grateful for them though she was, she'd always got the impression the locals were the ones keeping everything afloat.

Besides, she offered something Vicky Van's didn't, beyond homemade cakes and bulk discounts on scones: a place to sit, and more importantly, talk.

People really seemed to like Vicky too. Along with being a decade younger than Penelope, Vicky's personality was different from the deceased woman's in every way. After Julia's scouting mission when the van first popped up, Katie had asked what Vicky was like, and the word 'bubbly' had been the best descriptor.

The line moved quickly, as most people only opted for a drink and a quick chat. The cakes in the display case did look tempting at first glance, but Julia didn't know how much moisture could be in the sponges and brownies behind their plastic wrappers. At least Vicky wasn't trying to pass them off as her own.

"Julia." Vicky's face lit up when she shuffled to the front of the queue. "It's really good to see you again. I was in your café just the other day, as it happens."

"You were?" Julia swallowed the upwelling of guilt for pondering if Vicky's presence was affecting her bottom line. "I wish I could say I was just here for a friendly chat, but from one service woman to another, I'll be honest and tell you that I'm here on neighbourhood watch business." She held up the scones. "I did bring a bribe, though. Freshly baked last night."

Whether Vicky had been planning to take a fifteen-minute break, Julia didn't know, but she appreciated when Vicky slid down the shutter after serving the queue that had formed after Julia. She put a 'Be Right Back!' sign next to the sugar sachets before motioning for Julia to join her around the back of the van. It wasn't a kitchen, but the area between the van and the thick oak tree created a lovely shaded place to take a break, weather permitting.

"Is coffee alright?" Vicky passed her a polystyrene cup.

"Thank you."

After settling on two upturned plastic crates, Vicky unpacked a scone onto her lap and put the three ingredients together. She took a bite, and her lids fluttered before she immediately licked her lips. Julia sipped the coffee and tried to hold in her cough. It was somehow burnt and too weak all at once, but she smiled all the same.

"I've been wondering where I could get my hands on these," Vicky said through a mouthful. "I've seen people carrying them up and down the street all week."

From the numbers alone, Julia knew the scones were flying off the shelves, but since she wasn't working in the café, she hadn't witnessed them out in the wild. She'd eaten more than her fair share; the perks of café ownership.

"I should have known they'd be yours," said Vicky after another bite. "I've always enjoyed your baking."

"And here I thought it was my job to flatter you."

"It's true." Vicky laughed. "I admired your café a lot. Part of the reason I started this van, actually. I always liked the idea, and one day, I just thought, why not? And here I am. You've been so nice about it, too. Plenty to go around, isn't there?"

Julia nodded. She'd experienced suffocating competition in the form of a chain coffee shop once before, but that had been, albeit briefly, on the other side of the green and stealing her customers out from under her nose. Before it had closed, she'd wondered if she could continue, and she'd been nowhere near that since Vicky's Van parked up.

As long as Vicky didn't permanently move the van to the green.

"So, what's going on?" Vicky asked after devouring her first scone. "I haven't been keeping up with everything. I imagine things have fallen apart a bit since Penelope died."

"You could say that."

"Sounds like I got out at the right time."

"Then what you just said makes more sense." Julia laughed. "I haven't joined that group. It's a new group. It's a long story, but we've somehow found ourselves trying to solve Penelope's murder."

"Do neighbourhood watch groups do that?"

"My gran's does."

"Well, I'm sorry I can't help you there," Vicky said with a shrug. "I left weeks ago. Haven't been to any meetings. I've been kept out of the loop."

"So, you have no idea what they were all arguing

about in the village hall before Penelope's death?"

Tight-lipped as she cut open another scone, Vicky shook her head. A dead end. Of all the people to be interviewed, she'd landed the suspect who wasn't even part of the group anymore. Technically, she'd volunteered on account of vaguely knowing Vicky, but only because she was part of the Peridale's Eyes.

"Were you close to Penelope?" she asked, sensing an opportunity to get to know the victim better.

"Oh, we were friends," she said, with a nod. "For years, until . . . Well, I suppose we were always friends. We never really had a falling out, as such, but it's just different when you're no longer in the group that brought you together so often."

A cold prickle tinged her warm voice.

"And you left to focus on this?"

"I quickly realised I couldn't do both." Vicky slapped the metal van. "There were no hard feelings or anything."

Julia hadn't asked or suggested there were.

"What was Penelope like?" Julia asked, not trying to focus too hard on Vicky's face. "I was only ever on her receiving end. I didn't know much about the real woman."

Vicky took her time chewing, her distant gaze fixed somewhere on the trunk of the tree.

"She used to be an accountant," Vicky began,

returning the rest of the second scone to the box. "She retired a little later than I want to, and then jumped right in and started Peridale's Eyes. She was really passionate about it."

"Passionate is one word for it."

"I've been around since the first meeting," Vicky said, gaze once again distant. "We became quite friendly at water aerobics, and she asked me to join. I didn't have a business then. Worked at the hospital. Hardly exciting, is it? And the neighbourhood watch was exciting . . . at first. But it changed."

"Changed how?"

"It got really serious," Vicky whispered, clasping her fingers around her knee and glancing around as if they might somehow be overheard. "Penelope was always the leader, but she wasn't controlling. And then one day, she started treating it like a job. I thought she'd get bored, but she tightened her grip. She became obsessed with the strangest things. Like your parking, and people's garden fences being two inches out of property lines. I didn't enjoy all of that so much. We used to just . . . keep an eye on things. Lost cats, people in need, that sort of thing. Friendly neighbourhood stuff."

"And none of that made you want to leave before the coffee van?"

Vicky's gaze shifted from the tree to Julia. The

alertness in her expression while she said nothing made Julia shift on the plastic crate. Everything Vicky said would have been fine information to take back to her gran. It would have ticked a box that technically shouldn't have been a box to begin with. But what Julia saw in Vicky's demeanour conflicted with what she was hearing.

Could it be grief?

The lines around Vicky's eyes softened as she snapped back to bubbly attention.

"We were friends," she said with a shrug, checking her phone. "I tried to stand by her, but she didn't always make it easy. Listen, I need to get back. I have an hour of good trade left."

"Absolutely." Julia stood up with the coffee she'd barely touched. "I've already taken enough of your time. I appreciate it."

"Any time."

"There's one more thing," she said, following Vicky to the door at the side of the van. "I saw a slender young man leaving flowers at Penelope's – Well, it's not hers. Where she was . . . struck. I *think* I saw him laying flowers, at least. Any idea who that could be?"

"Slender?" Vicky shook her head. "Not off the top of my head, no. There's Desmond and Gus, but only one is slender and neither are young."

"Desmond?"

"You know Des?"

"No, but it seems you do. He's in the group, isn't he?"

Vicky nodded and stepped into the van. A line was already forming.

"Penelope's first husband."

"So, he wasn't in the group?"

"I know how it looks," Vicky said, lifting the shutter. "First husband and second husband in the same group? But they all got along fine. I think Des and Penelope ended on good terms. If you want to talk to him, he's just started part time at the library."

Carrying the coffee, Julia walked halfway back up the street before turning to look over her shoulder. Though her long-distance vision wasn't the best, she was sure Vicky was watching her. She turned to the shop she'd lingered outside of to disguise it by browsing, but of course she'd chosen to stop outside Trotter's Books boarded up window.

A distraction appeared as her father crossed the street towards her with a giddy spring in his step. He waved.

"Up to trouble?" he asked, pulling her into a bigger hug than usual. "Of course you are."

"Something like that. Little early for closing the antique shop, isn't it?

"I have an important meeting." He tugged at his crisp white collar and ran his fingers through his thick, blown-back hair. "I might as well tell you. I don't know how we've been keeping it secret for so long, but you know what Katie is like."

Brian paused to build tension, giving Julia just enough time to invent a genuine reaction to the second-hand news.

"We've had an offer on the manor."

"Oh wow!" she cried, slapping his arm. "That's amazing news!"

"Katie already told you, didn't she?"

"That obvious?"

"It was the eyes." He peered at her face. "Your mum used to look the same whenever she was trying to get one over on me. Usually when she was planning my birthday parties."

Julia smiled, still touched by the flowers he'd left by her grave. She wanted to ask about the occasion, but the gesture of visiting and talking about her was enough; it hadn't always been so easy for him.

"Things are finally looking up!" He beamed through a toothy grin. "All our worries are about to be over. We'll have enough to pay off the debt, and maybe even—"

"Dad," she interjected, resting her palm on his soft cheek. "Promise me you won't rush into anything?"

"When have I ever?" He gave her another tight squeeze that lifted her slightly off the ground. "Don't worry about a thing. Everything is about to get a whole lot better. Brian South is coming back."

Before she could ask where he'd been, the Brian South she'd grown accustomed to as of late hurried up the lane. Julia hoped he heeded her warning. Though he hadn't started the sinkhole of debt at the manor, his attempts at secretly fixing it had only made things worse.

Following in her father's footsteps, she made her way to the top of the lane. She sipped the coffee out of habit, but it went straight into a bin when she rounded the corner.

Staring down at Vicky's logo printed on the side of the small cup, Julia couldn't shake the feeling she'd just been lied to.

*Kept me out of the loop.*

*No hard feelings.*

*I tried to stand by her.*

Good friends parting on good terms, Vicky had claimed, but Julia suspected another version of events was scribbled between the lines. Part of Peridale's Eyes Vicky might no longer have been, but she had still given Julia plenty to think about.

And now she knew where to find Desmond Newton.

# 7

*L*ater that evening, gravel crunched under Julia's feet as she paced in the shadow of Wellington Manor. She stuck the phone high towards the clear sky, though from what she could see on the screen, the sudden drop in video quality wasn't her doing.

"Go back to the window," she called, unsure if Jessie was receiving her. "Back to the . . . window . . . *window* . . . Can you even hear me?"

Jittery pixels formed and dragged around the vague shape of a face like something pulled from Picasso's nightmares. All at once, it snapped into high-definition focus, the signal-ghost chased from the machine.

"*Muuuuum*?" Jessie moaned, as though she'd been saying it on loop. "Can you hear me now?"

"Yes!" she said. "Stay right there."

Jessie curled up cross-legged by the large corner windows, and when she settled, the light balance adjusted. With it came Julia's first clear look at the view through the windows.

"You alright, Mum?" Jessie asked, pulling her knees up. "You look like you're about to start drooling or something."

"The view," she said, trying to peer past Jessie. "It's so flat I almost didn't know what I was looking at."

A glance over the edge of her own phone revealed the rolling Cotswolds hills in every direction. When she looked back at the screen, the camera had flipped to focus on the window, and Jessie gave her a sweeping panoramic view of the flat cityscape stretching as far as she could see.

"We're right by the water," she said, zooming in on water cutting through the city. "It's pretty swanky."

Jessie turned the camera back onto her face as she flopped into a soft-looking brown leather armchair. The video jittered, but only for a second.

Apparently, five months was all it took for a nineteen-year-old to shape an identity different in so many ways to the one Julia had hugged goodbye.

"New piercings?" Julia asked, moving in closer to

count the gold studs and rings glittering up Jessie's ears.

"Tragus in Amsterdam," she pulled at one. "These two studs in Paris." She flapped her lobes and flipped her hair away. She pulled her ear forward to show a black ring in the top of the other. "Got this one this morning. Hurts like hell, but it looks cool."

*Cool.*

Julia couldn't disagree with that.

Relaxed, too.

"You're going to run out of space before you've even left Europe."

Julia turned to the kitchen window, through which she could see Sue with Olivia, the twins, and Vinnie all on her own. She waved 'two minutes' with her fingers and turned away before the guilt dragged her back inside. She hadn't managed to get Jessie on a video call all week. Even with so little a difference in time zone, they were living such different lives . . . and on such different schedules.

"We're going east after the first six months," Jessie said, yawning, dragging down her skin to check her undereye bags in the camera. "Then we're looping right back around. Do I look tired?"

"You're a teenager, so yes."

"Not for much longer," she said, wiggling a finger

in her ear as though digging for something. "Birthday in two weeks."

"And you still haven't given me your address so I can send you something."

"Who knows where we'll be in two weeks." Jessie shrugged. "And you don't have to. It's not an important birthday."

Julia couldn't find the words to describe how important and life-changing the upcoming decade would be for Jessie, but it didn't matter. Julia wasn't sure anything she said would sink into her daughter's tired brain; she'd been yawning for most of the call.

"Went to an insane nightclub last night," Jessie said, looking through the window and off into the city. "Alfie knew the DJ and got us into VIP. Ended in a fight though."

"You didn't."

"You always assume the worst of me." Jessie rolled her eyes. "It was Alfie."

That wasn't any better. Julia was trusting Jessie's older brother, a seasoned traveller, to stop things like fights from happening, not to wade into them.

"Just make sure you're staying—"

Jessie's eyes darted over the top of the phone as what sounded like a door opened somewhere in the apartment. She smiled before looking down and appearing to realise she was still on camera.

"Love you," she whispered into the microphone. "Gotta go."

And just like that, the call ended, and Julia left Berlin and returned to Peridale. Most of the video calls ended in a hurry. Some featured Alfie, and others the friends Jessie was making along the way. Once, Jessie had called her, handed Julia to a baker in France, and a strange but entertaining twenty-minute conversation about baking techniques had followed. Most calls came at a civilised hour, but some didn't. Those had livened up the late-night feeds in the early days, back when they'd missed each other terribly.

Julia still missed Jessie terribly.

She could tell Jessie was having too much fun to remember to miss home these days. And Julia was glad of it. When Jessie had first gone away, she'd called all the time, full of nerves and sometimes tears. She'd kept up to date with things going on in Peridale through social media, and most of the time was more in tune with the local gossip than Julia, who spent those first few months in a home-shaped bubble with Barker and their newborn. Jessie had stopped bringing things up, which meant she'd stopped checking, and sometimes she didn't even ask. On those days, Julia knew Jessie was probably living her life to the fullest.

"That girl is going to come home with more holes

than a pin cushion," Julia said, joining Sue in the grand kitchen currently doubling as a makeshift nursery.

"Huh?"

Sue immediately passed Olivia to Julia so she could tend to the twins fighting over the same toy horse.

"Jessie's got more piercings," Julia explained, eyeing her sister as she let Olivia bounce excitedly against her. "I didn't mean to be so long. Kept losing signal."

"It's fine." Sue pulled a screaming Pearl away from a screaming Dottie. "It's not you. I've just had a lot going on lately."

The girls continued to skreich while Vinnie lay on his front, thumping on a tablet computer, unbothered. The twins' wailing set off Olivia, whose higher pitch was an almost unbearable addition to the orchestra of infant chaos.

Dottie, Pearl, and Vinnie would all turn three this year.

Time moved too quickly.

Julia clung tighter to Olivia as her daughter's empty cries petered out.

*They grow up too quickly.*

When Sue had calmed the girls and placated them with separate toys, she collapsed against the island, arms stretched out, and exhaled. Julia suspected that if a pillow were handy, her sister might have screamed into it before going straight to sleep.

"First of all, I apologise for being a rubbish big sister," Julia said, rubbing Sue's back. "Something's going on, and I should have noticed before it got to this point."

"*You've* had a lot going on." Sue looked up and the sight of Olivia seemed to soothe her. "She couldn't even hold her head up properly not that long ago. At least mine can feed themselves."

"I haven't seen *you* as much lately, though."

"I know." Sue rested her forehead against the marble. "And I feel rubbish about it."

"Then we both feel rubbish about not being there for each other. What do you need?"

"A break?" Sue heaved a laugh. "I've been working flat-out shifts back-to-back. Today's the only day I've had off this week, so I took the kids out of the house just to give Neil a break. I can't juggle it all."

"Especially when you're trying to juggle concrete blocks," Julia said, widening the soothing circles. "Until I had Olivia, I really had no idea how hard it could be, and that's with one. *And* that's before we get to your job."

"Before you say it again, I can't go part time." She ran her fingers through her hair. "We're more understaffed than ever. There just aren't enough new nurses coming up. I'm stretched to the limit, and I'm supposed to be happy with pay rises counted in pennies."

"You can't keep this up."

"I know," she moaned, "but I *have* to."

"Neil has a job."

"For now," she said, pushing herself upright. "The council have slashed funding for the library again. Nobody has any idea how close that place came to shutting for good. Neil begged to keep it open, reduced his shifts, took a pay cut, halved the opening hours, and has to rely on volunteers to staff the place."

Julia thought of Des.

"My kids aren't the only ones I feel like I'm missing out on, but what choice do I have right now? In two years, they'll be in school, and maybe then—"

"You can't think like that," Julia jumped in, her stern big sister voice coming out as she resettled Olivia at her waist. "Here and now, not two years in the future. There's always another option. We'll all chip in, and—"

"It's my career, Julia," Sue snapped in her equally familiar little sister defensive tone. "*Years* of my life. It's not that simple."

"I never said it was." Julia kissed Sue on the top of

her head. "And I'm here for you. Any time, any place, always."

"I know."

"But I'll keep reminding you anyway."

They hugged until the clink of stilettoes echoed through the entrance hall, and they pulled away and walked to the arch.

"Weirdly, I've missed that sound," said Sue. "Feels odd to be back here."

"You're telling me."

Standing under the plastic-wrapped chandelier, Julia looked across the entrance hall as Katie made her way along the landing. The sitting room was still empty, just as it had been on the night Julia had discovered she was pregnant while burglars roamed the manor. The burglary had turned out to be an elaborate last-ditch insurance-fraud claim misguidedly cooked up by Katie.

A year later, the burglary situation put Katie's misstep into perspective. Somehow, Julia didn't think the explanation behind what was going on with Penelope would have such a simple solution.

"I found them!" Katie squealed, teetering down the stairs in sky-scraper heels carrying a cardboard box barely contained against her chest. "Oh, thanks, Sue."

Katie handed over the box as Sue met her halfway

before moving a hand to the bannister to support her the rest of the way down.

"Found these in the attic too," she said, grimacing as she made it to the bottom step. "I can't believe I used to wear these every day."

"Used to?" Sue laughed. "When did you stop?"

"I haven't worn heels like these in years." As Katie dragged them off her feet, the pink shimmer coating sparkled in the early evening sunlight. "When I was pregnant, I quickly realised I had to let them go. What do I do with them?"

"Keep them," Julia suggested, following them into the kitchen. "A souvenir of a long-lost time."

"Good idea." Katie slammed the heels onto the marble island before going to check on Vinnie, who now stood by the patio doors, looking out onto the grounds. "Anyway, I can't believe you thought I still wore heels that high. Haven't you noticed I've been toning down my look?"

As Katie leaned down to wipe Vinnie's runny nose, her tight t-shirt rode up, down, and sideways, revealing skin at every angle.

"Wear what you want until you can't," Sue said, admiring the shoes on the counter. "Sorry if I ever gave you a hard time about any of it."

"Look at us." Katie returned to the island. "Not that

long ago, you couldn't stand to be in the same room as me, and now here we all are, having birthed the next generation of our family. You'd think we planned it."

"We've come so far." Julia toasted with her tea before tossing back the last cold mouthful. "Did you find what you were looking for?"

"I did." Katie grinned, and pulled the box in close. "I wanted to come back for *these* the second I realised I'd left them here. Thought it was about time. Who knows how much longer we'll have keys to this place?"

"What is it?"

Katie bit her lip, her grin growing.

"All my glamour modelling shoots," she said, hugging the box. "Do you want to see them?"

Sue and Julia looked at each other and, so perfectly timed it seemed rehearsed, said, "Absolutely."

Early in their relationship, Julia had to get comfortable seeing her 'step-mother' almost nude. What used to be Katie's master bedroom upstairs had been lined with blown-up photographs, leaving nowhere to look without a hint of something.

Seeing them up close now, all spread out on the island while the kids were in their little worlds, Julia's reaction was different.

"You were fearless," said Julia. "It looks like you always lived on holiday."

"The magazines would fly us out," she said, showing them a particularly brave one perched on the edge of a rock while waves crashed moodily behind her. "They were never five-star places, and it didn't seem fun at the time, but looking back, it actually was. It's not like I could have done it forever. I would have been too old for them ten years ago, and most of those magazines don't even exist anymore."

"It's a time capsule of you at your peak," said Sue, tilting her head at one picture, "in every position on every beach around the world."

"Mostly Europe."

"Mostly Europe," Sue continued. "And you looked phenomenal doing it."

"I did, didn't I?" Katie beamed. "I much prefer myself now, though. I was such an annoying brat back then."

Sue looked about to react the same way she'd done with the shoes, but Julia gave a subtle headshake. Sue let the inevitable 'Only back then?' slide.

"Sometimes I wonder if I went too big." Katie stood to the side and pushed her chest out. "I used to be completely flat. What do you girls think?"

Sue and Julia shared an uncertain look, though

the right words between not lying and not hurting Katie's feelings didn't come as easily as the previous response had done. Gravel crunched outside, bursting their bubble in a flash.

"Nobody should be here," Katie said, almost to herself.

Picture still in hand, Katie crossed to the window as a car pulled up next to hers and Sue's.

"Your sneaky father."

Katie marched into the entrance hall as car doors slammed outside.

"What do we do?" Sue whispered. "The island is full of naked pictures of Katie."

"She does own the house."

Not wanting to leave the kids alone but also not wanting to miss the showdown, Julia and Sue hovered by the kitchen arch. Posed perfectly in the centre of the space, one hip popped, the picture clutched in her hand while her wrist leaned against her hip, Katie looked powerful, even barefoot.

"*Brian*!" Katie cried, clapping her hands together when the door creaked open. "What a *wonderful* surprise. And you have Mr Jacobson with you. Of course, why wouldn't you?"

Sue and Julia exchanged more glances, but their eyes went right back to the action.

"K-Katie." Their father walked in, arms out. "I

didn't know you were here. I've just come to show Mr Jacobson around again and—"

The handsome, suited man sank back, looking for all the world as though he was about to make a run for it.

"Brian." Katie held a finger in the air. "You promised we'd do everything together. You know my feelings on *this*."

Julia and Sue's heads tilted, mirroring Mr Jacobson's. Though the picture was curled in Katie's palm, she was so well lit on the beach it was hard not to see . . . everything.

"You're absolutely right, baby." Brian swooped in, blocking the picture as their potential buyer's eyes nearly popped out of his skull. "Mr Jacobson, can we reconvene at a more convenient time?"

The man left with little fuss, no doubt glad to be away from the confrontation. Katie and Brian's voices hushed to frenzied whispers, so Julia and Sue left them alone.

Just as Julia was wondering if the extended silence meant they'd killed each other, Katie returned to the kitchen and stood where she had been before. She whipped her blonde curls over her shoulder as she smoothed the picture on the island.

"I had this in my hand the whole time, didn't I?" she asked, gathering the rest of the shots as though on autopilot. "The man trying to buy my house just saw me naked."

"Yeah," Julia said, resting a hand on her shoulder. "That's about the long and short of it."

"Look at it this way." Sue joined in at Katie's other side. "You said it yourself, you were in all the magazines. A man his age? There's a good chance he's already seen it."

Julia held her breath, braced for the argument that would have come in a past life. Instead, they laughed. They laughed until the kids joined in for the sake of laughing.

Brian's head popped around the arch and he approached with palms outstretched. Julia gave him a 'what did I tell you earlier?' arched brow and tight eye, and he replied with an 'I know, I know' nod.

"At least it was one of my favourites?" Brian said, going in for a kiss but getting only Katie's cheek.

"Okay." Sue pointed two fingers at their dad. "*That* made it weird."

Julia hadn't intended to stay at the manor for long, but when Dot called to say Evelyn had insisted they move their meeting to eight in the evening, they ordered a Chinese takeaway and ate around the island, something they'd never have done when living in the place. Everybody stayed until life kicked back in and they were pulled in their separate directions.

When Julia discovered Sue was going to the library to pick up Neil, her plan to be dropped off at her gran's to set Olivia up before the meeting changed.

Neil emerged from the building and locked up. He waved to the car before patting a man talking on a phone on the shoulder.

"Night, Des," said Neil as he walked away. "See you tomorrow."

Sensing her chance to finally get her one interview with a *current* member of Peridale's Eyes, Julia climbed out of the car. After a quick hello and goodbye with Neil, Julia popped up the pram and waved off her waiting sister.

Julia hung back while Des finished on the phone. He was of average height and build, around the same age as Penelope, and dressed just as a sensible librarian would. She couldn't make out who Desmond was talking to, but he didn't seem happy.

She approached once he hung up the phone. "Desmond?"

"*What*?" he snapped, whipping around to face Julia. "What do you want?"

Faced with his fury, all Julia could do was freeze and pull back the pram. The lurch pulled Desmond to his senses, and his rage blinked away to reveal an expression as warm and open as Percy's.

"Forgive me," he said in a voice devoid of its earlier boom. "I hope I didn't scare you, I—"

He reached out a hand, and Julia pulled further away.

"Serves me right," he said, bowing in retreat. "My wife died recently. *Ex*-wife, I mean. According to her *new* husband, I didn't know the woman at all, and never mind we were married for forty years to his four. He's planning her funeral all wrong, and I just have to sit here and—" He clenched his fists but dropped them just as quick. "Just one of those days."

Des hesitated as though listening back to everything he'd just said. One of the main questions Julia had cooked up on the drive over had already been answered.

*Did Des and Gus get on as well as Vicky claimed?*

It didn't seem that way.

"You approached me," he remembered. "You know my name."

"Yes," she said, finally stepping forward. "My name is Julia. I own the café in the village."

"Ah, yes. The woman with the vintage car."

She paused, expecting a car-related tirade like those of his ex-wife, but the attack didn't come.

"I hoped to find you here. I'd like to ask some questions about Penelope," she said. "But I can see it's a bad time."

"What kinds of questions?"

"I'm part of a new neighbourhood—"

"Are you with *her*?" he snapped, pointing sharply at the library. "That *crazy* woman?"

Julia gulped.

"C-crazy woman?"

"Tall lady," he said, indicating a height. "Little white dog with a yellow bow."

"Ah, that would be my grandmother," Julia admitted, seeing no point in denying it. "And I apologise for everything and anything she might have said. She means no harm."

Des forced a disbelieving laugh before crossing the street. He pushed heavily on the door to the busy-as-ever Comfy Corner restaurant. A single finger went up to indicate 'one' to Mary, one of the owners, before the door swung shut.

"Auntie Leah was right," Julia whispered to Olivia as she set off to the meeting. "It's time to say something to Great-Granny Dot."

# 8

Thirty minutes after setting foot into the fish and chip shop on Mulberry Lane, Dot finally left with four plastic bags stuffed with paper-wrapped food. Next time she offered her as-yet-unnamed group a chippy supper at a late-night meeting, she'd make sure they all ordered the same thing.

Eager to discuss the case, she shot up the street past the mostly closed shops as darkness consumed the last of the lingering daylight. She couldn't believe she'd had to wait another two hours at Evelyn's bizarre insistence, especially since they were only meeting every two days.

Perhaps they should be meeting every day, especially while Penelope's killer was still on the loose. Not for much longer, if Dot had anything to do with it. Once Julia filled them in on her interview with Vicky, Dot would have a full page on her board for everyone in Peridale's Eyes.

And what were the police doing?

Twiddling their thumbs, no doubt.

Dot's Detective's couldn't have come at a better time.

Before she could decide if she would suggest the excellent name again, she rounded the corner and all thoughts of the investigation vanished.

Why was her cottage dark?

And what was the source of the faint flickering light behind the curtains?

Acutely aware of her heavy bags, she cut across the green and pushed through the gate at as close to a jog as she could manage. Ditching the food on the doorstep, Dot tapped the handle with the back of her hand. Cool to the touch, and her skin didn't melt off.

She opened the door, and a cloud of smoke hit her.

Rich, spicy smoke.

"*Percy*?" she bellowed into the cottage as she counted over twenty candles in the hallway alone. "What in heaven's name is going on?"

As Percy appeared at the top of the stairs and

scurried down, the soft flames lit up his shiny round head like a disco ball.

"You're back," he announced, fiddling with his glasses. "Was the chippy closed?"

"Food's on the doorstep." She glanced towards the kitchen where Evelyn, Amy, and Shilpa were talking amongst themselves. "I thought the cottage was on fire."

"Ah, I can see why you'd think that." Thumbs hooked through his red suspenders, Percy rocked on his heels with a chuckle. "We're about to have a séance!"

Dot tilted an ear at her husband, not quite believing she'd heard him say what she thought he said.

"A *what*?"

"Séance," he repeated, this time with a gulp. "It's where you contact the dead with—"

"I know what a séance is, Percy."

"It was Evelyn's idea."

"It wasn't going to be anyone else's, was it?"

Dot cut eyes down the hallway, and the three women quickly turned away; were they pretending to talk?

"Over my dead body are we having a séance under my roof."

"*Our*, roof, dear," he pointed out, tapping on his wedding band. "And everyone wants to do it."

"Everyone?"

She couldn't hide the disappointment in her voice.

"Aren't you a little curious?" he whispered, tickling her in the side with a finger. "Evelyn's always offering to do them, and nobody ever takes her up on it."

"And for good reason."

The urge to put her foot down, flick on the lights, and blow out the candles bubbled up like last night's strawberry jam.

"Well, if *everyone* wants to do it," she said, exhaling the pent-up irritation through her nostrils and letting her shoulders relax, "I suppose I don't have much choice."

"That's the spirit!"

"It's the *spirits* I'm afraid of." She forced a strained smile as she stared into the kitchen again; the women returned it. "Why couldn't we do it at the B&B? Evelyn's always inviting them in, but I like to keep them out. Why do you think I shut the curtains on funeral days? I don't want any spirits flying in here."

"It'll take more than curtains to keep the spirits out." Evelyn emerged from the kitchen. The candlelight caught the gold embroidered pattern across her scarlet kaftan and matching, bejewelled turban. "And it's your proximity to the church that makes this the perfect location. Can't you feel her? She never left the graveyard."

Evelyn floated into the sitting room, and Amy and Shilpa followed. Dot smiled and nodded at them, then spun to Percy and blocked his path before he could gleefully follow them in.

"If you, me, or the dogs start levitating off our beds with spinning heads throwing up pea soup," she said with an outstretched finger, "I'm holding you personally responsible."

He nudged her finger away and turned over her hand to kiss the back of it.

"My dear Dorothy," he said with another kiss. "I'd never let such a thing happen to you."

"I bet that woman in *The Exorcist* thought the same thing," she said, noticing Lady curled up in her bed through the dining room door, "and look what happened to *her* daughter."

Dot put the chips in the oven on the lowest temperature before joining everyone else in the sitting room. The furniture had been pushed to the sides to make room for a circle of cushions. Some were Dot's, and they blended in with the rest of the neutral floral décor just fine. The cushions Evelyn had brought – and there was no denying they belonged to Evelyn – clashed in every way, what with their bright colours, mirrored circles, bobbles, and strange, thick textures.

Julia, Johnny, and Julia's friend were all sitting cross-legged next to each other on one side, leaving the rest of them to pick from the remaining cushions.

"We'll never get that smell out of the walls," Dot whispered to Percy, nodding at the incense stick burning on the mantelpiece.

"Sit down, dear," he said, patting the cushion next to him. "I saved you the biggest one."

When they were all settled, Evelyn clinked a metal block against something resembling a turkey fork. It let out a strange sound, or more of a frequency, which tickled deep within Dot's ear. The room fell silent, and Evelyn ran the prongs around a stone bowl lying in the middle of the room.

"I do things a little differently," she said dreamily as she reached into her kaftan to pull out a matching scarlet velvet satchel. "Take one of each and pass it around."

Evelyn plucked two stones from the bag and passed it to Amy.

"Labradorite." Evelyn held up a dark stone that shifted blue and green in the light. "It will be serving a dual purpose tonight. It grounds the spirits, but it can also raise consciousness so we can make the right connections. It goes in your right hand, looking forward to future answers."

Dot dug around in the bag and pulled out two

stones with different textures. The dark labradorite was smooth as glass, while the other, a green stone, was rougher. She passed the bag to Shilpa, unable to believe she was going along with such charlatanry.

"Peridot." Evelyn held up the stone before clutching it in her left palm. "A great calming stone. The spirits can change the mood in a room very dramatically. Peridot, in our left hand, will protect us from the spirits of the past."

Dot groaned, catching the eyes of everyone. She coughed and looked down at the stones in her hands, wondering where in life she'd gone wrong to end up in this situation. It was a good job all the asylums had closed donkey's years ago.

"Grass cut from the location of her death," Evelyn continued, sprinkling green blades into the bowl, which already contained a blend of something like curry spices in the bottom. "Everyone should link arms. We're about to begin."

Clutching the stones in their appropriate hands, everyone linked arms. Dot slid hers through Percy's on her right and Shilpa to her left. Julia, Leah, and Johnny grinned like schoolchildren, whereas Amy's and Percy's faces were as white as the ghost they were about to contact. Shilpa seemed unbothered by the whole event, and Evelyn was in a world of her own – but when wasn't she?

"*Penelope*!" Evelyn cried, eyes clenched shut as her grip pulled Johnny and Amy closer . "I can see her."

"I don't like this already," whispered Amy.

Evelyn's groaning and swaying dragged the circle this way and that. Dot planted herself firm; she'd be doing no such thing, no matter how much Shilpa and Percy bashed into her on either side.

All at once, the noise and movement stopped. Evelyn's eyes popped open, staring right at Dot.

No, *through* Dot.

The angle at which she was sat meant that from Evelyn's position, the graveyard was directly in a straight line *through* Dot.

She didn't like that one bit.

Her grip tightened on the stones.

"Hello," Evelyn said with a weary smile. "Everyone, she's here. And she knows what happened to her, alright." Her face contorted. "It hurts. Her head hurts so much."

In the back of Dot's head, a twinge.

She wanted to turn around but, suddenly, she didn't dare.

Tighter Dot clung to the rocks.

"And angry," she turned so far to the left it looked like her neck might snap. "So much rage. *Betrayal.* She knows who killed her. Oh, she *knows*, and she didn't see it coming until she was already dead."

Evelyn's head snapped to the other side, and she nodded as though someone was talking to her over her shoulder.

On one side, Amy shivered like a cold church mouse.

On the other, Johnny seemed to be biting back laughter.

"It was quick," Evelyn said with a firm nod. "Yes, thankfully it was quick."

"Ask her who killed her," Shilpa urged.

"Someone she trusted." Evelyn's eyes squeezed shut even more tightly. "She doesn't want to say. The name has too much power. Oh, she feels so betrayed. What is it, Penelope? Why can't you tell me their name?"

"Convenient," whispered Dot.

More swaying and rocking followed, and this time Dot couldn't resist the movement. Dizzied, she watched as Evelyn's face, blurred by the candles, twisted and pulled around as her lips formed the abnormal shapes of words Dot couldn't make out.

"Ca . . . Ca . . ." Evelyn choked on the sounds. "Penelope, tell me. Please. Ca . . . Ca . . ."

The house creaked and Amy squeaked, her eyes shut tight. A breeze tickled Dot's neck. There was that gap under the back door. She wanted to turn to make sure, but she was frozen.

"She doesn't like the graveyard," Evelyn continued in a tone as soft as a child's. "It's too quiet at night."

"A name, Evelyn," Dot pushed.

Evelyn's head rolled back and more groaning followed. Dot was sure she could hear footsteps coming up behind her.

She *could*.

Soft creaks but creaks all the same.

*Turn around, Dorothy*!

Blinding light filled the room, as did a chorus of terrified screams.

"Are we dead?" Amy cried.

Dot spun around, letting go of the stones. With Olivia in his arms, Barker and his daughter stared down at them all through eyes squinting like they'd just awoken from naps.

"I thought you were having a meeting?"

"*Exactly* my thoughts!" Dot sprang to her feet and pulled Percy upright with both hands. "Get all these cushions up off the floor, and let's get the sofa back to where it belongs. I've had quite enough of that."

Dot retreated to the kitchen and retrieved their supper from the warm oven. She pulled open the cupboard to retrieve a stack of plates, but she couldn't quite bring her hands to reach for them.

"It wasn't real," she whispered to herself. "Just a trick."

Shaking her head until she was too dizzy to be scared, Dot pulled down the plates and set to work.

"That was an interesting experience," Julia said when she and Olivia joined Dot in the kitchen. "Now we know what it's like, I guess."

"Yes, *quite* the show." Dot pushed up her curls. "Food, and we can finally get to business."

"About that."

The controlled way Julia exhaled through her nose told Dot her granddaughter was about to tell her off for something. She busied herself with spreading out the plates.

"I've been hearing things."

"Not spirits, is it?" Dot asked. "Strange voices?"

"Gossip."

"About?"

"Your interviewing tactics." Julia peeled the bag off a stack of food with her free hand while Olivia tried to reach for Dot. "I know you're . . . *enthusiastic* about your group, but . . . did you throw a cup of tea in Ethel's face?"

"Someone said that?" She snorted. "This village! *This* is why Ethel needs to go. She's spreading lies."

"But you did crash their bridge meeting?"

"I was invited to join," she said. "A trial, as it were. And it was an illegal geriatric poker ring, not bridge, I'll have you know. We exchanged nothing more than cross words during an interview. If anything, Ethel has only made herself look guiltier by lying about what happened. And don't expect her cronies to back me up, either. They're all brainwashed. Ask Amy."

"It's not that I don't believe you, it's—"

"She's blood-thirsty!" Dot couldn't help herself. "She's clearly been desperate to take Penelope's place. It's pathetic. I exposed that, and now she's bothered about being caught out."

"And Gus?" Julia pushed. "And Des?"

"Gus was . . ." She paused, reaching for the right word. "A warm-up. I'll admit, it could have gone better. And Des? What are people saying about that? Did I punch him? Push him down the stairs? Switch out his heart pills for breath mints?"

"I don't know what you did," Julia said, throwing the plastic bags in the cupboard with the rest of Dot's never-ending 'bag for life' collection. "I tried to ask him some questions, and when he realised I was connected to you, he called you crazy and ran away from me."

"What a drama queen."

"His ex-wife was murdered."

"*Ex* for a reason." Dot rolled her eyes as she dumped the first steaming, soggy portion of fish and chips onto a plate. "And a suspect in a murder investigation."

"But still a human being. You know we're only looking for one person; the rest will be innocent."

"No one in *that* group is innocent."

"There's still a chance none of them murdered Penelope, Gran."

"There bloody isn't!" Two plates clacked together as Dot continued dumping out the food. "I understand why he might feel that way, but I did nothing wrong. I went to Vicky's Van and had the worst cup of tea ever, and she pointed me in Des's direction."

"She did the same to me. Why did you go to Vicky's Van?"

"To check that you'd conducted your interview."

"Oh, Gran."

"Which you did!" Dot cheered up. "I was very happy to hear that you're getting involved. But as nobody had claimed Des, I popped by the library to have a little chat with him. My grandson-in-law manages the place. I had a *right* to be there."

"What did you do?"

"Nothing."

"What did you do, Gran?"

"*Nothing.*" Dot huffed. "I only . . . talked to him. Tried to relate to him. I lost a husband once, you know. I've felt that pain. I pushed it too far. Perhaps."

She scratched at her hair. "Embellished. Made my grief sound more . . . recent."

"Gran . . ."

"He opened up!" she insisted. "I found out what they were arguing about in that meeting I overheard, and everyone else would know too if we hadn't settled on amateur dramatics hour."

Julia's eyes lit up.

"I thought you'd like to hear *that* part." Dot circled Julia's face with a finger. "Something about his grandson. He didn't say more than that. I didn't get the chance. He realised I was interviewing him. Neil blabbed the truth and asked me to leave. *Me*! I've a good mind to give him a lump of coal come Christmas. I never meant to upset the man."

"Did he say anything about Penelope?" Julia asked as Dot scooped up four served plates. "We still don't know much about her."

"Well, we now know she has a grandson since they were married for so long," she said. "And from the way Des talked about Penelope, he was still very much in love with her. *And* I learned that their marriage ended five years ago thanks to Penelope's wandering eye. He didn't say who it wandered to, but from the numbers, it can't have been too long afterwards that she married Gus."

The information silenced Julia.

"Ah, I thought you'd like that too." Dot pushed open the door with her hip. "I might not have been on my best behaviour, but I got something."

Back in the sitting room, everything was back to normal, though the incense smell still lingered. If it did stick, she'd be sending Evelyn the cleaning bill.

"All that swaying must have taken it out of her," she whispered to Percy as Evelyn fanned herself with an issue of *Cotswold Life*. "There's a couple more plates in the kitchen, dear."

Dot dished out the food from memory, only switching up Johnny and Julia's friend's orders. When they all sat – on the sofas this time – Shilpa cleared her throat, and Dot sensed another telling off was on its way.

"We've been talking," Shilpa said, wiping salt off her fingers with a napkin. "We all agree that we should be focusing on the break-ins, not the murder."

"The police are close," Barker spoke up through a mouthful of chips. "Christie thinks one of them will crack soon."

"Which is why we *all* think," Shilpa continued, looking around the room as though needing everyone's support, "that it would be best to try and solve the issue that will have the most impact. After talking to Julia about the flowers, I think it's safe to say the same culprit is behind all the break-ins and thieving going on lately."

Knowing she was outnumbered, Dot had to admit it wasn't the worst idea. Maybe she had gone too far with her storytelling. Upsetting the man certainly hadn't been her intention.

"Fine," she said as coolly as she could. "Have it your way."

"We don't have much to go on, though," said Julia, feeding Olivia rather than eating her own food. "Other than a new shoe."

"Seen anyone barefoot lately?" Barker asked. "Skinny lad?"

They all shook their heads.

"There's been another break-in, too," said Johnny, pulling out his phone. "It was on Peridale Chat. *Was* being the operative word. I can't seem to—"

"*Shoes*!" Evelyn announced, jumping up with her plate in her hands. "That's it!"

"Shoes killed Penelope?" Dot pinched between her eyes. "Evelyn, you had your chance for your little perfo—"

"My gardening shoes," she continued, putting the plate down and taking Dot's centre-stage spot at the mantelpiece. "I meant to do some weeding this morning, but my gardening shoes had gone missing."

"From where?" asked Julia.

"My shed," she whispered excitedly. "What if my visitor is the same person?"

Dot looked down at Evelyn's feet, tiny even poking out of her kaftan.

"They were a men's size eight," Evelyn explained, picking up the hem, "and a little roomy, but if I tied them tight enough, they hung on."

"Why would anyone want to wear their shoes too big?" asked Dot.

"A guest left them behind, and I couldn't reach them. Felt like a waste."

"Barker?" He was perched on the arm of Julia's chair, and she rested a hand on his knee. "What size were the white trainers?"

"Eight."

Like before, bright light flooded through Dot, though this time it was in her mind only. A fully formed plan landed like she'd already spent hours coming up with it. Oh, it was good.

"Then let's do something about it," Dot announced, taking her turn to jump up. She budged Evelyn from the mantlepiece and back into her seat. "You said it yourself. It's probably the same person. They could have killed Penelope, too."

"Unlikely," Barker said firmly. "Just going off the distance between the graveyard and Leah's cottage, he would have had to teleport. They happened at almost the same time."

"Then we put the break-in case to bed," Dot said, pointing at Johnny's phone. "And when everyone on that silly little internet group sees that it was *us* that solved it, Peridale's Eyes will be a thing of the past. What are they doing about anything right now?"

The group looked amongst themselves and, just as they'd done on the night of her victorious first meeting, she sensed they were hanging on every word she spoke.

"I'm in," said Leah. "Johnny?"

"Sure," he said, still scrolling. "I still can't find it though. Or any of them, for that matter."

"Do you have a plan, Gran?"

"Oh, yes," Dot said, straightening her brooch. "And we're doing it tonight. I hope none of you have places to be, because it's going to be a late one."

And she had just the outfit in mind.

## 9

$\mathcal{I}$t had been one of those glorious nights where Olivia drifted off without much fuss. Her gran had assured her that it would be easy to leave if Olivia was already asleep. Leaning into the cot to brush her daughter's soft pink cheek, Julia already knew that not to be true.

While pregnant with Olivia, Julia had hoped the whispers of 'mother's guilt' wouldn't be as bad as the women around her had alluded to, but she couldn't deny how much it prickled. After some trial and error in the early days, at least it was easier to manage now.

"Your life can't revolve around a baby!" Dot had said one day in Olivia's third week home after Julia had exhausted herself trying to keep every plate spinning by herself. "The faster you learn to hand over the baby when you need to, the sooner you'll realise how much easier that help makes everything else."

As it turned out, it really did take a village.

Handing over the reins so she could rest her mind and body did help, and Julia had grown to cherish the support those that cared about her offered.

During the daytime, anyway.

Julia had avoided everything and anything that might involve leaving Olivia past sunset. Subconsciously, perhaps, but Julia hadn't yet been ready to take that first step of walking away from the cot instead of lying down next to it.

"Do it before she's six months," Dot had warned as Julia prepared to leave her gran's cottage after the séance, "or you just never might."

Most of the time, Julia felt like she knew none of the moves to the dance of motherhood. At others, she had to do them wrong several times to know when she was veering off track.

Today, she was certain this move was the right one.

"We'll be fine," Barker said softly from the doorway, backlit by the hallway light. "I'm more worried about you. I know your gran agreed to only get a picture, but you know what she's like. A picture might be enough for the police, but for her? I'm not so sure."

"I won't even leave the B&B." Julia switched on the star nightlight on the bedside table, casting the trio of stones in a dancing wash of colour. "You know where everything is?"

"If I don't, I'll find it."

Not the answer she'd hoped for.

"We'll be fine," he repeated, laughing as he pulled her in. "If we're lucky, she'll have another magnificent all-through-the-night sleep. Have you noticed we've been having more of those?"

Julia nodded, although it had taken the rough night after Penelope's death to see the contrast; sleeping hadn't been Olivia's favourite pastime.

"If she wakes up—"

"We'll be *fine*." He kissed her again. "Trust me."

"I do," she said.

She'd tried to explain the insidiousness of mother's guilt to Barker. He seemed to understand, though she could tell whatever version he felt wasn't quite the same.

"Be careful," he urged, planting one last kiss on her at the front door. "I told Christie the lot of you were up to something. All you have to do is scream, and he'll be across."

"Didn't he ask questions?"

"He's got a lot on his mind," Barker said, whispering despite Johnny and Leah being all the way across the lane and out of earshot. "The Chief Superintendent is breathing down his neck to wrap up the Penelope case."

Heaving her backpack over her shoulder, Julia went on her way. She crossed the lane, deciding it might be easier if she didn't glance back.

"I can't believe we're doing this." Johnny kicked away from the stone wall and balanced on his crutches. His camera dangled around his neck. "Your gran is going to get us all killed, I swear."

"Might finally get offered a cup of Evelyn's special tea," Leah agreed, picking up her backpack and unlocking her car. "I heard someone talking about how they'd been nothing but happy since popping by for a visit."

"Really?" Johnny rested a hand on his stomach. "It just had me up all night with the—" He cleared his throat. "Should we get going? Any later and Dot will fetch for us."

Julia checked her watch. They were late. Only by five minutes, but she'd been in a world of her own by the cot.

She looked back at the cottage.

"I'll take the blame," she said, pulling her gaze

away from her cosy home as she ducked into Leah's car. "Something tells me this will be the least of what she has on her mind tonight."

Julia took the front while Johnny stretched out along the backseat. Leah's car was as 'modern executive' as they came, and it always had a new car smell strong enough to knock Julia sick if she didn't open the window a crack on long journeys. She hadn't realised the wedding planning industry paid so well until Leah changed her car for the third time in the near two years since she'd inherited her mother's house. Julia smiled. Maybe Leah traded them in whenever that new car smell started to wane.

The drive was short, and before long they turned out of the green and past The Plough. As if Julia needed a reminder of how late it was, the pub was busy brushing out the last of the stagger-legged customers.

"Guys . . ." Johnny pulled forward through the front seats. "A-are those . . . green glowing eyes?"

The light of an overhead streetlamp blinded Julia as Leah slowed to a crawl. Through her squint, she also saw green eyes. Two pairs – and they were staring right at them.

Leah hit a stone in the road before slowing to a halt, flashing the dark-clad owners of the green eyes long enough for Julia to figure out what was going on. They jumped out of the car and approached the dark duo: one tall and slender, the other round and squat.

"What do you think?" Dot lifted away the green eyes, leaving her own visible through the dark green camouflage makeup. "I've been waiting for a reason to pull these bad boys out."

"Gran . . ." Julia took in the outfits and blew out a sigh. "I honestly have no words."

"Are those stab-proof vests?" Johnny asked. He reached out with one crutch and tapped their boots. The clunk revealed steel toes.

"Bulletproof, too." Percy popped up his night vision goggles and knocked on the black vest. "Quite something, aren't they?"

Dot and Percy were padded or covered in hard panels, all black, from head to toe. Dot had never been one to shy away from a costume, and their Wizard-of-Oz-themed wedding proved she and Percy were well suited in that regard. Still, this topped them all.

Julia had to take a picture.

"Did you say you were *waiting* to pull these out?" Julia asked, zipping the picture to Jessie without explanation. "For what possible occasion?"

"We saw a documentary." Dot removed a black

helmet and unleashed her grey curls. "Didn't expect it to be so warm in there. And you may be pulling those faces, but knife crime is on the up, nationally! You'd all do yourselves a favour to invest in protective gear."

"We bought it for late-night dog walks," Percy whispered, leaning in, "but after we almost gave Father David a heart attack when we took them out for a test drive, we felt rather silly."

"They've found their use." Dot removed a glove and knocked on the hard plastic helmet. "If Penelope had been wearing one of these, she might have stood a chance. Johnny, good to see you brought the camera like I asked."

Dot held out her hand, and just so Johnny knew she was waiting, tapped her steel-toed boot against the shiny stone pavement. Johnny's hand tightened around the camera, and the strap remained firmly around his neck.

"I'll take good care of it," Dot insisted, summoning the device – or Johnny's co-operation – by clapping her fingers against her palm. "We'll need something with a good lens if we're to snap the winning shot of Evelyn's shed-dweller stealing her food."

"We'll be in the bushes," added Percy with a twinkle in his eye. "Hence the camouflage."

"I was going to wait for that until we explained

The Plan, dear." Dot's lips pursed as her fingers began their insistent clapping again. "Camera, Johnathan!"

Groaning under his breath, Johnny pulled the large piece of equipment from around his neck. He hesitated, and both he and Dot held on for dear life to the middle of the strap.

"They're not easy to use."

"Point and click, Johnny." She tugged it away from him. "And I'll take excellent care of it. I'll treat it like a baby."

*Baby.*

A pang of guilt caught Julia off-guard.

To distract herself, Julia lifted her phone and spotted two new text messages from Jessie: *???*, followed by three yellow faces crying tears of laughter. Julia shot back a quick explanation, and in all caps, Jessie replied with: *THEY GOT THOSE TO WALK THE DOGS???*

Dot spun on her heels and marched up to the front door, snapping pictures of the front garden, complete with blinding flash, as she went. Above, guests twitched at their curtains.

"Shilpa's not coming," Dot revealed as they filed through the front door. "She can't handle the late nights, so it's just the nine of us."

"Nine?" Julia asked. "Shouldn't there be seven?"

Lady and Bruce ran through the sitting room door after Dot pushed it open and pursed her lips so tightly the greasy makeup settled into the lines around her mouth.

"Honestly, Julia," Dot tutted. "You didn't think we were leaving them at home, did you?"

*Home.*

She tucked her phone away.

If those texts from Jessie hadn't given her a moment to reflect, Barker might already have had his first check-in text message of the night.

After the dogs' excitement wore off, they followed Dot and Percy into the sitting room. A couple were reading in the front armchairs, but the incoming elderly stormtroopers diverted their concentration.

The light from their reading lights faded out to near darkness at the back, where another couple of armchairs sat before a matching bay window, currently occupied by Evelyn and Amy. They were sipping tea and giggling, stopping when they saw Dot. As per Dot's request, Evelyn was in a dark kaftan, and Amy looked almost unrecognisable in deep navies instead of her signature pastels. Behind them, the window looked out onto a wildflower garden cut by a path leading to the shed squarely in the middle.

And in perfect view of the armchairs.

"Gather round, gather round!" Dot clapped her hands together as Percy hurried in with her presentation board. "The plan is really quite simple."

The visible page showed the original list of suspects, all with reams of information jotted beneath them. Before Julia could focus enough to read any of it, Dot flipped. Five pages of notes later, she landed on a crudely drawn cross-section of the house, complete with garden and shed.

Simple, it was not.

"Amy and Evelyn will take the first watch upstairs," Dot explained, circling two drawings of women in chairs before running along one of the many coloured lines pointing to the shed. "Both eyes out at all times. Julia and Johnny will be taking watch at this bay window, also maintaining full sight of the shed. Percy and I will be in the bushes outside."

Percy opened a box recycled from one of the café's boxes of overstocked flour and passed around binoculars and walkie-talkies.

"What do *I* do?" Leah asked, accepting her gadgets.

"Yes!" Dot pushed down the pointer. "Yes, Julia's friend, it's . . . it's your job to make sure nobody falls asleep. That sounds right. And if anyone needs anything, you go and get it."

"Leah can cover bathroom breaks too," Percy suggested.

"Good observation." Dot agreed with a nod. "The five of you will take turns in that role. I'll let you decide the details amongst yourselves. Now, enough chat. From this moment on, we act as though he could turn up at any moment."

Dot and Percy marched through the living area and out of view. The two readers waited a moment before following behind, no doubt to get safely to their beds and away from the madness they'd just overheard. Through the windows, Dot and Percy waved before retreating into the bushes on either side of the shed.

"Testing, testing." Dot's voice crackled through all the walkie-talkies, static interference whining at the edges. "Over."

"Received," said Julia.

Evelyn and Amy retreated upstairs with the equipment and a prepared tray of more strangely-scented tea, along with scones from the café.

"Received?" Dot pushed.

"Received," Julia repeated, trying to swallow a chuckle. "*Over*."

"Can you see us?" asked Percy. "Over."

"Negative," Amy replied from upstairs. "This is quite fun. Oh, my finger is still on the . . . *Over*."

Julia arranged herself at the window, unzipping her bag.

"Leftovers from the café," she explained when Johnny limped over. "Switch with Leah for the first watch."

"But your gran said—"

"Take whatever you want," she urged with a smile, wiggling the bag temptingly. "And give us at least fifteen minutes."

"Fine." Glaring over his glasses, he dug in the back and pulled out a clear box holding a slice of carrot cake and another containing a custard slice. "You're up to something."

"Women's things."

Balancing the boxes, Johnny went on his way without pushing the subject further. Not that she expected him to; the glimmer of confusion in men's eyes as they wondered what those words could mean always tickled her.

"Sit down," she said after beckoning Leah over. "Reach into my bag of goodies and see what you pull out."

Leah pulled out a brownie and sank into the chair by the window. Julia wasn't hungry, but she waited for Leah to take a bite before offering a warning shot via a throat clearing.

"The other day," she started in a whisper, aware of

Johnny's presence by the front bay windows, "before Katie came into the kitchen—"

"When I almost had a breakdown?" Leah forced a dismissive laugh between bites. "Is that why I'm sat here and Johnny isn't?"

"I wanted to check in."

"I'm fine." Her glance at Johnny as he shuffled through a pack of Evelyn's tarot cards said otherwise. "You never really know someone until you live with them."

"That doesn't sound good."

Leah's gaze lingered on Johnny as his shuffling escaped him. An explosion of cards fluttered around him and onto the carpet. He sent them both a red-faced smile and got on with retrieving them as best his awkward stiff ankle allowed.

"Do you think there's a chance Johnny is" – Leah took another bite, and mumbled through the mouthful – "seeing someone else?"

"*Johnny*?" Julia tried not to laugh. "No way. C'mon, Leah. It's Johnny. He wouldn't do that. Unless . . . have you found something?"

"Not as such," she said, looking at the brownie as though it had lost all temptation "He keeps hiding his phone from me."

"Oh."

"Upside down on surfaces," she whispered.

"Everything I've read online . . . it's not a good sign. I would never have noticed if I hadn't been forced to stay with him."

"Have you talked to him about—"

"You're right." Leah shifted to face the window. "Lack of sleep mixed with always looking over my shoulder doesn't have me at my best. I'm glad we're finally focusing on this, at least."

Julia let her gaze linger on Leah before turning her head and looking into the garden. Contrary to her gran's warning, she hadn't managed to keep her eyes on the unmoving shed for more than a few seconds at a time. To make up for it, they spent the next fifteen minutes looking straight ahead in silence. Other than some light rustling in the bushes, there was nothing to report.

"Melinda Newton," Leah said out of the blue. "I knew there was something I wanted to tell you. Johnny gave me access to the paper's digital archive, and I found it instantly. Turns out she *is* Penelope's daughter. Or was. She did die. Twenty years ago, during childbirth."

"That's awful," Julia said. "Towards the end, I couldn't stop my mind lingering on the possibility of that scenario. Sue and Katie said they were the same, but only afterwards. Did the poor baby survive?"

"The article I read was from back then," she said

with a nod, "but her baby boy was alive at the time of her obituary. No idea if it fits in anywhere. Unsettling to know that people we went to school with died at twenty. Four years after we left school to experience life, and then – *poof* – gone, just like that."

Julia returned her focus to the shed, acknowledging the nudges her brain was trying to make.

Melinda's surviving son.

Desmond and Penelope's argument-causing grandson.

Leah's shoeless burglar.

Evelyn's gardening shoes' new owner.

Shilpa's shoplifter.

The boy forcing back tears at the spot where Penelope died.

If they weren't all the same person, Julia would eat her hat.

"Julia!" Leah hissed, slapping the back of her hand against Julia's arm. She left it there as she picked up the small binoculars with the other. "I think I see someone."

Leaning forward, Julia squinted into the dark. To the left of the shed, she saw the flicker of movement that Leah had caught. A figure emerged from the blackness at the bottom of the garden and slipped straight into the shed.

"Did you see that?" Amy whispered through the walkie-talkies. "He's here! *Over.*"

A bright flash emerged from the bushes, and another, and another. Green eyes followed the flashing as a slender, dark figure charged at the shed, camera first.

"*Gran!*" Julia cried into the walkie-talkie. "What are you *doing*?"

Dot slammed the shed door and bolted it with a padlock.

"You didn't say 'over'," said Dot through the walkie-talkie. "And nice job, Amy. You didn't give me much choice there, did you? He surely heard your message, over."

"Sorry, Dot," said Amy meekly. "Over."

Though Julia had promised she would stay in the B&B, she wasn't about to sit by and watch as the shed bounced from side to side. If nothing else, it wouldn't take much to break the old wood.

"This has gone too far!" Evelyn bombed down the staircase in a flurry of fabric as Julia and Leah rushed into the kitchen. "A picture, you said!"

"A citizen's arrest," Dot corrected, meeting them halfway up the path, helmet tucked under her arm as she yanked off her gloves. "Percy? Are you coming out?"

Percy dove out of the bushes with heavy lids and a

sway in his step. Pulling off his night-vision goggles, he yawned at the shed, squinting as though confirming that it was really rocking and not just a leftover of the nap he'd obviously been having.

"Gran . . ."

"For goodness's sake, Julia!" Dot planted both hands on her hips. "Isn't this what everyone wants? We've *caught* him. The village can rest easy now."

"No, Dot!" Evelyn stomped her foot on the paving stone. "No, no, *no*! This isn't right. You can't just lock someone up in a shed."

"I just did." Dot fluffed out her curls. "Now, is someone going to call the police, or do I have to do everything myself?"

Dot pushed through the gathered crowd and entered the B&B with Percy at her heels. Johnny appeared at the back door, as sleepy-eyed as Percy had been.

"Shilpa was right," Evelyn said, her watery eyes fixed on the shed. "She said Dot would go too far tonight."

Evelyn whooshed her kaftan around and ran back into the B&B. Johnny reached them, his gaze fixed on the shed. Julia hadn't noticed the thrashing stop. She turned, her heart skipping a beat. He was at the window next to the door and staring right at them. Or she assumed he was; she couldn't see his eyes for the shadow cast by his peaked cap.

"I'm going to talk to him," she said.

"What?" Leah pulled her back. "You're insane."

"The police will be here in seconds," she said, freeing her arm. "He's not trying to escape anymore. Let me talk to him."

The shed drew Julia down the garden path, and the click of crutches told her Johnny was right behind her. The face came into focus, and though he looked up, the shadows around his eyes still didn't clear.

He looked far too young to be so exhausted.

"I'm sorry about my grandmother," she said.

"Then open the door," he commanded through gritted teeth, the bones of his jaw tautening sallow skin. "Don't make me ask again."

Ah, the tough guy act.

In her early days with Jessie, Julia had seen that act a lot. She'd caught Jessie stealing from her café via a trap she'd set up, though she hadn't locked Jessie anywhere. She'd offered the lost, angry teenager a bed, a shower, and a home.

The more she paid attention, the more she saw Jessie everywhere. They were the system's lost children – and this boy was a child, despite his weary, hollow eyes.

"I saw you recently," she said, "in the graveyard.

Only from the back, but I saw you. Did you lay those flowers? For your grandmother?"

His eyes lit up, focusing harshly on Julia. The bones of his jaw appeared again, and it wasn't hard to imagine his clenched fists. She'd seen that enough times too.

"I don't know your story," she said softly, ducking to meet his downcast eyes. "I don't claim to. Those flowers you stole and left. 'You were right'. What does that mean?"

The jaw tightened further and he turned away, exposing a sprawling tattoo of a single word on his neck.

Cal.

"Callum?" Leah asked, stepping forward. "Callum Newton?"

The fury in his eyes was confirmation enough that Leah had hit the nail on the head. Julia was about to ask how she'd made that connection when she remembered Melinda and her baby. It had been years since she'd seen the legend who burnt down the girls' toilets, but Julia still recalled the deep line in her narrow chin; she was looking right at it again.

"I didn't kill her," he said, his voice scratchy and deep. "If that's what you think."

"It isn't," she said, remembering Barker's comment

about the distance. "But you have been breaking into people's houses?"

The silence that followed said it all.

"Mine being one of them," Leah said shakily, stepping back into the safety of Johnny's open arm. "The nightmares I've had because of you."

Callum rolled his head back and laughed. Bony shoulders shook beneath a tracksuit zip-up, like at the graveyard.

Maybe he hadn't been crying at all?

"Why?" Leah pushed in a louder voice. "Why would you do something like that to honest, hardworking people?"

"You people always think you're honest," he said, deeper still. "You walk around thinking you're safe, only looking at people like me out of the corner of your eye. I didn't *break* into your house. You left the back door unlocked."

Leah inhaled as though to rebuke the claim, but the breath stopped dead as her expression revealed her doubts.

"Still doesn't answer why," she muttered, stepping further back. "It's not right."

He laughed again, though like Leah's breath, he cut it short. Clenched fists beat against the frame, shaking the shed's structure. A light shone from the

B&B, casting Callum in a distant light just bright enough for Julia to see and understand the 'why'.

Like Jessie's ears after travelling, his forearms were covered in tiny pinprick holes, though his weren't for piercings. All at once, she realised she was out of her depth.

"I'm sorry," she said, unable to meet his gaze when his thrashing paused. "The police will be here soon."

Leaving the garden, Julia returned to the B&B. By the back window, Dot and Percy were enjoying glasses of Baileys.

"It's okay to celebrate, dears," Dot said, raising her glass. "The village can sleep soundly tonight."

Hurried knocking at the door pulled Julia into the hallway before she could say something she regretted. Shilpa, though not here, had been right, as had Barker. Naively, Julia had hoped a picture would be enough for her gran.

"Where is he?" Christie urged, flanked by uniformed officers. "I had to see this for myself."

"Shed. He's in a bad way, so go easy on him. Please."

"Ah, Detective Inspector." Dot rose immediately, hand outstretched and either not noticing or ignoring DI Christie's slack-jawed examination of their outfits. "To ease the worries felt by some of my fellow group members, a citizen's arrest is perfectly legal when someone has been caught in the act of committing a crime or is about to flee the scene of one, is it not?"

"Technically, yes," he said, looking through the back window, "but *that* is obstruction of justice."

The DI and his officers sprinted through the house, leaving the rest of them to gaze out after them. Dot's knuckles beat against the window as Evelyn's bolt cutters slid through the padlock. It sprang off, and without a second glance, Callum vanished into the darkness behind the shed as the two officers bit at his heels.

"I can't believe it," Dot muttered, pushing her hands into her curls. "I . . . we . . . we had him. We *had* him."

Once again, Dot pushed through the crowd, and she and Evelyn met in the hallway. Julia had witnessed many of Evelyn's moods, but she'd never before seen a nose-crinkling snarl scrunch up the mystic's face.

"You silly woman!" Dot cried, tossing her hands out. "I have a right mind to—" A hand rose and immediately dropped. "Why, Evelyn? *Why*?"

"*No!*" Evelyn repeated, finger outstretched. "Why did you do that? A *picture*, you said. I would never have agreed to any of this if I'd known your true intentions."

"You're talking as though I planned it!" Dot tossed a hand to Amy. "I wouldn't have had to if she didn't choose her perfect moment to have us rumbled. It was him before us. Tell them, Detective Inspector," she said, waving Christie over from the back door. "Tell them I was within my rights as a concerned citizen."

"And what about his rights?" Evelyn's snarl vanished, pulled down by a wobbling lip. "I only wanted to *help* him."

"And now you've doomed us all," Dot said, lifting her gaze to the corner of the ceiling. "Our one shot, and we blew it."

Evelyn slipped away and walked to the bottom of the stairs. Clutching the bannister, she looked down at DI Christie.

"Are you going to arrest me?"

"Unless you have absolute proof that was the burglar," he said, clearly as frustrated as Dot, "I don't see how I can."

"Ha!" Dot pulled up the camera. "I have . . . Johnny?"

"That button."

"Ah, yes." Dot pressed it and began flicking through the images. "One of them will be clear. Surely *one* of them . . ."

But they were all blurry enough to have DI Christie and his officers retreat through the front door with a warning to call the police if he showed up again—not that any of them expected Evelyn would do it.

"Dorothy," Evelyn said from halfway up the stairs. "I would like you to leave my home. The energy you are giving off right now is turning my stomach."

"Evelyn, I—"

"And I quit." She reached into her kaftan with one hand before glancing over her shoulder at Dot. "You might want to burn this in your cottage. Penelope's spirit was still lingering when I left."

Evelyn tossed a bundle of sage at Dot's feet before continuing up to bed with heavy footsteps.

"We had him," she whispered almost to herself as she picked up the dried herb. "We *had* him."

Whether or not it was radiating from her gran, something in the air had Julia packing up her things and waiting in the car.

"I think she wants to talk to you," Leah said when she was behind the wheel. "Should I set off?"

Julia nodded, watching the outlines of her gran and Percy shrink in the rear-view mirror. Though she'd feared it would happen, she still wished her earlier warning to her gran hadn't fallen on deaf ears.

"She's still got my camera," Johnny groaned when Leah pulled up outside Julia's cottage. "Julia—"

"I'll get it back."

"When?"

"When I know what to say to my gran," she said with a sigh. "Goodnight. I'm . . . sorry."

She was getting awfully tired of apologising for her grandmother.

As they left to drive back to Johnny's cottage on the other side of the village, Julia retreated into the darkness of her own. After changing into the previous night's pyjamas in the bathroom, she pushed open the bedroom door.

Olivia was where she'd left her, sleeping on her back with her arms spread out as though no time had passed. Barker was on Julia's side of the bed, nearest Olivia, with reading glasses perched on the end of his nose and a book – Stephen King's *Mr Mercedes* – open on his chest.

She hated to wake him, but she'd never fall asleep on his side; she'd only keep sitting up and checking. She folded his reading glasses and placed the book on his bedside table still open to the page where he'd drifted off. She stirred him with a kiss.

"I thought you'd be later," he mumbled as he crawled under the sheets. "How did it go?"

"You were right," she said, running the back of her finger across Olivia's cheek. "A picture wasn't enough."

Barker grumbled something, but his was only a whistle-stop visit to The Land of the Awake. While he snored lightly, Julia settled on her warmed side and, facing Olivia, wondered how their night had gone.

Realising it didn't even matter and that everything had been fine, Julia let her eyes close. Regardless of how her evening had turned out, she was glad to have pulled off that plaster.

## 10

----

*H*arsh morning sunlight burst through the white fluffy clouds, the first since the transition to cheerier spring weather. Julia's end of the video call flipped its contrast, washing her out except for eyes, lips, and nostrils, and bright enough to make Jessie, in her much darker setting, squint.

"Where are you?" asked Julia, dragging Olivia's pram into the shade of The Comfy Corner's overhanging roof. "It looks like a tunnel."

"*Berliner Unterwelten,*" Jessie said with a tight-throated inflection that made her pronunciation sound surprisingly spot-on, at least to Julia's untrained ear. "Second World War tunnels and bunkers. It's all still here under the city."

"You've not—"

"Broken in?" Jessie cut in with a snort. "You've got break-ins on the brain, Mum. I'm here with a tour group."

"I can go if you're busy?"

"No," she whispered, looking ahead as she set off after the tour group. "I need to hear the rest of this story."

Julia leaned against a British Telecom 'Fibre broadband here!' green metal cabinet that had popped up since her last visit to the restaurant, glad to have Jessie for a little longer. Unlike their last one, this had been Julia's call to make. She'd awoken needing a Jessie pick-me-up.

"The padlock sprang off, and he sprinted away before the police could get him."

"Why does Evelyn even have bolt cutters?"

"The same reason my gran has a bulletproof vest and night-vision goggles."

"Another normal day in Peridale." Jessie's laugh echoed around the tunnel, drifting off in slow stutters. "I miss the place."

"We miss you too," Julia said, swallowing a lump. "And *then* Evelyn quit the group."

"And you haven't spoken to Dot since?"

Julia shook her head. She wasn't proud to admit she'd ignored the ringing phone as she was locking the cottage door that morning. Not wanting to leave

Olivia on the doorstep had been a factor, but mostly she'd had a feeling the call was coming from her gran, and she hadn't wanted to take it.

"I don't know what to say to her," she admitted, looking up as the sun drifted behind the white clouds again, turning them a brilliant silver; in the shade, the video remained consistent. "I've thought of little else since this morning, and all I can conclude is that she thought she was doing the right thing. I get why she thought that, but . . ."

"She should have told you."

"Exactly."

"I know she said it was spur of the moment," Jessie said as she glanced into a room before continuing her walk through the tunnel, "but wouldn't she have taken that padlock with her?"

"I hadn't even considered that."

"Your brain is going to jelly without me there to keep you on your toes." Jessie winked into the camera. "Whatever the reason, it took guts to do it."

"I can't deny that."

"Stupid, but brave."

Jessie's side to side eye darting suggested she'd reached a junction in the tunnel, and her sudden stillness suggested even more.

"Are you lost?"

"Nope," she said merrily. "Maybe . . . a little. It's fine. I'll find Alfie. We're talking again now, so—"

Julia's heart dropped.

"You weren't talking?"

"It was nothing." Jessie sighed, clenching one eye as if pained and wishing she hadn't said anything. "It's sorted. We're fine. After that fight, we . . . Oh, I can hear them." Her hair, longer than Julia had seen it in a while, floated around the piercings as she hurried towards the voices Julia could just pick up. "Listen, I should probably go."

"Convenient timing," Julia said with mock firmness. "Just promise me you're being safe."

"Sounds like it's more dangerous *there* lately," Jessie said. "In that article that everyone is talking about online, it sounds like you're all up to your neck in . . . *Alfie*, I'm coming!" She motioned off camera. "Let me have a look at her before I go."

Julia flipped the camera into Olivia's pram, wondering what article she'd missed, and surprised Jessie was still checking in on the village after all. Jessie's expression melted like it always did when Olivia was on camera. Olivia was in one of her peaceful 'content to lie here and stare up at the clouds' moods and didn't seem to notice.

"She's growing so quickly," Jessie said as Julia

flipped the camera back. "She actually looks like a person now."

"What did she look like before?"

"All babies sort of look like bald old men," Jessie said, bringing the camera closer. "Sort of like Percy. Love you, gotta go."

Jessie kissed the air in front of the camera as she hung up, and Julia left the tunnels under Berlin and returned to Peridale. Across the street, Neil waved as he cleaned the windows of the library. She waved back just as she caught the glimmer of a pink and turquoise sari in the newly gleaming reflection.

"Sorry I'm late!" Shilpa waved as she hurried. "The line at the post office multiplied every time I looked up."

"Managed to sneak in a quick call with Jessie," she said, pushing away from the cabinet. "Almost got her lost in a World War II tunnel in Berlin."

"My Jayesh was *just* in Germany."

Shilpa pulled open the door to The Comfy Corner restaurant and helped Julia lift the pram over the doorframe – always easier with someone at the other end.

"Oh, I was wondering when I'd get my turn!" Mary exclaimed, rushing to the pram and waving her husband over from behind the bar. "Todd, Julia's brought little baby Olivia in!"

Olivia's face lit up. The attention was just what the silence had needed. Mary immediately had her smiling, and after asking permission, scooped her out for a cuddle while Julia set them up at a table.

"I know you said it was usually quiet around this time, but I didn't expect it to be empty," Julia whispered to Shilpa as she removed Olivia's sit-up play seat from the bottom of the pram. "Did you say Jayesh was still travelling?"

"Him and Poppy have done the world over and can't seem to get enough," she said, settling across from Julia and grabbing a menu. "He's stopped giving me dates for his return because he kept missing them. It would be nice if they made one of those flights a trip home, but who am I to stop their fun?"

Julia stared through her menu as she mentally worked out how long it had been since Shilpa's son and his girlfriend had left the village. It was after Poppy's father died during the debut of the Christmas nativity play Dot had starred in. How many Christmases ago was that? Was it the one when Sue had the twins?

"Two and a half years?" Both Julia's brows arched toward her hairline. "That's . . . a long time."

"They'd likely be back if it weren't for that huge inheritance Poppy's father left her," Shilpa said quickly, almost apologetically. "Jessie's home for Christmas, isn't that right?"

Julia summoned a smile and nodded, wondering if it was that obvious where her mind had gone. Mary brought Olivia back and settled her into the play chair Julia had set up next to her on the bench. With a gurgling grin, Olivia continued staring at Mary with her most adoring eyes.

"Isn't she just the most precious little button you've ever seen," Mary said, pulling a notepad from her apron. "And I must say, it's good to see you again, Julia, and looking so well! Any drinks? And can I talk you through the specials?"

They both ordered lemonades and chicken Caesar salads; the latter salad on Mary's near insistence for Todd's new homemade dressing alone. Mary went on her way, and Shilpa pulled her seat in, clearing her throat.

"You probably know why I asked to meet for early lunch," she said, resting her hands on the table. "I don't blame you. I couldn't blame you. You and your gran are alike in many ways, and very different in others. Most of the time, I find I can forgive her shortcomings because I see her heart. And to tell you the truth, she can be rather amusing. But after seeing Evelyn this morning, I *must* say something."

Mary rushed in with the drinks, and they both

smiled, bowing their heads until she left. As loveable as Mary and Todd were, the locals all knew the walls at The Comfy Corner had ears.

"I can't disagree," Julia replied. "As much as I don't like what she did at the shed, it's not so much that—"

"It's the fact she didn't tell anyone *before* she did it," Shilpa jumped in, taking the words right from Julia's mouth. "And it's not just that. She didn't let Percy talk to Gus, she barged in on Amy's interview, and don't even get me started on her ruining Evelyn's séance. This is not why I signed up for the group. It doesn't have to be like that."

"I tried telling her."

"If she won't listen to you, nobody stands a chance." Shilpa sighed before taking a lemonade break and a steadying breath. "Evelyn was a shell of herself this morning. She's far too sensitive for the Dots of the world. She felt such compassion for the boy, regardless of how little she knew about him. Have you read that article?"

"Jessie mentioned that too," she said, patting for her phone. "What's it about?"

"Everyone's going on about it," Shilpa said, checking her watch. "It's better if you read . . ."

Shilpa's eyes drifted to the door seconds before it opened. As though destiny had blown them through the door, Dot and Percy hurried in with Lady and Bruce at their feet.

"Usual table please, Mary, and two bowls of—"

Dot's confident steps faltered when she noticed them in their corner. Percy collided with her, too preoccupied with squinting at the specials board.

"Julia," she said, stiffening and presenting an unnatural smile, "and *Shilpa*. What a surprise."

And just like that, the air became suffocatingly uncomfortable.

"Julia and I were just about to have lunch," said Shilpa with unexpected firmness.

"During the quiet hour?" Dot looked around the restaurant as though she knew exactly what they were there to talk about. "Only time Mary and Todd say we can bring these in. It's the early-early-bird dog special."

Julia waited for a dig about her 'NO DOGS' sign or phantom hatred, but neither came; she almost wished they had, just so she knew things were normal between them.

But Dot's eyes couldn't quite focus on her.

Julia's hopes that her gran hadn't noticed her quick getaway the night before evaporated. As good an actress as her gran could be, every expressive line on her face told her story.

"About last night," Dot started, pushing up her

curls just as Lady attempted to bound up to Julia. "*Sit!*"

The dog did as she was told and promptly gobbled the treat that appeared at Dot's fingertips. Percy did the same with Bruce, though it took a little bottom-pushing to get him all the way down into a sit.

"Since you brought it up," Shilpa said, pushing back her chair so she could turn sideways and address Dot, "I want you to know I'm really not happy about how you treated Evelyn last night."

"I just want to start fresh," Dot insisted with a nod that told Julia her gran had spent the night convincing herself she'd done little, if anything, wrong. "I will go and talk to Evelyn when—"

"Please, don't," Shilpa cut in. "She doesn't want to see you right now."

"And she told you that for a fact, did she?"

"Yes," Shilpa replied firmly, cutting off Dot's attempt at a laugh. "This morning, before I left her in bed, barely making a lick of sense and surrounded by about a hundred crystals."

"That's just Evelyn."

Julia wished Dot had left out the dismissive waft of her hand.

"No. That's just Evelyn when she comes across someone like *you*," Shilpa said, standing and retrieving her purse from her bag. "Sorry, Julia. I've lost my appetite. I wanted you to pass a message to your gran, but since she's here, I'll tell her myself." She tucked a five-pound note under her barely touched lemonade and turned to Dot. "Like Evelyn, I quit."

"Shilpa," Dot said, stepping back. "I'm sorry. I . . . let's just talk about this. I made *one* mistake."

Shilpa looked prepared to repeat the list all things she'd said to Julia, but instead, she dropped her head. Evidently, Dot *thinking* she'd only made one mistake was bad enough.

"Julia, I really wish you had taken on the leadership," Shilpa said as she pushed in her chair. "I can't imagine we would have got here if you had."

As the door closed behind Shilpa, Julia couldn't take the compliment, especially since it was wrapped around an insult aimed at her gran. She understood Shilpa's frustration and the seemingly blank stare in her gran's glassy eyes equally well.

Julia could almost hear the penny dropping.

"I was hoping to see you," said Dot, her voice small and dry. "I did call. I . . . I *am* sorry, Julia. I . . . I . . . Oh, this is so silly!"

Dot stiffened and stared at the ceiling. Some might have thought she was trying to summon divine intervention, but Julia knew she was holding back tears.

"Gran, you didn't do anything to me," she said. "And you didn't do anything *to* Evelyn either. But she's upset nonetheless, and with good reason."

"I thought I was doing the right thing," she said, blinking hard. "My father used to say—"

The blink ended, and tears rolled down Dot's cheeks before she made for the exit with Lady trotting behind.

"She's not storming off," Percy explained as he hovered on the spot, clearly eager to go. "She doesn't like people seeing her cry."

"I know," she replied softly. "Go on, Percy."

He thanked her with a quick bow and hurried after her with cries of "My Dorothy!" Shilpa's assessment revealed that she had a decent grasp on Julia's gran, but she knew nothing of the side Dot only let her family see.

"Two chicken Caesar salads coming right—" Mary stopped and looked around. "Shilpa in the loo?"

"Might have to take those to go," she said, already retrieving her purse. "Family drama."

"Say no more." Mary looked down at the salads. "Unless . . . you want to?"

On another day, Julia might have indulged Mary with a tale.

Today, she had to go after her gran.

Leaving The Comfy Corner with a paper bag of

boxed chicken salads dangling from the pram's handle, Julia turned right, ready to go straight to her gran's cottage. The vision she had of Dot crying in the sitting room vanished with the sound of her gran's voice. From the volume alone, it wasn't difficult to figure out she was in the library.

"Your gran has lost it," Neil whispered to Julia as she rushed through the front doors. "Doesn't she know she's screaming in a library of all places?"

While Neil looked after Olivia at the front desk, Julia followed her gran's voice to the world travel section. Dot and Percy stood with leads in hand and chests puffed out, and they weren't alone.

From the description her gran had given, Julia assumed the woman mirroring their stance was Ethel White. The description hadn't been wholly accurate. From their slight frames to their outfits, Ethel and Dot could have been sisters, even despite the lilac tinge to Ethel's hair and her being closer to Percy in height.

"Dot's Detective's?" Ethel laughed. "That's your name?"

"*Yes*." Dot snapped. "And when we start recruiting again—"

"*Nobody* will want to join your group." Ethel looked her up and down. "Dotty Old Dot has gained quite a reputation for questionable behaviour in some circles as of late."

"No doubt thanks to *your* gossiping."

"I do *not* gossip," Ethel insisted. "I'm merely a keen observer."

The words could have been pulled right from Dot's mouth, which probably explained why they only seemed to enrage her further. Julia wasn't sure if she preferred this or the crying.

"Gran." Julia stepped between them to neutralise the tension. "Ethel, is it?"

"Yes," she said, glaring. "And *you* are?"

"Don't you speak to my granddaughter like that!"

Julia held up an arm as Dot tried to circle around her, and Ethel did the same on the other side. Behind the lilac hair, two men Julia had assumed were browsing stepped forward.

"Ethel, calm down," said one with the familiarity of a friend. "If she said she didn't write the article, maybe she didn't."

Was Julia the only person in Peridale to have left the house before the paper arrived?

The other man smiled at Julia, and she recognised Desmond. She took another look at the man who'd spoken: Gus, no doubt. The widower and the ex could stand to be in the same room, at least.

"She *had* to have written it," Ethel lamented. "It was too accurate. She must have had the village hall bugged."

"For *your* information, your little tiff happened *before* I started my group," Dot said smugly, tiptoeing around Julia's arm. "And I overheard all that drama, which means anyone could have."

"But the newspaper editor *is* in *your* group," Ethel pointed out. "So, if it wasn't you, how did he find out about everything?"

"Does it matter?" Desmond sighed. "We've admitted it to the police now, which means we can get on with our lives and focus on Penelope's funeral."

"But it makes us all look guilty!" Ethel continued shrilly. "You're okay with that?"

"Yes, because *I* know I didn't kill Penelope," he said, stepping around her to exit the aisle. "It sounds like you have a guilty conscience, Ethel."

"Nobody asked you, Desmond." Ethel dismissed him with a shake of her hand. "Might as well tell you this now to save on the lunch I was going to buy you. You're out of the Eyes. Now you'll have all the time in the world for your *other* group."

Desmond waved over his head as though he couldn't care less and busied himself unloading a book trolley.

"Maybe it's time to give it up, Ethel," said Gus, pulling out a book, reading the spine, and returning it. "Like you said, that article was a hit piece."

"Likewise, nobody asked you." Ethel rubbed at her

temples. "You're out too. No point keeping Penelope's sidekick around. You probably knew everything she did. I need fresh blood."

"Penelope always knew you wanted her spot as leader," Gus said as he passed her. "The difference is that people actually saw Penelope as a leader. She didn't have to pry it from someone's cold, dead hands."

Like an angry French bulldog, Ethel screwed up her face as Gus walked away.

"Give my love to Vicky, won't you?" she called after him.

Gus stopped in his tracks and stared over his shoulder, though only from the corner of his eye. Ethel's pleased-as-punch grin showed she'd hit the nerve she'd intended.

"This is *far* from over," Ethel said as she and Dot both stepped around Julia at the same time to eliminate her from the equation. "My new group is meeting me across the road in twenty minutes, so you've just done me a favour by showing up here and mouthing off. Then again, isn't that what you do best?"

"If Penelope was covered in her killer's fingerprints, next to a signed confession, beside a video tape of it happening, your bridge club still wouldn't be able to figure it out."

"That's what you *think*, Dorothy?"

Ethel stepped up.

"It's what I *know*, Ethel."

Dot stepped up.

Julia sighed, waiting for a referee to pass them boxing mitts and mouthguards before ringing a bell.

"This is *on*," Ethel said, eyes darting to Percy and Julia before snapping back onto Dot. "And you're the first suspect. Don't think people haven't noticed how quickly you jumped in to take her place."

"Likewise." Dot fired back. "And this was already on, you just hadn't finished sleeping to notice."

"Watch your back, Dorothy," said Ethel, extending a warning finger. "It's a small village."

"And you watch your—" Dot called after her as she quickly walked away. "And you watch – and you watch *your* back . . . Can she hear me?"

"I think she's gone," Julia said, letting out her held breath. "Dare I ask?"

"They were coming in *here* while we were coming out of *there*," Percy explained in a whisper. "She was right about it being a small village."

"The only thing she's right about," said Dot, floating back down to the ground. "The cheek of the woman! I *wish* I had written that article."

"What *is* this article?"

"How have you not seen it?" asked Dot. "Some

anonymous person wrote in exposing Penelope's agenda. It finally all makes sense."

Leaving them with the dogs, Julia returned to the front desk, where Neil was entertaining Olivia with the mechanism of the library stamp and a sheet of paper. As she'd hoped, the latest issue of *The Peridale Post* rested on the counter. She'd walked right by it on her way in, too distracted by her gran's voice to even look at the headline:

## THE LIES OF PERIDALE'S EYES!
*Shocking secret crime-rising agenda of neighbourhood watch group exposed*!

There was no time to focus on Johnny's wordplay, for the front page was one of the more unusual she'd ever seen. With a clipboard acting as the background, five faces were mocked up in polaroid frames, each with a heading. The unsmiling, professional picture of Penelope that looked suited to her days as an accountant read 'MURDERED!', while pictures of Desmond, Gus, and Ethel had 'SUSPECT!' above them.

On the right side of the clipboard, the picture under 'BURGLAR!' caught Julia off-guard. The deep line in the chin and the small print underneath confirmed that it was Callum, but she'd never have recognised this slightly younger, fresher-faced version who bore little resemblance to the shadow of a man she'd encountered through the shed window the night before. He was on the softer side of a normal weight, too.

And if the headline wasn't eye-catching enough, Johnny had printed The Agenda in the middle of the clipboard, right there on the front page:

Until her death, Penelope Newton, 72, used her position as leader of local neighbourhood watch group, Peridale's Eyes, to distract and deceive you. From what? Her grandson, Callum Newton, 20, and his insatiable need to break into YOUR homes! *Story continues on page 5 . . .*

"You heard Ethel," Dot said, leaning against the desk. "It's accurate, and this time she can't deny she said it. I'd say she's just outed herself as the culprit. If not her, it's one of the group. They all found out about this at the village hall. *That's* what I overheard. Someone exposed Penelope to her group before revealing everything in the paper."

"The article doesn't say who," Percy chipped in, "but I'd bet a gold coin it was the anonymous person who sent this in."

"What do you say about a meeting at mine tonight, Julia?" Dot asked, her face far too hopeful. "We could try and regroup to get to the bottom of this?"

Thumbing through the paper to get to the fifth page, Julia wondered if honesty would be the best policy right now. Though she'd decided earlier that she was done with the meetings and whatever was left with the group, after Shilpa's declaration, she just couldn't be another quitter.

"Maybe let the dust settle for a day?" she suggested. "See how everyone feels tomorrow."

"*Tomorrow*?" Dot shook her head. "No, we must act *now*. There's both a burglar and a killer out there right now, and it's almost worse that they're not one and the same. Now we know they're connected."

"I think I'm going to be busy tonight," Julia said, opening the paper and flattening it out. "I have a thing with Olivia."

"Why don't we go home, my love?" Percy suggested, tugging Dot towards the door. "Put the kettle on and see what's on the telly?"

"Telly?" Dot pulled away from him. "Thing? What thing? I don't . . . Oh, I see. Yes, I understand."

And from the pain in her eyes, it was clear that her gran *did* understand what Julia had wanted to avoid saying. Dot left, and this time, Percy followed her without trying to claim Dot wasn't storming out; if he had, it would have been a lie.

"You did the right thing," Neil said, passing Olivia across the desk as the phone rang, "and I wouldn't believe everything you read in the paper. Desmond is a decent guy, and from how he described it to me, Penelope was just trying to look out for her only grandson."

Neil picked up the phone, and Julia stared at a picture Johnny had found of Penelope, Desmond, and Callum. Taken in a happier time, they were all smiling at the camera. Callum was around ten or eleven. Next to that photo was a school picture of Melinda Newton identical to the ones Julia had of herself from around that time.

"Not just her only grandson," she whispered as she set Olivia down in the pram. "Her last connection to her daughter."

"I'm glad someone understands," Desmond said over Julia's shoulder, and she noticed the line in his chin for the first time. "Penelope was only doing what she thought was best." He examined the photo Julia had been staring at. "Melinda hated that picture. Said it made her face look too round or something." He chuckled, and in a darker tone, said, "Whoever wrote that article has quite the imagination, though I will admit some bits are correct."

"Only some?"

"It's more what *isn't* there," he said. "How's your friend's ankle?"

Without waiting for a response, Desmond pushed the book trolley away and vanished into the library. As Julia folded up the paper to pore over in private, she wondered what Johnny's ankle had to do with anything, and why Desmond's delivery had made it sound like a warning.

## 11

*J*ulia was halfway up the lane that led to her cottage before turning around and heading back to the village. A day alone with only Olivia's babbling, the cartoons, and her thoughts didn't appeal to Julia after the friction with her gran.

Thankfully, it wasn't her only option.

While Barker typed away at his desk, and after a quick nappy change for Olivia, Julia settled into the cushions of the antique red chesterfield in the corner. To her surprise, the old cellar under her café had become one of her favourite spots to escape the hustle and bustle of the village above.

Thanks to Barker's secret talent for interior design, little of the cellar's starkness remained. A porch and door had been built where a trapdoor, once hidden by paving stones, led down a staircase into the space as big as the footprint of the building upstairs. He'd panelled and papered the walls, hung Cotswold landscapes in thick gold frames, installed a new floor, covered it in rugs, and then covered those with warm-toned furniture all bought from her father's antique shop.

A ceiling-grazing Kentia palm loomed from the corner where Julia had once discovered the body of Evelyn's long-missing daughter. On the B&B owner's request, a selection of crystals and stones poked out from the soil. Learning the fate of her daughter was the last and only time Julia had seen Evelyn so distressed until the padlock appeared on the shed. Julia could feel the lack of Evelyn's warmth in the air.

Storm clouds could block even the brightest sunshine.

But the storm in the cellar had cleared.

Olivia's content gurgling attested to that.

Maybe it was Julia's imagination, but Olivia always seemed calmer in her daddy's office. Dot swore it was the below-ground peace; Barker, the soft lights; and Evelyn declared that Olivia had been a private investigator, like Barker, in a previous life and still loved the smell of the old wood.

Julia would happily retreat to the red chesterfield

whether or not Barker was in, though she preferred when he was. Seeing her husband in his element, deep in a case and scratching at his hair with a pen, warmed her heart.

Today, he was scratching extra deep as he compiled his findings for the Wellington Manor case. He hadn't told her the results, and she hadn't asked, aware of the line of being too closely related to Katie.

An hour of floor play and eye training with animal puppets, just like Sue had shown her, wore Olivia out to the point where reclining in her slightly bouncy lounge seat was enough entertainment for her. Kicking off her shoes, Julia pulled her notepad and pen from her bag and scanned the numbers she'd copied from Katie's email over rushed corn flakes that morning. Over three hundred scones sold so far, with the trio-sampler box making up the bulk of the sales. A fair few had been sold in the stand she hadn't known her father had set up in his shop, and Barker taking a crateload and a card machine to the station had nudged them into a small profit.

Scribbling away, she worked out that if they bought extra butter, were content with a little leftover flour, and froze half the strawberries, the last batch could be the final one. It wasn't difficult to work out. Fractions and ratios were some of the few maths lessons from school that she'd used enough over the years to know them by heart.

But her pen scribbled on.

Page after page.

Numbers tumbled through her stream of thoughts, but they were ages, dates, and times, rather than grams, millilitres, and quantities.

The crack of Barker's joints as he stretched his arms over his head brought her back. She flicked to the next page in her pad, the last before she'd need to pull a fresh one from the dining room drawer at home.

"Time to get Katie," he said, closing his laptop as he rose and rolled his neck from side to side. "Sounds quiet up there."

Julia pointed her ear towards the ceiling. At some point in her trance, the peak afternoon bustle had faded to the late afternoon stragglers to the solitary sweeping and scraping of chair legs moving around on tiles.

Barker fetched Katie, leaving Julia to pick up Olivia, who'd drifted off in the calm, for her next feed. When she'd latched on, Julia flipped to the last page, where she'd summarised her final thoughts.

Or rather, written the questions she hoped to answer.

*What did 'You were right' on the flowers mean?*

*Why did Ethel tell Gus to send her love to Vicky?*

*Why did Desmond mention Johnny's ankle?*

*How did Evelyn correctly pull out 'Ca . . . ' during her séance?*

"Johnny's upstairs for you," said Barker as Katie followed him down the wooden staircase. "He seems . . . excited."

"Practically doing back flips." Katie tugged off her apron, and the chesterfield let out a sigh as she collapsed back into the cracked leather. "If I hear the word 'agenda' one more time, I'm going to scream. I still don't fully understand what it means."

"Well, there can be two meanings—"

Katie's fingers went into her ears, and she gargled gibberish. Olivia laughed and bobbed her head, no doubt sensing a kindred spirit.

"Now," Katie said, rubbing her hands together and reaching for Olivia as her feeding ended, "you can leave the burping to Granny Katie. Can't get Vinnie over my shoulder for a back rub these days."

"Katie, Olivia," he said, offering the chair across from his desk as he tucked in. "If you'll take a seat, then I'll show you my—"

"You come here." Katie produced Olivia's first burp. "We're comfy."

Leaving Olivia in Katie's capable hands, Julia headed upstairs. As promised, Johnny was waiting for her by the string of postcards. His nose was so close to the latest one, he looked as though he was trying to smell the tulips through the paper.

"Did you see it?" he asked giddily, rushing over to meet her at the counter. "Also, notice anything?"

Johnny performed a small spin, repeating it twice with increased speed before Julia spotted the obvious.

"Crutches!" she cried, pointing at his leg. "Cast!"

"I'm a free man!" He gave his leg a wiggle. "Two months of being confined. I'm back! Let me tell you, it never felt so good to wash my leg. Anyway, did you see it?"

"If you mean your scandalous front page, then yes." She offered a slight bow. "I hope you're going to frame that one. You've caused quite the stir."

"They had to do a second lunchtime press." Grinning, he scratched at his uncharacteristically stubbly jaw; Johnny was usually clean-shaven to within an inch of his life. "Hasn't happened in *years*, and the higher-ups have noticed. Who knew a little rejig would have such an impact?"

"How long have you been working on this?"

"Since about twenty minutes after we dropped you off last night?" He collapsed into a chair, his blink dragging out until he shook his head and forced his eyes open. "Haven't slept."

"Explains . . . a lot." She hovered by the coffee machine but thought better of it. "Camomile tea!"

After making a quick cup, she set it in front of Johnny and sat across from him. Leftover copies of *The Peridale Post* were scattered around the empty tables, though it was likely most villagers would save a copy; this was one they'd be talking about for a while.

"Who's your anonymous source?"

He grinned, biting back a laugh.

"Johnny . . ."

She hoped Percy hadn't bet that gold coin.

"Made them up," he whispered. "And don't give me that look. Everything I said was based on the information we've been gathering all week." He sniffed the steaming tea. "It smells like a hamster cage."

"You never had a hamster."

"It's not hard to imagine." He took a sip, and it dribbled back into the cup. "Tastes hot."

"Johnny, relax." She slapped his arm. "You're acting like . . . Well, you're acting like you haven't slept, which makes sense. Not so easy to hide at our age."

"What do you mean?" He looked at his reflection in the back of the spoon like he couldn't see his red eyes and ashen skin. "And how could I? When Leah and I got back to my place, I couldn't stop thinking about everything I read on Dot's board, so I went back."

"To the B&B?"

"Snuck in." He sipped the still-steaming tea and winced. "Door wasn't locked, but people are always coming and going." He grimaced at whatever he saw on her face and said, "Relax, I was there for five minutes, and besides, Dot left my camera there, remember? I took pictures of Dot's notes and went straight home. I had to work in the bathroom so the light wouldn't distract Leah."

"You didn't sit too close to the cleaning products, by any chance?"

"Huh?" He blew on the hot liquid before risking another sip. "Whatever. Turns out your gran had the agenda all laid out. She was just too close to see it. Pieced together my version, it made the most sense, so I wrote it up and sent it off."

"So, essentially, it's a work of fiction?"

"That's *exactly* what my boss said," he recalled, "right before he fired me."

"*Fired* you?"

"Relax." He repeated, fanning out his palms and leaning weirdly in the chair like he could barely keep himself upright. "Because when they heard that the three of them, the leftover Peridale's Eyes—"

"It's just Ethel and her bridge club now."

"Maybe, but then Ethel, Gus, and Desmond walked into the station and confessed to everything in the paper." A yawn longer than any Julia had ever seen split Johnny's face in two, giving her a sustained look at his tonsils. "Penelope was covering for Callum, her beloved grandson, and she used the group to stir people up about parking and whatever else. Classic distraction techni – *Look*!"

Johnny pointed across the café, and Julia spun.

"See," he said. "It's easy to distract people. I thought she was just harassing you and a few others, but the more I dug into it last night, the more people I found. Start talking to people about Penelope, and I'd bet the bonus they're about to give me that they have a dispute."

"Not personal, then."

"Like half the people in the village, it turns out you're just a low-level criminal breaking a law only Penelope cared to check for. All while she was covering for a grandson breaking much more serious ones."

"So, you had your job back at noon?" She glanced at the clock on the wall. "And you're still awake near six in the evening for what reason?"

"After the three of them waltzed in to verify everything I'd figured out and confess that they'd been keeping their discovery of Callum's break-ins a secret since their bust-up, the police wanted to talk to me. Naturally. I had to claim confidentiality for my source. I thought they were going to lock me up, but it seemed to be enough."

"Let me get this straight." Julia's brows furrowed. "You stayed up *all* night, wrote an exposé that just happened to be correct, were fired, tore the group apart, rehired, and lied to the police."

"And I sold a record number of papers doing it." His sip of tea turned into a lip-curling slurp. "And I didn't *lie*, I just *chose* not to tell the truth."

"By telling them nothing?"

"Exactly!" He slapped both hands on the table. "You get it."

"You sound deranged."

"I sound like a *journalist*," he said, digging into his pocket. "No. Today, I *feel* like an editor. *The Peridale Post*: a dying paper no more. Johnny Watson saves the day."

"You know you haven't solved the murder, right?"

"As good as," he said, digging deeper. "And that's not all."

"I'm not sure I can take another—"

Johnny pulled a small black box with gold trim from his jacket. With a snap, he popped back the lid. A large, pear-shaped diamond glittered against a solid gold band.

"Julia—"

"Johnny, I thought we were past—"

"It's not for you, you wally!" He kicked her lightly under the table. "Just happened to *arrive* today. I've been planning this for months, and now I'm too excited to sleep. Then I realised I didn't want to sleep, and that I wanted to propose tonight, so I had two energy drinks."

"When was that?"

"About ten minutes before I came here?" he said with a hard sniff. "What do you think?"

"First of all, this is gorgeous," she said, taking the box and turning it so the stone glinted under the light. "Knowing Leah, this looks like it was designed for her."

"It was," Johnny said, pulling out his phone. "I've been back and forth with the jeweller all month as they've been working on cutting it perfectly. Been saving up all year for *the* ring." He turned his phone to show her the image on it. "Designed it to be a blend of all the rings she had saved on her 'My Wedding' Pinterest board. Do you think she'll like it?"

Julia rested her hand on her chest, fighting back tears of joy . . . and a bit of relief at knowing he was neither seeing someone else nor trying to propose to her.

"I think she'll love it, and I don't doubt she'll say

yes," Julia said. She took a deep breath, preparing to deliver the middle of her compliment sandwich. "But I need you to promise me one tiny thing."

He clicked his fingers and pointed two finger guns at her.

"Shoot!"

"*Two* things," she said, returning the ring. "Never do *that* again, and whatever you do, do not propose to her today."

"Wh—"

"You *both* deserve a special moment when you're not so . . . excited."

Julia reached out and rested her hand against his. He was clammy and cold, and he trembled like a washing machine warming up for the big final spin.

"Really?" He investigated the spoon again. "Am I that bad?"

"You've been better."

"That's what friends are for, I guess." He jutted his chin at the spoon before letting it clatter against the table. "Special. You're right. So, I won't propose. Not tonight. I'll go figure out a way to make it special."

"You'll go home," she ordered, "and you'll drink as much water as you can stomach, have a shower, and crawl into bed. And if you have any alarms set, you'll turn them off so you can sleep as much as you need."

"What a strange day," he said, a little more calmly.

"You should have seen what they were saying about me on Peridale Chat. Someone called me a legend."

After patting himself down, he pulled his phone from the back pocket of his trousers. As he tapped on the screen, his ever-drifting brows dropped into a deep crease.

"It's gone," he muttered, scrolling quicker. "All traces of it. It's just pictures of landscapes, people complaining about the council and the buses, and ads for old tat nobody wants to buy."

He showed her a local lady's post. She was trying to sell a mirror cracked in three places for forty-five British pounds, claiming it was in 'decent condition.'

"Can they censor groups?" she asked. "Seems to be happening a lot lately."

"You still haven't accepted my invite request."

"I talk to my fellow villagers quite enough, thank you."

"Admins can censor," he said, more focused now that he had a task. "Well, well, well! Would you *look* at that. The picture grows *clearer* still. What a turn up for the books. An absolute—"

"Johnny!"

"Right." He slid the phone across the table. "Turns out Penelope wasn't the only one going out of her way to protect her grandson."

Four people, two women, two men, and all at least

fifty plus from their profile pictures, were listed as admins. Only one name was familiar.

"Desmond," she read aloud, pushing the phone back. "You're not the only one who's had a strange day. I saw him at the library, and he mentioned you. Asked how your ankle was. Before I could say a word, he walked off."

"Weird."

"Very." Her fingers drummed against the tabletop. "Does Desmond have any connection to your ankle? Any vested interest?"

"Don't even know the guy."

"Then why bring it up?" Her mind flicked through the pages of notes. "Could be nothing."

"He *is* seventy," he said, rising. "Speaking of old people, what's going on with your gran? I heard Evelyn and Shilpa quit the group and now your gran's in meltdown mode."

"First of all, I'm going to tell her you used the line 'speaking of old people' to bring her up," she said. "And secondly, I wish I knew. This whole group thing has got to her."

"Who didn't see *that* coming?" He yanked open the door so hard it banged into the wall. "Saying that, none of today would have happened if she hadn't put everything together in her only-Dot way. Maybe I'll go and tell her that?"

"*Maybe* you'll go home like I said, and you promised."

Johnny inhaled the cool early evening air, and a smile spread from ear to ear as he released it.

"Today's been a good day."

"I'm glad it has been for some." Her mind returned to the question about Desmond, the one that was gnawing at her the most. "Desmond seems to think you have quite the imagination."

He leaned into a deep bow.

"But he also thinks you're missing something," she said. Johnny snapped straight. "He made a point of mentioning it."

"Was he taunting you?"

"Maybe." Standing on the café's doorstep, she folded her arms against the light breeze. "From what I've seen, he has a quick temper."

"Whatever it is," he said, stepping backwards and tripping off the pavement and into the road, "I'm sure the police are close after today."

"I'm sure they are." She waved him off. "Go home, Johnny. Sleep. I mean it."

Alone in the café, Julia continued closing for the day where Katie had left off. Her months off hadn't tampered with the autopilot she'd honed over the years, and her hands and mind were equally busy as one dealt with closing and the other spun with questions.

With the café gleaming, she settled at the counter and pulled out one of the salads leftover from her fateful lunch. Katie crept through the back door, clutching the folder Barker had spent all afternoon compiling to her chest.

"What did Johnny want?" she asked in a small voice as she took the stool next to Julia.

"It's a secret for now," she said, eyes on the folder as Katie set it down. "He was . . . something. I've just spent fifteen minutes in a Jim Carey film."

"Which one?"

"All of them."

Fingers plucking at the edge of the folder, Katie let out a muted laugh.

"Good news?" Julia asked. "Bad news?

"It's . . . news." After a moment's hesitation, she flipped the folder open. "I asked Barker to look into James Jacobson thinking he'd turn out to be some con man or gangster or . . . I don't even know."

"And what is he?"

"A property developer with an offer still on the table," she said, cheeks flushing pink. "Even after the photograph *incident*."

"Developer?"

"He has a track record of buying stately homes

and manors." She spread out glossy photographs, some like Wellington Manor and others twice as grand. "He turns them into luxury apartments."

"Apartments." Julia nodded, not wanting to put Katie off the only offer on the table. "It has the space."

"My dad would kill me if he found out I'd sold the manor to be turned into flats." She flopped her head onto her folded arms and mumbled, "What do I do, Julia?"

As much as Katie had grown, she still looked to others for guidance and advice more than anyone else Julia knew. That Katie wasn't afraid to ask was one of the reasons Julia liked her, but it also meant Julia's words held weight she wasn't comfortable with. The scone overstock numbers paled in comparison to the debt figures her father had shown her.

"As sad as it is, your dad isn't here anymore," Julia said softly, resting a hand on the back of Katie's crispy blonde bun. "And let's not forget *he* left you with this debt. How likely are you to pay it off without selling the manor?"

"From the money I make here and nails on the side?" She counted on her fingers. "Three thousand years? But another buyer could come along next week and keep it the same."

"Or you might be waiting another year or more. I've seen enough episodes of *Grand Designs* and

*Location, Location, Location* over these last five months to know nothing moves quickly with houses like that."

"I know, I know," she groaned, fanning out more pictures, this time of apartments. "And he does a great job. They're stunning."

"I can't disagree there."

"I need to talk to your father," she said, gathering up the documents. "I hope he didn't know about this."

After a hug that lingered a little longer than usual, Katie left through the back door. Before long, Barker emerged with Olivia, all wrapped up and ready to go home.

"Are you okay to strap her in her seat?" Julia asked, squishing sideways past Barker's car, which, to Penelope's credit, did make the lane a tighter squeeze. "I won't be long."

One short walk across the green later, Julia knocked on her gran's door, hoping to banish another storm cloud before the day ended.

"Who is it?" Percy sang through the door.

"It's Julia."

"Oh, hello, love." There was a long pause. "It's . . . it might not be the *best* time."

"Percy, can I come in and—"

"Why don't you come back tomorrow, my love?" he called, the cheery timbre of his voice barely holding together. "Best to let the dust settle, like you said."

Julia reached into her pocket and pulled out her keys. She had one for the front door, but the message was clear. Besides, knowing her gran and Percy, there was no telling how many chains and bolts on the other side would render her key useless.

"Hugo Scott, MP, on the council came in handy," said Barker as Julia climbed in the car to Olivia's delighted raspberries. "I should help prove that politicians' private pictures are faked more often."

"Are they faked *that* often?"

"Good point." He started the engine with a press of a button on the dashboard. "According to Mr Scott, it's unlikely planning permission for the apartments would be denied, especially after Katie's attempt at turning it into a spa."

"I forgot about that."

"I still wish she'd built that pool," he said with a sigh. "From the sounds of it, as long as the outside structure isn't compromised and any important details are preserved as per listed status requests, the rest can be sliced and diced. I talked to an old detective pal from back in the day. He's an architect now, and he reckons you could fit four large apartments in there easily, six if they want them small, and that's not including the attic, which seems to go on forever. Do you think Katie will balk?"

"I'm not sure what choice she has."

"Whatever happens," he whispered, reversing out of the spot, "they're not moving in with us again."

"Deal. And now that you're finished with the manor case, I need a fresh pair of eyes on some notes I made earlier. Will you help me, Inspector?"

"Oh, Miss Julia!" he said in his best Belgian accent, twiddling a non-existent moustache. "I would be 'appy to lend my little grey cells to your case."

The Poirot impression raised a giggle from Olivia, and one glance through the rear-view mirror provided a ray of sunshine to brighten the gloom of the day.

By hook or by crook, tomorrow she would clear those clouds above her gran's cottage.

## 12

Dot teased back the curtain at her bedroom window as Barker's car drove away. She wasn't one to avoid her granddaughter, but she wasn't entirely herself today. Who she was, exactly, she hadn't yet figured out. How many hours of reflection would it take now that she'd seen herself through everyone else's eyes?

The woman they quit.

The woman who *pushed* them to quit.

"I should have been the wizard," Dot said when Percy crept onto the top step with a wheeze. "At our wedding, you were the wizard, and I was Dorothy Gale, but what if *I'm* the wizard? I didn't save everyone from the witch. I was just some sad, shrivelled-up old man behind a smoke-and-mirror show."

"My Dorothy," he said, waltzing in with the bundle of burning sage. "*I* am the shrivelled-up old man in this relationship, and your name *is* Dorothy. Perhaps she saved the day, but she wasn't innocent. Lest we forget the poor witch her house landed on, and the other she threw a bucket of water over."

"They deserved it."

"They probably didn't think so." He fanned her all over with the woodsy, stinking sage. "And the Wizard still got them home in the end. He didn't give up when the curtain was pulled back on him, did he?"

"This is where *I* give up." She let the curtain fall and retreated to her bed. "Julia must hate me."

"She doesn't hate you." He twirled the smoking sage around his head in a circle. "I only heard concern in her voice. Wasn't easy to send her on her way, but I did for you."

Percy planted a kiss on her curls, bringing the sage alarmingly close.

"Alright, now." She coughed and fanned her hand. "I feel like Julia's profiterole tower when she spun it with sugar. What are you doing?"

"The energy," he whispered, glancing around. "Evelyn said she sensed that Penelope had lingered. Nothing has been the same since the séance."

"As much as I'd like to blame Evelyn's swaying and crystals for what's going on," she said, returning to the window and pulling it up to let in the fresh air, "only I am to blame. But I appreciate the effort."

Percy dumped the sage in the glass of water usually reserved for his teeth on the bedside table between their twin beds. With a dog each, they stretched out on their beds and watched the evening air dance the curtains.

"I'm embarrassed, Percy," Dot said, turning away from the window after a period of stillness. "Ashamed, even. That look in Julia's eyes. How could I have gone about everything so wrong? I should have listened. She tried to warn me to pull in the reins, but I was far too distracted with my own notions to pay her any mind."

"It's best not to torture yourself."

"She looked so disappointed."

"C'mon, Dorothy."

"And the rest of them." Dot pulled Lady onto her lap and adjusted her bow as she settled. "I brought everyone together to become a group, and what did I do? What I *always* do. *I* claimed centre stage."

"You do have a certain star quality."

"I know that." She pushed up her curls. "But perhaps there's a time and a place."

"Now, I don't like your tone," he said, sitting up and throwing his legs over the bed, a firm finger pointed her way. "The Dorothy South I married wouldn't give up so easily. What about what you said to Ethel in the library?"

"I was hardly going to tell her everything had fallen apart. Could you imagine the ammunition it would have given her? And that's when I thought I still had Julia on my side. Now, I have no one."

"You have me until my dying breath," he said with a wink. "And Johnny, Leah, and Amy are still members, as far as we know. It's not over yet, and it's not about sides. Ethel may be against you, but Evelyn and Shilpa aren't, and they won't stay upset forever. In the meantime, you can't stay cooped up in the cottage."

"Can't I?"

"Dorothy . . ."

"'Everyone is the hero of their own story', my father used to say," she recited. "It's like I heard his voice when Amy crackled through the walkie-talkie. I panicked. Us or him, I thought."

"No true harm was done," he said, "and the boy is still on the loose, ready to strike again. But now his face is on the front page of the paper, so people know who to look out for. That's down to you in part, my dear. Celebrate that because it's something. This is nothing more than an opportunity to learn."

"What's the lesson?"

"We'll figure that out as we go." He hopped off the

bed and walked to the wardrobe, Bruce tight on his heels. "Now, are you going to wallow in bed for the rest of the evening feeling sorry for yourself, or will you accompany me to my choir rehearsal?"

"Do I have to?"

"Yes." He put her shoes at the bottom of her bed. "The fresh air will do you good."

After readying themselves and the dogs, they walked the short distance to the church arm in arm. Dot didn't know how far the gossip had spread, or what people were saying, or if what they thought they knew about her was even real, but she donned a disguise just in case.

"It's not too much?" she asked, checking that the silk scarf was tied under her neck. "And the sunglasses?"

"You look like Audrey Hepburn in her heyday."

"Percy, your glasses are full of smudges."

He pulled them off and wiped them on the fresh, crisp shirt held tight behind his suspenders. Sliding them back on, he said, "Still Audrey Hepburn to me."

"What did I do to deserve you, Percy Cropper?"

"You gave me a chance, dear. That's all it was."

Once again, Dot lingered by the photograph of her father, watching as the choir members filed in one by one. Rather than subjecting herself to their stares and whispering, she observed them in the reflection of the picture's glass.

Only one member made her turn.

"Gus?" she said quietly, motioning him over. "Can I have a word? It's me, Dot."

"Yes, I know," he said, giving her an odd look. "If this is about what happened in the library, I—"

"I'm sorry for how I talked to you at the last rehearsal," she said, nodding through the arch as she removed her sunglasses. "It was too soon after your wife's passing to be so . . . forward."

"Thank you," he said with a smile more genuine than the one he'd offered the first time she'd approached him. "I appreciate that. Maybe you're not so much like Ethel after all. She'd never apologise."

Dot didn't think she was like Ethel at all, but Gus didn't linger long enough for her to ask why he'd make such a comparison. It felt good to apologise, but it was only the first of many. Turning to the picture, she remembered her ambition when last she'd stood in this spot – minus the scarf and glasses.

"I gave being the hero a shot," she whispered to her father. "Didn't quite work out the way I hoped."

"And what was it you'd hoped for?"

Dot's sunglasses flew off as she spun towards the startling voice. Father David scooped them up and handed them back as he once again joined her in standing before the photograph.

"Whispers on the wind tell me your new neighbourhood watch team has fractured?" he asked as she slipped her glasses back on. "How did you hope it would turn out?"

"With glory?" She sighed. "My moment in the sun? Who knows what I was thinking, Father? Perhaps I wasn't thinking at all, and that's where I strayed."

"The ego wants what the ego wants," he said, "but a reason to start a neighbourhood watch it is not."

"It's fine. I'm giving it up."

"Now, I didn't say you should do that."

"Shouldn't I?"

"Maybe you should?" He shrugged. "It's not for me to say. Perhaps it's not even for *you* to say since the group isn't yours to claim."

"That's the problem," she said, removing the glasses again. "I only saw myself. I confess, I have been a terrible friend."

"I'll take your confession, though we are Church of England and not Catholic," he reminded her with a wink. "I'll listen all the same, any time. If you believe in something, giving up truly isn't an option."

"I believed in being the hero."

"Another terrible reason to want to help people."

"It's something silly my father used to say to me," she admitted. "'You're the hero of your own story, Dorothy, and nobody tries to be the hero more than you.'"

Father David reflected as the choir reached their first glorious crescendo. In the mix, Percy's voice stuck out to Dot's ear; she knew it the best.

"I can't claim to know what your father intended with those words," he began, "but a part of that saying is missing. Being the hero of your own story isn't necessarily a bad thing, but there's always a chance that in doing so, you're becoming the villain of someone else's."

Dot opened her mouth to protest, but the words didn't come. How many years had she waited to learn that lesson, and why hadn't it been obvious to her before?

"He only used to say it when I was rebelling," she revealed with a fond smile. "I was always up to something."

"Only good trouble, I hope."

Father David picked up a full box of tinned food from the donations station and went back into the church. Dot sank into the chair, struggling to process this revelation. She had a stronger than ever urge to apologise to everyone for her bullish ways.

But the dust did need to settle first.

It wasn't like she didn't have enough to be getting on with. There were, after all, a burglar and a killer on the loose.

Oh. And Bruce, too.

"Oi!" She ran after the little French bulldog as he trotted through the open doors, his lead trailing behind him. "Where do you think you're running off to?"

Stumpy tail in the air, he wiggled around the corner. Dot walked as fast as her legs would carry her without breaking into a run. Though Bruce was big as a football and about as clever, his dumpy legs could pick up speed if he tried.

"Finally," she said, slowing when he paused to cock his leg against a tree next to the village hall. "Don't you dare think about running off again, you little scamp."

Dot scooped up the lead and jumped back when she noticed a woman sitting behind the tree Bruce was still emptying his bladder against. She immediately recognised Vicky from the coffee van and crammed her sunglasses back on.

"Sorry about him," Dot said when Bruce finally pulled away as the woman stood. "He just goes wherever he pleases."

"I shouldn't have been sat down there anyway." She forced a laugh, though the inky mascara settling in the lines around her sixty-something eyes told a different story. "I was just having . . . a moment."

"Yes, we all have those," Dot said. "I can do you one better than the grass."

Dot sat on a nearby bench in the church grounds, and as Lady and Bruce stood patiently, Vicky settled next to her. She wasn't sure if the disguise was working or if Vicky even remembered her brief visit to the coffee van, but perhaps it didn't matter. Vicky had left Peridale's Eyes at the right time.

So why the tears?

"Would you look at me." Vicky pulled a packet of tissues from her bag and blew her nose. "I think I've just been dumped."

"Oh, no!"

"If our relationship was even anything to begin with," she said, budging closer on the bench. "Why are men like this?"

"Oh, I know," Dot replied, covering the wedding rings from both happy marriages. "Total pigs."

"Exactly!" She laughed. "It's nice to know someone gets it. They string you along, lie to you, and then cut you loose when you've served your purpose. I've had it. I thought he was different, but they're all the same. All. The. Same."

Ethel's parting words to Gus wriggled free and rattled around her mind.

"Give my love to Vicky, won't you?" she'd called after him.

Dot took Vicky in. Plain, age appropriate, with an air of desperation . . . or at least a need to be liked. Prime target for an affair if the midweek television dramas were to be believed. If Penelope had hopped from Desmond to Gus, it wasn't difficult to imagine Gus hopping to a model a decade younger, especially one right under his nose in the neighbourhood watch group.

"You lose them how you get them," Dot stated. "It's never easy being the other woman."

"I never said I was."

Hadn't she?

Had she put her foot in it again already?

Dot scrambled for something, anything to say. Glancing at her hands, the lines and age spots inspired her.

"When you get to *my* age," she said from deep in her chest, as wisely as she could muster, "you can tell these things."

Vicky nodded, the bomb defused despite the age gap between them being no more than twenty-five years. Still, Dot remembered being that age. She thought she'd known herself then, had it all figured out.

*The fool.*

"He's part of the choir," Vicky volunteered, looking over at the church as the peppy lyrics of 'All Things Bright and Beautiful' swelled forth. "I thought he asked me here to finally watch a rehearsal. I've always loved singing, but he didn't even let me past the front door. I'm so . . . humiliated."

"Sweetheart," Dot asked, reaching out and scooping up Vicky's hand. "Is it Gus?"

Vicky's confused look turned to a nod that gave way to more tears. She blew her nose again, and Dot could only pat her hand and wait for them to stop.

"How did you know?"

"A feeling," she said, summoning her wise voice once more. "You'll understand one day. No point crying over it. Like you said, it might not have been anything, anyway."

"We never even kissed," she admitted, dabbing the corners of her eyes though it only made the mess of mascara worse. "It was more . . . emotional."

"Sometimes they feel more real."

"You actually get it." Vicky let out a sigh of relief. "I've felt so alone. I loved him but . . . he belonged to someone else. He said he'd leave her."

"They never do."

"I shouldn't have fallen for it at my age," she said, rubbing under her eyes and finally ridding herself of the mascara mess. "Although maybe my age is why I fell for it. It's not like men are lining up around the corner."

"That's not true," Dot said, squeezing her hand. "There's always a line at your coffee van."

At least Vicky could find a chuckle, even in her state.

"After all that stuff in the paper," Dot whispered, pushing her shoulder against Vicky's, "he's done you a favour."

"Right?" Vicky huffed. "That wasn't even the *half* of it."

"There was more?"

"*So* much more."

"Worse than a break-in?"

"I-I shouldn't say. I promised him."

"Promised a man who never kissed you and left you out here to cry alone?"

Vicky frowned, and once again, Dot thought she'd gone too far. She surprised her with a nod that kept going until she let go of Dot's hand and rose.

"You're absolutely right." Still nodding, she blew her nose again. "I've spent *all* day slaving away in that van, and the one time I think he's invited me to be part of his life now that *she* isn't in the way, he tells me it's over. *Done.* No refunds. He thinks just because it's the anniversary of his son's death I won't make a scene. Six months! He strung me along for *six* months!

I'm going to go in there . . . and give him a piece of my mind."

"Alright, now." Dot fanned her hands. "Best not to get carried away."

"You're right." Vicky tossed the tissue into a nearby bin and snapped her fingers. "I won't go in there. I'll get *revenge*."

"Yes." Dot stood. "Wait, *no*, that's not what I meant."

"I'm going to *ruin* his life like he *ruined* mine."

"How about a cup of tea back at—"

"Thank you." Vicky squeezed her into a rocking hug, the dogs crammed between them. "You're a great listener. You've really helped."

If this one came to bite Dot on the behind, she wasn't sure how she'd explain it, other than somehow ending up riding a runaway train on which she wasn't even a passenger.

As Vicky marched across the village green to do who knew what, Dot and the dogs returned to the church as rehearsals ended. As on her previous visit, the crowd orbited around Gus and his outpouring of grief. This time, Percy was in the fray, and there were smiles instead of hostility.

If they'd been playing dominos, her debut interview with Gus had been the wobbly one that sent all the others crashing down.

"Get anything?"

"Afraid not, Dorothy," he said, pushing up his glasses before accepting Bruce's lead. "He was rather preoccupied with his son, Shawn, today. But he always is this time of year."

"Forget that," she whispered, looking around to make sure they were alone. "Let me tell you something you didn't know. Turns out Gus and Vicky were having an emotional affair, and Ethel knew about it."

"'Give my love to Vicky!'"

"Exactly." Dot leaned in, her smile growing. "The way she was talking, she seems over the moon that Penelope isn't in the picture even if she didn't get what she wanted. Gus just dumped her."

"She's back."

"Who?" Dot looked around.

"My Dorothy." He pinched her cheek. "All you needed was a whiff of a clue and you're ready to go again."

Taking in the grand church, Dot puffed out her chest. She was ready. Pulling off the glasses and scarf, she released a heavy breath.

"Back home," she said, looping her arm through Percy's as they walked down the aisle. "I think we need to start with a fresh sheet of paper and a new point of view. And Percy? From now on, I may need you to tell me if I'm stepping over the line."

"A-are you sure about that?"

"Yes."

"Then I shall give it my best shot." He cleared his throat. "I would have quite liked to interview Gus myself at the last rehearsal."

"Steady on," Dot said as they left the church. "Let's start fresh now."

"Right you are, dear."

Dot gazed out at the village as the sun slipped from the sky and declared another day done. She loved her village, and that was enough for her, no matter what people said about her or the lack of moments in the sun.

"Tomorrow," she said to Percy. "Tomorrow we take a burglar and a murderer off the streets for the sake of this village. And then we get our team back together. It's not over until it's over."

## 13

———

Waiting for Barker by the front door, with Olivia already in her pram, Julia tapped her foot. He'd had a whole morning to find his reading glasses. As had all too frequently become the case in the year since he'd gained the prescription, opening the front door had triggered what Julia dubbed the 'psycho specs search'.

"Really, Barker?" She leaned away as a scatter cushion flew from the sitting room and sent Mowgli on a skidding dash towards the safety of under the bed. "Every time."

"Ah, ha! Left them in the paper." Emerging with a pat of his shirt pocket, he climbed over the mess he'd created. "Want me to quickly—"

"No, no." She pushed the pram over the threshold.

"We'll sort it later. Let's get going."

Speedy exits from the cottage had been a rarity since Olivia's arrival. If they weren't rushing off to an appointment, they were hurrying back because they'd forgotten something. Julia had learned to be thorough with the pram-packing, but there was always something. She almost missed the waddling slowness of late pregnancy.

Once again, she had no time to slow-waddle and enjoy the morning birdsong as yet another perfect spring morning played out around her. They rushed a wave to Leah as she pruned her rose bushes but didn't stop to chat. When speed was necessary, Julia found she could take advantage of the winding lane down to the village in such a way that it was quicker trundling with the pram than packing and unpacking the car at either end.

"I think she's enjoying it." Barker jogged to keep up, wiggling a finger at Olivia. "Is this fun? *Is it*? Yes?"

"She loves it," Julia said, taking a wide berth around a pothole she'd learned to avoid. "I think it's the bumpiness."

The lane's exit and the village green came into view, as did Johnny on his way up. Olivia's vibrating gurgles smoothed as Julia slowed to a halt. Catching her breath, she ran a hand down her windblown hair and met Johnny in the middle.

"Sorry for yesterday," he said, shielding his eyes from the sun. "Someone should tell Shilpa how dangerous that two-for-one offer is."

"I don't think it was the energy drinks," Julia said with a smile. "Up to Leah's?"

"I was on my way to you, actually." His brows dropped, sending Julia's heart plummeting with them. "I've not had the greatest morning."

"She didn't say—"

"No." He shook his head quickly, glancing at Barker as though to check if she'd told him; she hadn't. "It's not that. I . . . I think I've just found out who my hit-and-run driver was."

Julia and Barker glanced at each other as he pulled something from his cross-body messenger bag. He unfolded a sheet of paper. Orange letters on a black background stitched together a single word – a name – like something from a film. There was a picture of a car, too, cut from a glossy magazine.

"Unless I'm missing something, it's a pretty clear message," he said, handing it over to Barker's outstretched hand. "Callum. Do you think that's why Desmond asked? Because he knew his grandson was the driver?"

Closer inspection revealed black-tinged water droplets and the halved ring of a coffee stain. Even without those clues, Julia knew who'd put together the letter. She opened her handbag and did what Barker had dubbed her 'psycho bag dig'. Under a bottle of peppermint chewing gum, her fingers closed around the shiny paper of the flyer. It had crumpled into something resembling a wonky flattened paper airplane, but it was still perfectly legible. She held it next to Johnny's art project.

The cut-out letters were identical.

"'Vicky's Van Grand Opening,'" Barker read aloud. "'Come on down to Mulberrry La—' Wait. Mulberry with three r's?"

"Which is why I know this flyer didn't make it into circulation," she said, dragging the pram to the side as a car slowed to pass. "First time I spoke to Vicky, these were hot off the press, and I noticed too. She said she was glad I'd spared her the embarrassment, and unless she sent them out anyway—"

Julia dove in again and pulled out the more professionally designed, less creased, and correctly spelled flyer Vicky had opted for. This one had a 20% off coupon attached to the bottom.

"Then it had to be Vicky," Johnny said, taking it back. "I don't get it. Why would she send me this? And how does she know?"

"Have you shown the police?"

"I wanted to see what you thought first," he said,

folding it before putting it away. "I'm on my way there now, and I can tell them where to look."

"Then we know where we need to start," Julia said to Barker as she set off again. "We talk to Vicky first, and then we go to the library like we planned. Johnny, station."

They walked to the bottom of the lane together, after which Johnny sped ahead and left them behind. When Julia reached the village green and glanced at her café to check how busy it was, movement in the alley drew her eye.

"What on Earth . . ."

"Ah!" Ethel ducked under the 'ILLEGAL PARKING' sign strung up between the café and the post office in front of Katie's pink Fiat 500. "Just the woman we wanted to see!"

Another of the women took over holding the string while a gang of conservatively dressed pensioners rushed out and arranged themselves around Ethel. Holding either end of what looked like a large bedsheet, two women spread out in front of the café. 'ILLEGAL PARKING' written in red paint on the white sheet blocked the view through the window.

"You can't do that," Barker called, overtaking Julia.

"We have a *right* to protest!" A megaphone appeared at Ethel's lips on the final word. "Peridale's Eyes stands against *illegal* parking, and we want to make sure everyone in this village knows the *truth* about this alley. It's a *public* right of way!"

Julia bit her tongue and denied Ethel the reaction she was no doubt gunning for. Penelope might have been vaguely irritating when she popped up with her complaints, but she had never made it personal.

"You might have a right to protest," Barker called, pulling one of the women away from the café's door so Father David could leave, "but you *don't* have a right to block entry to someone's business."

One of the women whispered something into Ethel's ear, and the words 'former detective' crackled through the megaphone. Ethel batted the woman away like a fly and scanned Barker from the tips of his shoes to the top of his head.

"*Illegal parking!*" she cried through the megaphone with a rallying cheer. "Is this what you all want for *your* village? Peridale's Eyes stands against *illegal* parking, and we are recruiting for—"

Ethel's voice fell abruptly silent as a pair of scissors cut through the sheet from behind. Reaching up until her apron was as short as her top, Katie sheared through the fabric and stepped through the slit she'd made. A click of her keys unlocked her car and she climbed in, slammed the door, and started the engine. Blaring the horn, she crawled forward, and the protestors scattered like ants.

Ethel stood her ground, forcing Katie to drive around her. She parked on the row adjacent, where the short-lived Happy Bean chain coffee shop remained abandoned years after its failed attempt to steal Julia's customers.

"Ten till four!" Katie cried, pointing at the sign jutting from the pavement. "Get a life, woman! There are *real* things to protest about."

Ethel checked her watch.

"Ladies, it's ten minutes to ten." She clicked her fingers and pointed them at the pink car. "*Illegal parking! Illegal parking!*"

Ethel's eyes darted between Julia and Dot's cottage. If Dot was in and could hear it, she had yet to rise to the taunting bait.

But Julia had one thing to say.

Or rather, one question to ask.

"Ethel?" she called, leaving Olivia with Barker. "Did you know Callum was behind the hit and run that put my friend in a cast for two months?"

Ethel's tight-throated stutter through the megaphone was the only answer Julia required. Ethel stared blankly outwards, as though summoning a denial or an excuse.

"*Illegal parking!*" she continued, turning so her angle to Dot's cottage was blatant. "Peridale's Eyes does not stand—"

Julia tuned out, turning to the café as Katie scooped up the abandoned halves of the sheet. She returned to the counter to mild applause from the four morning customers.

"Something is trying to stop us getting to the library to talk to Desmond," Barker said as they hurried past The Plough.

"Or something wanted us to have some more information before we got there." She glanced at the B&B next door. "We're starting to sound like Evelyn."

Once they reached the top of Mulberry Lane, they glanced down and saw the shutter pulled low over the van's serving window. The street was already getting busy for the day, but the lack of people lingering around the van indicated there wasn't a 'BE RIGHT BACK!' sign today.

"Do you know where she lives?"

"Not a clue," Julia replied. "And it was *my* job to interview her."

Thankfully, the library was open, though today was one of the slashed opening days. Using the pram, she pushed open the loose door and the library's insulation cut off the last crackle of the distant megaphone.

"If you're here for your brother-in-law," Desmond began from behind the desk as they walked in, lifting his gaze from his book, "he's had to take the day off."

"Is he alright?"

"No idea." He closed the book. "Didn't go into detail. If you're here for me, I'm not in the mood to answer more questions, thank you."

Barker gave Julia a sideways squint that read as 'Want me to take the lead on this one?' She shook her head.

"There's no point beating around the bush," she said after pulling Olivia's fist from her mouth and exchanging it with a plastic chomping ring still cold from the freezer. "I know your grandson was behind the hit and run, and I know you know."

"Ah, yes," he said with a nod. "I gave a little too much away with my question yesterday, which was why I didn't stick around."

"So, it's true?"

"If you know, then it's out there." He nodded, sighing heavily. "I wish it weren't, but it is. Maybe I let on more than I should have because I subconsciously wanted this to be over, but yes, he did it, and I knew. But I only found out when the others did at that last meeting."

"The true source of the argument?"

"They were upset about the break-ins, naturally," he said with another sigh, "but the hit and runs really pushed it over the edge."

"Hit and run*s*? Plural?"

"Did I say that?" He tapped his head. "Slip of the tongue. Old brain."

Julia had seen her grandmother try that trick enough times to know it didn't always sell the way she thought it did, and she didn't buy Desmond's veiled attempt at deception any more than she did her gran's.

"Want what to be over?" Barker pushed. "Penelope's murder case or the things Callum has done?"

"Both?" He busied his hands with gathering books behind the counter. "They're not connected. And before you ask, no, I didn't kill Penelope."

Barker and Julia glanced at each other. After going over their notes, Desmond had emerged as a prime suspect, and though they hadn't been able to put their finger on why, they'd had a few theories.

"Where were you the night Penelope was murdered?" Barker asked, his detective inspector tone never too far away.

"Not that I *have* to tell you," he said, turning a tight smile on Barker, "but I have an alibi your successor referred to as 'iron-clad'. I'm one of Peridale Chat's admins and founding members. On the night in question, I was moderating a question-and-answer session with a local musician."

"Jack the Strummer?" Barker asked.

"Yes."

"I didn't comment, but I read along with the Q&A," Barker told Julia. Turning back to Desmond, he raised a questioning brow. "The police traced all the internet records?"

"Right back to my house." He dropped the books onto the counter. "Now, you could cook up a story about me paying someone to be there or rigging some elaborate button-pushing mechanism so I could be in two places at once, but I know the truth. I wouldn't have, and didn't, touch a hair on Penelope's head."

"You still loved her," said Julia.

"Yes." He squinted at her. "I did. For all her faults, I went to bed beside her and woke up next to her for forty years. I thought I'd die first, and she'd have to live without me. I never suspected we'd divorce, but it was what she wanted. Ask anyone; I didn't stand in her way."

"But you would have taken her back?"

"In a heartbeat." He scooped up the books and stepped back. "Penelope was a loyal and kind woman to those closest to her, but very few were lucky enough to be in her inner circle. I never left it; she just fell out of love with me. We were still friends. We shared a daughter and a grandchild. She only did what she thought was best. I pray you never find out what it's like to love a troubled addict. Their eyes beg for forgiveness while they take with both hands. We were getting him help, getting him on the straight and narrow, but the accidents sent him back to rock bottom. We lost all control of him. We thought there was nowhere else for him to fall, but I've grown to learn that rock bottom always has a trapdoor to take you deeper."

Desmond loaded the books onto a trolley and pushed them into the library, empty aside from a woman with three children in the kids' corner.

"Two things," Barker said as they left. "Hit and runs? Accidents? One slip of the tongue maybe, but two?"

"I noticed that." She ducked into the shade of the library. "The second thing?"

"He knew the entire time about what Callum did," he whispered. "He had to, or how else could he have known the accidents were what sent Callum to rock bottom?"

"Do you think he killed her?"

"No."

"Me neither." She reached the top of the street and looked around, at a loss for where to turn. "What are we missing, Barker? Even discounting Desmond, we're still left with Ethel, Gus, and Vicky."

"Ethel's still my number one," he said, taking over pushing the pram to give Julia a break. "And it's not like we don't know where to find her."

"And Jack the Strummer?"

"Oh." Barker's cheeks tinged red. "Gothic guitar music. It's . . . you wouldn't get it. He's popular locally."

Wondering how Jack the Strummer and his gothic guitar had passed her by, Julia followed behind until they reached the green. Ethel had ceased her protest now that the parking rules applied to the small section of road. Julia's disappointment didn't last for long, though.

Barker gestured towards the green. "Your gran seems in better spirits."

They hurried ahead and caught up with Dot, Percy, and Amy as they cut across the village green in the direction of the graveyard. Julia walked around the edge to avoid the bad combination of wheels, grass, and having to weave through picnickers and kids playing football.

From her gran's smile alone, Julia could tell the storm cloud had blown over.

"Julia, you'll never believe what I found out yesterday," she announced giddily, cutting to the corner to meet on the road outside of the church. "Vicky and Gus are – or I should say *were* – having an emotional affair."

"*She* did it!" Percy revealed as he caught up. "She had to. It's all there."

"Lines up with what we've just found out," Julia

said, waiting for Amy Clark to catch up; a stray ball heading her way had sent her off course. "Callum was behind Johnny's hit and run, and presumably at least one more. From the looks of it, Vicky knew, and she told Johnny."

"The *revenge*!" Dot's fingers snapped. "Yesterday, I *accidentally* sent her off on a revenge mission against Gus."

"We think Vicky killed Penelope," said Amy.

"To get Gus to herself," added Percy.

"And she wanted to get revenge on him for dumping her," Dot finished. "And now that we know what she did, it's all there. Motive and opportunity! We were just on our way to the graveyard to write down the name on the headstone. Or, rather, the murder weapon."

"We've compiled a file." Amy pulled it from her cardigan. "We're going to take it to the police."

"But not for the glory," Dot insisted. "For accuracy. We don't want to leave anything out."

"Is that one of my folders?" asked Barker.

"We've been in your office all morning," said Dot as she crossed the road. "Peaceful down there, isn't it? And before you ask if we broke in, we found your key under the plant pot."

"Technically trespassing," he said, tipping his head from side to side. "But I'll let it slide. This time."

Dot, Percy, and Amy slipped through the half-open church gate, leaving Barker to drag it fully wide for Julia and the pram.

"She probably didn't even hear Ethel," he said. "You can only really make out what's going on in the café."

"Let's keep it that way," she whispered. "She's in a good mood."

Julia negotiated the headstones and found the trio at Gerald Martin's final resting place – not that he'd had much rest of late. While Amy wrote down the details, Dot crouched and read the cards. Percy kept the dogs entertained and let their sniffing lead him away.

"Only forty," Dot said with a sigh, pulling the card from the crinkling wrap around the stolen white and pink flowers. "Did you ever find out why Callum left this?"

"No," she said, slowing to a halt next to them. "Maybe it doesn't matter? If you're right about Vicky, it answers a lot of questions."

"He's still out there, though."

"Half the battle with burglaries is the who," Barker pointed out, leaning over the headstone from behind. "Once the police have an identity, it's hard to evade them, especially since Callum's still at it."

"I saw that on Peridale Chat this morning," Amy

said with a shake of her head. "Made off with jewellery three doors down from me."

"Aaaaand Desmond's already deleted it," Barker said after a quick check. "We should have asked him about that."

"D-Dorothy?" Percy waved from three rows down. "A word?"

Dot pushed herself up and scurried after him. Amy finished writing her notes and slapped the pad shut before flipping to a checklist at the back written in her gran's hand. She ticked off 'Graveyard name', but 'Apologise to Evelyn', 'Apologise to Shilpa', 'Apologise to Julia', 'Give file to police', and 'Save the day' remained unchecked. Julia took the pen from Amy and gladly ticked off the one regarding her.

Dot slowly made her way back to them in a diagonal line, touching the headstones to either side as she passed. Coming up behind Amy, Dot gently grabbed her by her pastel-clad shoulders and mimicked the movement of hitting someone's head on the stone. Shutting her eyes with a shudder, Amy straightened as Dot continued and pointed back at Percy in the general direction of the unseen green.

"She came from over there," Dot revealed, scanning the graveyard. "Yes, that's it. *That's* why Gerald Martin."

"Gran?"

"It's a straight line," she explained, gesturing towards Percy. "Gerald Martin is slap bang in the middle if you want to go from there to the front gates. Do you think she'd have been running? Would she have known?"

"It's a great theory," said Julia as Barker joined Percy, "but where's it come from?"

Barker looked down at the headstone Percy was hovering beside. His eyes lit up as he summoned Julia. With Dot and Amy following behind, she pushed the pram on a perfect diagonal through the slabs of rock. These old graves didn't have as many flowers, but the one near Percy and Barker was decorated with a fresh bouquet of sunflowers.

Born 1970.

Died 1983.

'RIP Our ray of sunshine.'

If forty was too young, and twenty was no life, thirteen was a cruel blip.

"The *name*, Julia." Percy urged, pointing above the dates. "Gerald Martin might have meant nothing, but this one certainly matters."

Julia read the name, and though it seemed to take her longer than anyone else to connect the dots, a line formed between the points. Like Barker's, her eyes attempted to leap from their sockets.

"Shawn *Morris*," Dot whispered, looking around.

"Amy, you might want to shred that file. We were a *little* off. I only know one Morris with a dead son."

Percy crouched and turned over the tag.

"'*Love, Dad.*'"

"Today is the anniversary of Gus Morris's son's death," Dot said after a dry gulp.

"What do we do, my Dorothy?"

"We gather Peridale's Eyes," she said, looking in the direction of the village hall. "Where it all started. Julia and Barker, find Vicky. Percy, call Gus and tell him there's urgent choir business. Amy, go to the library and get Desmond here." Stiffening, she adjusted her brooch. "I'll get Ethel."

Barely able to believe they might finally have something, Julia stopped at the café to drop Olivia with Katie. Her visit stopped flying when she turned to see Johnny crying at the corner table, just out of the window's view.

"Tell me she didn't say—"

"Why do you keep asking if she's said no?" Johnny blubbered up at her as he scrubbed his eyes with a napkin. "And no, it's got nothing to do with that. I shouldn't even be crying. I don't even know her."

"Know who?"

"Abigail Smith." He pulled up his phone and showed a teenage girl's smiling school picture; much more modern than the one she'd recently seen of

Melinda, but the same uniform. "Hit an hour after me in Riverswick. Apparently they've known for weeks that the same car did both, but nobody bothered to let me know. I had to look up the articles in the *Riverswick Chronicle*."

"Did she—"

"Survive?" He sighed and looked through the window. "She's been in a coma ever since. I don't know if you'd call that surviving."

Julia thought back to the eyes she'd seen through the dirty window in Evelyn's garden shed. So much pain, but even Julia hadn't foreseen how deep that wound had cut.

No wonder his arm had looked like it did.

"Get into your paper's database and find out everything you can about this boy," she said, scribbling the details on the edge of a paper abandoned on the crossword page at the next table. "Village hall in half an hour."

"Is it about to kick off?" he whispered a little too excitedly. "About time!"

"Let's just say that if you bring your camera," she said, giving in and matching his excitement for a second, "you're going to have another bestselling issue."

## 14

———

"Over here," Julia whispered to her dad when he finally gave up trying to sell a hunched-over woman with a cane a brass drinks trolley. "Do you know where Vicky is?"

"Has she still not opened up?" He rushed over, his blow-dried hair as bouncy as ever. "Missing out on some good trade today. I flogged a wardrobe I've been trying to sell for years this morning, and I almost sold that woman a drinks trolley."

He'd been nowhere near, but Julia wasn't going to squash his self-esteem, so she smiled with him, though her jaw clenched with each passing second spent standing around.

"I'm in a bit of a rush," she said. "Don't suppose you know where she lives?"

"You know, I haven't the foggiest idea." He chuckled, inhaling with a sense of ease that Julia, with pure adrenaline storming through her system, couldn't imagine. "Funny though – doesn't that look like a washing line?"

They ducked into the shade of the large tree and looked up at the string hanging from an antenna on the van to a thick branch.

"Pegs," he said. "You know, I could have sworn I heard someone in there this morning. Scared me half to death because I was up with the crow for a delivery."

"Delivery with the crow?" Julia's insides squirmed. "Nothing dodgy, I hope?"

"All above-board," he said with a wink. "Trust me, there's nothing to worry about."

If her father had a catchphrase, that was fast becoming it. The trouble was that him speaking the words almost always led to something to worry about.

"What did you hear?"

"Sounded like laughing or crying or both at once," he said as they turned to the van. Its coffee-bean colour gleamed in spots as the sun shone through the tree's leaves. "And this is going to sound odd, but I could have sworn I heard cutting. Like when you're at the barbers."

"Or paper?"

"Could have been."

Julia walked around to the door and, after clearing her throat loud enough that someone might hear, gave it three sharp knocks. Glass bottles clanged together.

"Closed," Vicky croaked. "There's a café round the corner."

"Actually," she said, injecting cheeriness into her voice, "it's Julia."

Julia waited so long for a response she felt awkward saying anything else; it was obvious she was being ignored. Something clicked inside, and the door opened. Vicky threw up her hand against the pinpoints of light, squinting like a vampire emerging from their tomb at the wrong end of the day.

Julia had experienced enough heavy nights to know what the aftereffects looked like. The two empty bottles of red wine on the floor next to the sleeping bag only confirmed it. Scissors and cut up flyers covered where she usually prepared the drinks.

"Oh, Vicky." Julia exhaled through her nose and smiled as the adrenaline suddenly cleared. "Are you sleeping in your van?"

"No?" She collapsed into a heap on the step. "Oh, what's the point? Yes, I am. I sold my house for this business."

"Oh, dear."

"I *really* wanted to make it work," she sobbed. "I thought it was all falling into place. Love, work, success. I was so tired of the same old, same old. New Vicky, I thought." She looked over her shoulder. "New Vicky is a loser."

"Hard times befall us all, love," Brian called from around the corner, although he declined to step forward when Julia gestured for him to emerge. "You'll make it back. You're busy every day."

"Not for much longer," she grunted, rubbing at eyes caked in dried, slept-in, and cried-in mascara. "I couldn't sleep, so I had a scroll on Peridale Chat. They all *hate* me. One person left a comment saying it was the worst coffee they'd ever tasted, and then bam, everyone chimed in. This is a failure. I'm a failure."

"Now, that's not true," Julia said. "You just have to learn to do it better, that's all. If I'd given up after my first bad review, do you think I'd still be here?"

"Three people said I was *nothing* compared to your café," she said, eyes watering. "My life is over."

"Cheer up, love," Brian called. "Can't be that bad."

Maybe it was a good idea he didn't step forward after all. Julia's next look sent him tiptoeing back to his shop with a tight-jawed apology.

"Look, we can talk about this for as long as you want, coffee and scones on me, and I'll even show you how to make a decent espresso." Julia scooped her hand around Vicky's. "But right now, I really need you to come with me and not ask why."

Whether it was the offer of a lesson, the shoulder to cry on, or the wine, Vicky let Julia lead her away. As though it had taken just as long to convince Desmond, Amy and her charge met them at the top of the street.

"I simply don't understand," Desmond called after Amy as she scurried ahead, a pastel blur. "What urgent library business?"

"The urgentest of urgent," Amy called sweetly over her shoulder. "Don't worry. All will make sense when we get there."

"Is this about the closure?"

"If you like."

Desmond's face fell. It seemed the gossip machine hadn't distorted or stretched news of the library's difficulties. Julia hoped it was because the council and everyone involved had done an amazing job of keeping things under wraps and not that people didn't care. Secrets never stayed secret for long in Peridale. For Sue and Neil, she hoped it was the former. And for Olivia, as well. She'd been hearing nonstop about how amazing Neil's toddler reading hours were.

The four of them joined up, though Amy only gave Julia a polite nod as they all walked in the same direction at the same speed. Desmond gritted his jaw at Julia as though to say, 'I hope you're not involved', but she couldn't blame him. She did keep popping up at his volunteering job to ask questions – with and without her 'crazy-lady' gran.

One interview.

Who had she been kidding?

"Wait here!"

Amy bolted up the path to the B&B and tugged the sing-song doorbell. Evelyn appeared in a mouth-watering peach kaftan and soft pink jewels. Her smile had returned, though it faltered when Amy told her the plan. Evelyn glanced at Julia before tugging the door shut behind her.

"What *is* going on?" Desmond hissed, though he kept pace with them when they sped up near the green. "You've all lost the plot."

"Girls?" Shilpa called, looking up as she restocked the flower stand in front of the post office. "Anything I should know about?"

"Urgent post office business at the village hall," Amy said with a wink she didn't try to hide.

"You said it was library business."

"Library *and* post office." Amy flapped her hand, tangled in her own tale. "It's a very complicated and serious matter."

Shilpa hurried along, her pale pink sari so

complementary to Evelyn's peach it looked co-ordinated. They looked so summery; Julia could already taste the return of iced drinks at the café.

Across the green, Percy emerged from the church with Gus. Dot was the closest to the village hall. Though Julia led Vicky up the street by the hand, Dot was dragging Ethel along like a reluctant dog. Percy rushed over with waving hands before Julia needed to step in.

Now that it would be obvious what they were doing, Julia expected Vicky and Desmond to make their bids for freedom, but they were either curious to find out what was going on or so confused they were going along with things unwittingly.

In the village hall, Father David was wiping down a large metal soup vat at a long table set up against a wall.

"You going to be long, Father?" Dot asked as the others milled about awkwardly.

"Have I missed a meeting on the schedule?" He checked his watch. "This is when I run a soup kitchen here for those in need of it. It was in the Parish newsletter."

"Ah, yes." Dot blushed. "I remember."

Julia didn't know if anyone read the Parish newsletter, but she'd heard the news from Father David's lips late last year while still pregnant and working. The café had been ordering and donating an extra box of carrots and potatoes every week since.

"I'm finished here, anyway. Ran out today, but nobody's been in for a while." He looked up and smiled into the crowd, and it parted around Desmond. "I'm sorry, Mr Newton, but I thought I should tell you: I'm on my way to the police station. Your grandson was in here again. He was hungry, and I wasn't going to turn him away. I tried to persuade him to do the right thing and hand himself in, and he said he would, but he didn't seem to be going that way when he left."

"It's okay, Father," Desmond said with a slow nod. "Well, nothing about any of this is *okay*, but there's little else anyone can do for him now."

"Don't give up on him, Desmond," Father David urged with kind firmness as he carried out his soup vat. "He'll still need a grandfather from inside prison."

When Father David left, the polite stillness they'd all been maintaining vanished. Ethel ripped away from Dot and turned in front of the stage. Two feet back, and she'd be right in the spotlight . . . if it was on.

"Will somebody tell me what is going on?" Ethel demanded, pushing up her lilac curls in a gesture alarmingly like Dot's. "And if anyone says the word *supergroup*, I won't be held responsible for my actions."

"Oh, I *really* wish it was you," Dot said, moving Ethel to the side and taking her spot at centre stage. "We did what you couldn't. We've figured it out. Not that I'm gloating or anything."

"You are," Ethel fired back.

"Am not."

"Figured out *what*, you dotty . . . Dot?"

"We know which of you killed Penelope," Dot stated, clasping her hands and looking around the group. She lifted her steepled fingers and pointed. "Vicky."

Vicky looked around, batting lashes ready to smudge the mascara she hadn't been able to wipe away on the walk over.

Dot's clasped pointed fingers went up to her lips, and her eyes closed. The silence stretched out cruelly until the door behind them creaked. They all spun as Johnny snuck in apologetically.

"Yes?" Vicky pushed.

"It wasn't you."

Vicky breathed a sigh of relief as though she'd somehow feared she might have killed Penelope.

"What gameshow is this?" Johnny whispered to Julia. "*I'm a Murder Suspect, Get Me Out of Here*?"

"We *thought* it was you," Dot admitted as she

paced a wider arc than her own sitting room allowed. "Oh, yes, we can admit when we've been wrong. That's what a balanced and calm group would do."

"What were you saying about gloating?" Desmond forced a laugh that didn't catch on. "Will you get on with it? I didn't have time to write a sign for the library."

Desmond glanced at Amy, who was too busy following Dot's pendulum pacing to notice.

"It would have made sense," she continued with a finger wag. "The scorned adulteress head over heels in love with her friend's husband. Engaged in an affair of words with a man who couldn't have cared less about her. A man ready to dispose of her, even after the wife exited stage left."

Dot paused to dramatically point stage left, no doubt revelling in her moment. As eloquent as she was, Julia could feel the knife sinking into Vicky's chest as she listened to a compilation of her recent lows in front of an audience.

"You could have met her at the graveyard, and with one hit – *bam*!" She repeated the move she'd performed on Amy, though at a more realistic speed. "Everything you ever wanted – or thought you wanted – in a single moment."

"Vicky and Gus were having an affair?" asked Desmond quietly.

"Everyone knew that," snapped Ethel, rolling her eyes at him.

"I didn't," Evelyn whispered.

"Me neither," said Shilpa.

"You ladies have missed a lot." Dot ceased pacing and took a moment to smile at them. "It's good to see you."

They returned her smile, and even though they had much to discuss, Julia had a feeling they weren't all enemies just yet. She leaned forward to look at Gus, sitting at the end of the row, but he seemed the least invested in listening.

"And then *you*." Dot rolled her eyes at Ethel. "The mediocre poker player ready to snatch her neighbourhood watch crown mere seconds after her leader's death."

"So were you."

"I came up with my idea *before* she died," Dot corrected, glancing back at the stage as though she could see the flowers on the other side of the open window through which she'd heard everything. "But no, as much joy as it would bring me to see the police cart you off, it wasn't you."

"I know it wasn't me!" Ethel's hands planted on her hips. "Is this going somewhere?"

"Let me set the scene, Ethel."

"Just get on with it, Dorothy."

"I will if you shut up, Ethel."

"Please." Ethel's curtsy dripped with sarcasm. "Continue."

Julia saw the moment her gran caught herself before snapping another automatic reply. Dot stretched out a finger and, once again, everyone turned. This time, they faced Desmond.

"*You* were trickier," she admitted, blowing out her cheeks. "Killed Penelope so nobody else could have her? But why in the graveyard? And why now?"

"Well, it wasn't me."

"Yes, I know." Dot whispered with a twitch of her brooch. "I was explaining *why*."

"Maybe just explain *who* it was," Ethel cried.

"Isn't it obvious?" Dot called back, both women squaring up like boxers again. "There's only one person left."

Julia leaned forward to observe Gus's reaction, but he'd gone. She spun around, as did everyone else, one by one. Gus froze and turned.

Click.

Flash.

Julia could practically hear Johnny's brain cooking up the headline.

"I just remembered," he said with a laugh. "I have a very important appointment."

"*Boys!*" Dot cried. "I said you'd know when I was

giving you the cue. *This* is the cue." She sighed her disappointment. "Amateurs."

The red curtain on the stage parted to reveal DI Christie and his brigade. Julia whirled back to the door just in time to see Gus open it, revealing two uniformed officers waiting in the foyer.

"Everyone who isn't Julia South-Brown," DI Christie called through a megaphone, "please exit through the rear."

Desmond, Vicky, and Ethel were the first to scurry for the doors, slipping past the officers. Julia was sure that, in time, DI Christie would pull each of the former Peridale's Eyes into the station to ask why they'd kept the hit-and-run secret.

"Actually, Detective Inspector," Julia said, stepping back and holding up her hands before anyone else left. "We're a team. If you want to hear this, we all stay."

Christie sighed, pinched between his brows, and lowered the megaphone. He snapped at some officers and a chair appeared in the middle of the hall, where Gus was sat to have his hands cuffed behind his back.

"Today's the anniversary of his son's death," Julia whispered to the DI. "Go easy on him."

"He's a murderer."

"A fact of which I'm fully aware," she replied, "but

which makes no odds to what I just said. Where'd you get that megaphone from?"

"Ethel came in screaming about parking or something," he said, looking down at it. "I couldn't be bothered with the noise, so I rattled my handcuffs at her. She dropped it and ran pretty much right into your gran's hands. That's when Dot reluctantly told me what was going on. She promised a show, and she didn't disappoint."

"It's not over yet, Detective," Dot said as she set up a chair across from, but at a considerable distance from, Gus. "And I only agreed to have you spring out if we got to talk to him before you shipped him off to his cell."

"Does she forget *we're* the police?" Christie whispered to Julia.

"My grandmother is an authority unto herself."

"She's something, alright." Christie clicked on the megaphone and lifted it to his mouth. "Action, Dot. You have five minutes."

"Ten."

"Six."

"*Ten.*"

"Nine."

"*Ten!*"

"Fine." Christie patted his pockets. "Unbelievable. I can see it right *there* on the desk.

How am I supposed to get through this without nicotine?"

Dot took her seat and, after adjusting her skirt hem for most of the first thirty seconds, clasped her hands against her knee and stared at Gus. He stared back, his gaze vacant.

"Why?" Dot asked. "We know you were at your son's grave, and we know you struck her as she was leaving."

Dot paused, but Gus didn't raise his voice to deny her claims.

"Was it because Penelope pushed your lover out of the group?" Dot ducked to meet his eyes. "Did it send you over the edge?"

"Lover?" He snorted. "I wouldn't go that far. She paid me attention, and I liked it. That was all. Vicky's desperate."

"You strung her along."

"She strung herself along."

"Was Penelope not paying you enough attention?" Dot pushed. "Spending too much time being pals with her ex-husband? I notice she kept his name, and here they were, running around this place covering up their grandson's messes. I bet you felt pushed to the side lines."

Gus blinked back tears, but not before one tumbled down his cheek.

"I think I might be able to explain the why," Johnny said as he stepped forward and pulled a notepad from his bag. "Julia asked me to look into Shawn Morris, your son."

Gus stared up through his brows, his jaw clenched tight.

"He died in 1983, aged thirteen," Johnny said, lowering the pad. "He'd have been fifty last week if not for that young girl who decided she was fine to drive home from the disco after one too many glasses of Cinzano Bianco."

"Four years," Gus said, laughing up at the ceiling. "They gave her *four years*, and then she got out and started a new life. I heard she moved to Canada. Shawn had these moose pyjamas that his nan bought him for his tenth birthday. I said I'd take him to see a real one at the zoo when we could afford it, and he laughed and said zoos didn't have moose. So we agreed we'd go somewhere to see them in the wild." His fond smile soured. "Canada has moose. She got to see them. *He* never got the chance."

The creaking floorboard under his chair was the only noise in the silent village hall. It was so uncomfortable, Julia strained to pick up on a mower – something, anything – outside.

"I had no idea," Dot said, choking back tears as

she dabbed under her eyes. "But Johnny's ankle surely wasn't—"

"There's a girl, gran." Julia swallowed her own tears. "She was hit in Riverswick the same night as Johnny."

"Abigail Smith," Gus said, his gaze once again distant. "I went to see her after Penelope told me. Her parents are torn up. She's just tubes in a bed because of him. And Penelope knew. She *knew*, and she did everything in her power to make sure nobody else found out."

"How did *you* find out?"

"Penelope knew how to pick her moments," he said, glancing up at the ceiling. "Every birthday, I lay an extra plate for Shawn. It used to be every day. I'd put food on it, thinking it was helping me cope. It made things worse, so I did it less, until eventually it became just a birthday thing. I liked the ritual of it. I set the plate out, wished him happy birthday, and was ready to go on with my day, unaware of everything my wife was keeping from me."

The tears gave way to a snarl.

"She's lucky I didn't kill her then," he said darkly. "She insisted she had to tell someone, and in her words, 'Today's the perfect day for it since it's fresh in my mind'. She thought I'd know what to do because that's how my son died. What sort of person makes that connection? She told me all about the night two months earlier when Callum turned up crying. I was away visiting my sister in Wales. He told her he'd hit two people. Then he passed out. By morning, he claimed not to remember a thing that had happened the night before. So, she didn't tell him."

"What?" Dot gasped.

"He knows what he did." Gus chewed the inside of his lip. "I never bought his act. Even at his worst, she desperately clung onto her memory of that little smiling boy everyone saw in the paper. She refused to see the man he'd become. When she looked at him, she saw Melinda; he knew that, and he used it. I hated him for it. And I hated her for falling for it every time, giving him *our* money, letting him sleep under *our* roof, bringing trouble to *our* door. But *this*? I couldn't believe it. I came for the meeting, and Ethel was already here. I told her everything. I wanted everyone to know."

"And it caused an argument?"

"Penelope tried to wriggle out of it," he continued, looking over his shoulder as though that's where it had happened. "Of course she ran to Desmond's open arms when nobody was on her side."

"And the graveyard?"

"I always go on his birthday," he said, lowering his gaze to the floor again, "and on the anniversary.

They're too close together, and it's always the worst week of the year. Maybe if she'd told me about it back when it happened, I might have spoken some sense into her. Maybe if she hadn't turned up in the graveyard, she might still be alive."

"You didn't invite her?" Dot asked.

"I wanted nothing to do with the woman." He shook his head. "I was sickened. I couldn't look past it."

"The phone call?" Christie remembered aloud. "Someone called Penelope from a withheld number half an hour before she died. We assumed it was whoever killed her, inviting her to the graveyard."

"Callum," he said bitterly. "Called from a phone box begging for more money for a fix. Last one, he claimed. No such thing. She said no. She told me as soon as she got to the graveyard, like I should be proud of her?"

"Explains why he ended up at Leah's," said Johnny.

"Penelope knew I'd be there." He pushed his hands through his hair. "She hadn't even come to reason with me, to talk to me; she came to *threaten* me. After everything she'd done, she said she'd tell everyone I was having an affair with Vicky if I spoke up about Callum. Everyone else in the group had agreed to keep their mouths shut because of how it would make them look, but how could I? I told her to leave, but as she did, she told me not to wait up because she was taking Desmond's sofa for the night. I snapped. It was over before I could reason with myself. I ran into the forest, and . . . well, here we are. What a week."

"And you kept her secret," Julia said, "because if you'd told the police the truth about the hit and run—"

"I'd eventually have ended up here," he said, tugging at the handcuffs. "Not how I expected. I thought the police finding out about the break-ins might keep them preoccupied, but your group has proven to be a worthy successor. You had me fooled there, Percy, with that rehearsal emergency."

"Sorry, old pal."

"It's alright." He shrugged. "This secret has exhausted me. It's worn me down to nothing. I don't know how Penelope managed it these last two months."

Christie stepped forward with a grunting cough and Dot rose from the chair. Like her gran, Julia wasn't sure what else there was to say. The excitement had evaporated and the adrenaline drained; Gus's story was a sobering dunk in an ice bath, and it was hard to feel triumphant after hearing it.

"I'm not saying I'm on his side," Johnny whispered

as they moved aside to allow the officers to lead him out, "but I'm definitely not on Penelope's."

Going by the surreptitious eye dabbing amongst her fellow neighbourhood watch members, they'd all been touched by Gus's story. It had been too raw to be a fabrication, and the admission saw him walking out of the hall with a lighter step than the one he'd had while walking to the chair.

"The worst part of all this?" Gus called over his shoulder, grinding the procession to a halt. "When I was running through the forest, I crossed paths with Callum. Penelope's precious grandson has known all week. He could have gone to the police any time. After everything she did for him, he chose to protect himself. Thought that needed to be said."

The officers left and, after clearing away the chairs, the group was left alone with DI Christie.

"Well done," he said, offering Dot his hand. "I can see where Julia gets it."

Dot beamed as she heartily shook his hand.

"Were you really close to figuring it out that whole time?" Julia whispered to him before he left.

"Not in the slightest," he replied with a wink. "I kept telling Barker that because I knew he'd tell you lot, and it turns out, I was right."

The door swung shut behind Christie, leaving them alone.

"Well, now that we're all here," Dot began, a note of hesitation in her tone, "Why don't—"

"Leah's not here," Johnny cut in.

"Isn't she?" Dot looked around. "Well, almost everyone. Why don't we go to the café for our first debriefing? We . . . well, we have a lot to talk about."

"I think that's a good idea," said Shilpa, looping arms with Dot. "Well done. That was marvellous to watch."

"Quite the show," Evelyn said, rushing to catch up on the other side. "How did you . . ."

With Amy and Percy trailing behind, Julia and Johnny took up the rear at a slower pace , hanging back by the door when Desmond approached. Had he been waiting there the whole time?

"I'm sorry, but I knew," he admitted, nodding at Johnny's ankle. "Penelope told me a few weeks afterwards when I asked her about Callum's increasingly erratic behaviour. I'm sorry. I'm truly sorry. But I can put things right. I'm going to tell the police he's been sleeping in my conservatory. We aren't on speaking terms, and I can barely bring myself to look at him, but he's still my grandson. Still Melinda's son. I . . . I couldn't turn him in, but . . ."

"What else is there to do?" Julia finished.

"Exactly." He smiled sadly. "Turns out I was wrong

about them not being connected. I knew I never liked Gus, but I could never put my finger on why."

Desmond turned to leave, but Julia thought back to her list of questions.

Two had been answered.

Two remained.

"The flowers," she called, drawing him back in. "At the graveyard. I think Callum left them. The card said 'You were right', and I can't figure out why. Did Penelope know Gus was going to kill her?"

"I can't see how," he said, shaking his head. "She trusted him and loved him, for whatever reason. I never saw it, but then again, people said the same thing to me about her before our separation." Pausing, he considered his next words. "Penelope was always telling Callum that he'd get someone killed. Maybe that's what he meant? He insisted he was in control, even after the car accidents. I don't think even he believed that, but somehow, she did. Enough that we've ended up here. Never in her wildest dreams would she have imagined that death would be hers. I'll figure out a way to sleep at night. I just hope Callum is able to do the same."

Desmond headed towards the station.

"When you put it like that," she said, setting off with a sigh, "I suppose Callum did kill his grandmother, in a roundabout way."

"Be careful who you cover for, I guess."

They joined everyone in the café, growing busy at a rate Katie couldn't keep up with. With Barker holding the baby and Dot holding court, Julia threw on an apron and prepared to do what she did best.

"Did it really happen like that?" Barker whispered to Julia as she hurried around him to clear a table as three more people peeled away from the crowd gathered at the door and made their way towards it. "It all sounds quite dramatic."

"For once," she whispered, kissing Olivia on the head, "that's *exactly* how it all happened."

# 15

On the first Sunday following Gus's arrest and the day after the funeral – rearranged to Desmond's account of what Penelope wanted – Julia flicked through the latest issue of *The Peridale Post* in the café's kitchen. She glanced over at the final scone from the final batch, but she couldn't quite stomach it.

"If I never see another," she said to herself, pushing it away, "it'll only be too soon."

Returning to the paper, she devoured Johnny's riveting write up of the events. He chronicled everything, bringing together the stories of Shawn Morris, Abigail Smith, himself, along with the murder, burglaries, and hit and runs. The headline "HIT-AND-RUN HEADSTONE HORROR!" ensured he'd have another great week of newspaper sales. Julia was glad this paper had circulated, for even poor Gerald Martin – once a keen gardener and artist and not just a miner – had a moment to shine.

Johnny's account, including his discovery of the crucial information that had tied everything together just moments before the village hall reveal, painted him as the hero of the piece. In the end, there was no denying that the title of hero belonged to Dot, if for her delivery alone.

She stopped reading when it dove into Callum's reasons for robbing houses. In Peridale, his methods related to how he'd chosen to fund his drug addiction had been a hotter topic than what happened to the girl in Riverswick, though she imagined it was the other way around over there. Most people had written him off, but Julia couldn't. She'd looked into his eyes and seen the pain there. Pain from losing his mother, or something else? It didn't matter. He was one person Julia couldn't help. She'd kept her thoughts to herself though.

Through the grapevine, she'd heard that, much like the night he'd hit Johnny, Callum claimed he didn't remember seeing Gus in Howarth Forest. She didn't spend too long thinking about whether she believed that. Going by Gus's account of the boy, it was probably a lie. However long he spent behind bars, she hoped he used the time wisely. As Gus had pointed out, he'd probably be out in a few years.

Maybe even four.

Ironic, since Gus was looking at a much longer stretch.

The back door opened slowly, and Barker walked in with a napping Olivia draped over his shoulder. He glanced into the café before passing her over.

"I have to get to my meeting," he whispered, "but she's just had a fresh change. How are they getting on in there?"

"No arguments yet." She closed the paper, up to when the police arrested Callum in the conservatory after staking it out for two nights after Desmond's confession. "I think they're wrapping up."

Chair legs scraped across the café's floor, and after a round of handshakes, James Jacobson, even more handsome in daylight, and his lawyer left. When the bell rang, Katie made her way into Julia's arms.

"It's happening," she said. She pulled away and sank into the nearest stool. "I thought I'd feel upset, but I'm relieved."

"Here, here." Brian dabbed at his forehead with his pocket square. "Don't suppose you have any whisky down in your office, Barker?"

"Sure," he said, checking his watch. "A quick one."

When they were alone, Katie let out another breath, and smiled.

"I'm free," she said, closed eyes tilted towards the light. "The woman in those magazine pictures never thought she'd be able to live without a mansion and designer bags and a housekeeper. The old Katie was clinging onto the last shred of hope that the old life would be coming back, but it's not, and I don't want it. The age of Wellingtons at Wellington Manor is over." She opened her eyes and rested her hand on Julia's. "Thanks for letting us use the café, by the way. I didn't fancy taking them to our new place. After seeing his property portfolio, it's a shoebox in comparison."

"But you're happy there?"

"Happier than I've been in a long time," she said, looking around the café. "You know, this is another thing I never thought I'd be able to do. A job. A real, proper, hardworking job. I know my dad would hate what we just did, but I still wish he could have seen this version of me. Then again, I suppose he's just set up my new, less expensive future."

"Did you manage to get the offer up?"

"We wiggled it a little," she said playfully, leaning in. "Enough to pay off every last penny of the debt, with leftover for Vinnie's future and our retirement. And we're going to pay a year's bills up front, just to be safe."

"That's wise."

"We're figuring this money stuff out. It's too easy to spend it when you think it will never run out, and nearly impossible to learn to stop when it does."

"But you're here."

"We are," she said. "Although, there is one *big* thing we want to do, and since he upped the offer, I think we can manage it." Her shiny teeth pushed into her plump pink lower lip, pulling back a smile. "I think we're going to buy a place where I can finally start my nail salon."

"Really?"

"We talked about it so long ago," she said, pulling the stool closer. "You'd barely found out you were pregnant. I wasn't ready then, even if I had been able to afford it, but now?" She looked around the kitchen and nodded. "If I can handle a busy Saturday shift in the café, I can handle anything."

"That's my secret."

"I've learned so much," she said. "I'm ready. And I think the village is ready. I've been juggling clients while working here, and now that I'm qualified, people seem to trust me."

"And you're *really* good at it."

Katie looked down at her nails. Julia knew Katie was keeping them shorter than she liked for the sake of the café, but they were pink and perfectly manicured, nonetheless.

"I suppose I am."

"Not to mention baking scones," she said, pushing the final one to Katie. "And selling them. I can't believe you shifted that last hundred so quickly."

"There was some bowls championship cup thing going on in Riverswick, so I loaded my car and headed over. Cleared me out, and I didn't even get to everyone."

"You're thinking like a businesswoman now. Though you might want to keep Vinnie away from the inventory orders." Julia lifted the paper and slid a white envelope across the table. "Your cut of the scones profit. Call it a bonus. You've worked hard, and you deserve it."

"Thank you." Katie tucked the envelope into her jeans. "I should get your father home before he drinks half that bottle with Barker. He's been walking on cloud nine all day. Besides, we've left Vinnie with your gran. Doesn't your meeting start soon?"

"Thanks for the reminder," she said before draining her leftover peppermint and liquorice tea. "I think it will be the last one for me, but I promised I'd be there."

Leaving Barker to get off to a first meeting with a potential new client claiming to have been framed for stealing his business's charity money, Julia crossed the green with Katie and her father. After they left with Vinnie, only the same people who'd been present for the first group meeting remained in the sitting room. Julia took the same place between Shilpa and Amy.

"I know we said we were done after the Penelope case," Dot began, standing at the mantlepiece, "and I know it wasn't smooth sailing."

"But we've all been talking," Percy added, "and, well . . ."

"We want to give it a go," said Shilpa while a giggling Olivia tugged at her bangles. "Properly, this time. Honestly and openly, with no bulldozing and no stepping on each other's toes."

"Equally," added Evelyn. "And for the good of the people."

"And for fun along the way," said Amy. "But mainly to help."

"Julia?" Dot stared at her eagerly. "What do you say? Are you in or—"

The doorbell cut her off, and Dot rushed off to fetch Johnny and Leah. This time, they walked in arm in arm, their smiles stretching all the way from Leah's left ear to Johnny's right.

Leah's hand shot up with a squeal.

The pear-shaped diamond glinted in the light for all it was worth.

"Bloody hell." Dot grabbed Leah's hand. "Look at the size of that thing, Leah!"

Leah's smile grew wider; Dot remembered her name.

"She said yes!" Johnny said, winking at Julia. "We're getting married!"

"Oh, I do love a wedding." Evelyn hugged herself. "And you're the perfect person for it! A wedding planner planning her own wedding."

"*Finally.*" Leah's elbow gently sank into Johnny's side. "Which is why I think I'm out of the group."

"Oh." Dot released her hand. "Well, it was lovely to have you. Johnny?"

Shrugging off his jacket, he perched on the arm of the sofa.

"I think I'll stay," he said. "As long as you don't ask to borrow my camera again. I'm going to be needing it for all this investigative journalism we're about to do."

"That's the spirit!" Dot rushed to the mantlepiece again. "Think of the headlines . . . and of all the good we can do. Of course."

"It *is* nice to read about yourself in the paper though," Shilpa admitted in a whisper. "I really liked the section about the guy whose grave . . ."

As they talked about the article, Julia joined Leah in the hallway. They clung to each other, their bond beyond the need for words.

"I feel so silly," Leah whispered as she pulled away. "I should have known Johnny didn't have a wandering eye."

"With the money he must have spent on that thing? I should say he's not looking at anyone else."

"It's perfect, isn't it?" Leah held it up, turning her hand this way and that to admire the sparkle. "It's like he pulled it right from my brain."

If Johnny hadn't told Leah about his Pinterest browsing, Julia was content to let the romantic mystery remain.

"Bridesmaid?"

"Oh, absolutely." Julia hugged her again. "And Roxy?"

"How could I not?" Leah stepped back and checked her watch before pulling open the door. "Speaking of the devil, I should go and tell her in person before I post the picture. I think she's just got back from her teacher training week." She laughed and shook her head. "To think this isn't even the wildest thing that happened this week! Feels good to sleep at home again, I'll tell you that much."

After a moment spent admiring the ring in natural sunlight – practically blinding, it was – Julia returned to the house. The garden gate opened before Julia shut the door. Ethel approached, her usual swagger a little more reserved.

"W-would it be possible to speak to your grandmother?"

"Sitting room," Julia said, holding open the door. "Play nice."

Ethel's appearance in the doorway silenced the chatter within. By the time Julia sank into her spot and took Olivia from a wary-looking Johnny, she could have heard a pin drop halfway across the village.

"Having a meeting?" she asked, looking around the room. "Of course you are. You did a great job, I suppose. Makes sense you'd continue."

"I told you we'd solve it," Dot said, folding her arms. "What do you want, Ethel?"

"I was . . . I was just . . . I-I don't suppose you have room for another?"

Percy choked on his tea.

"That's not what I was expecting." Dot looked around the room as if searching for a response in their faces. "I-I don't know what to say."

"Do you have room in your heart to forgive a little old lady like me?"

Ethel batted her lashes until a spluttering laugh emerged and she bent over to release it.

"Oh, your face was a *picture*, Dorothy!" Ethel wiped away a tear as she straightened. "As if I'd want to join your group."

"Very funny."

"I thought so." Ethel's chuckle slowed. "Yes, you did *fine* this time, but did you think Peridale's Eyes were going to roll over and die? *Ha*! We'll be doing no such thing."

"Neither will we."

"Fine."

"Fine."

"Then I'll guess we'll see who comes out on top." Dot strode to Ethel with an outstretched hand. "May the best woman – I mean, may the best *team* – win."

"Yes." Ethel accepted Dot's hand. "I think the best team *will* win."

"It's not you."

"It's certainly not you."

"It is."

"It isn't."

"We'll see." Dot released Ethel's hand and opened the sitting room door wide. "Now if you don't mind, get out of my house. We're having a meeting. A private meeting."

"I was just leaving." Ethel turned. "I have my own meeting to get to."

"Really?"

"Really."

"Then you should go."

"I *am* going."

"Good."

"I'll see you around, Dorothy." With two fingers, Ethel pointed at her eyes and then around the room. "Remember, Peridale's Eyes are always watching."

"Go and get an eye test."

Dot gave Ethel a slight shove down the hallway.

"Oh, and Ethel?" Dot called after her. "I threw all of those poker games, so you better start ... you better ..."

The slamming door silenced Dot, and dusting her hands, she strode back to the fireplace.

"Now that I've taken the rubbish out," she said, returning to her place. "You can't say no after that, Julia."

"Actually," Julia said. "I wasn't going to say no. I thought a lot about what you said, about doing things for good. If that's where we'll focus, I'd be happy to join."

"I still think Julia should be the leader," said Shilpa.

"Maybe we don't need one?" Johnny suggested. "We seemed to get more done when we all used our strengths and followed our intuition."

"And I don't quite think I'm cut out for it," Dot admitted, examining her nails. "It really was demanding." She glanced up. "But is this it? Is this our group?"

"I think it is, dear." Percy looped his arm around her waist. "We still don't have a name."

"I was thinking about that," Julia said, removing a lock of her hair from Olivia's fist before Olivia removed it from her scalp; she'd have to start wearing it up more. "At our first meeting, you told us to keep our ears to the ground. Random, but it came to me in the bath last night. Ear to the Ground isn't a bad name?"

"Hmmm." Dot tapped her chin. "It's good . . . but it could be snappier."

"Since there's Peridale's Eyes," Percy said, rocking back on his heels and hooking his thumbs through his suspenders. "How about . . . Peridale's *Ears*?"

Dot went to snort but stopped midway. As though it was meant to be, they all shared the same questioning smile.

"It is simple," Evelyn said. "I like it."

"Me too," Amy agreed. "Eyes vs. Ears has a nice ring."

"Maybe they're always watching," Shilpa said. "But *we're* the listeners."

"It'll work well in the paper," Johnny said.

"Then Peridale's Ears it is," Julia said, standing up. "Let's get this coffee table out of the way and take our first official group picture. Johnny, get the camera on that dresser and set up a timer."

Dragging out the word 'ears', they grinned as the camera clicked a few shots of the group posed in front of the fireplace with Olivia, their honorary member, front and centre.

"I had a feeling today would turn out wonderfully!" Evelyn reached into her satchel. "Here, everyone take a lapis lazuli."

She passed around the pouch, and they each claimed a deep blue stone flecked with gold.

"What does this one do?" asked Dot, with none of her usual derision for Evelyn's mystic ways as she rolled the stone in the light.

"Thank you for asking." Evelyn rested her hand on her chest. "Lapis lazuli is the friendship stone. It strengthens old bonds and helps new ones grow with compassion, consciousness, and lack of judgement."

Dot pulled Evelyn into a hug, and though it was a little stiff and included some patting, it was more than enough to set Evelyn to beaming. Their friendship had hit rock bottom, but they'd found the ladder before the trapdoor opened to claim them.

"Great meeting everyone," Shilpa announced, already heading for the door. "Same time next week?"

As they readied to leave, Julia pulled out her notepad, already turned to the final question she'd yet to cross out. Her lips parted to ask Evelyn how she'd known to say 'Ca...' during the séance . . . but closed again as she decided against it.

Some things should remain a mystery.

Evelyn was one of them.

Peridale's Ears dispersed through the village, but Julia and Olivia hung back. After Dot and Percy had the coffee table where it belonged, Julia stayed for another cup of tea, and some plain, light, and fluffy Victoria sponge, a welcome change after countless heavy scones with cream and jam.

They hadn't talked about the day they'd crossed wires, and they hadn't needed to. Julia had seen the change in her gran's attitude, and as difficult as the ride had been, they'd reached their destination.

"I'm excited," Dot whispered, hugging her at the front door as Julia prepared to leave. "I was so sure you'd say no."

"If you asked me the day after the village hall showdown, I might have," she admitted. "But I learned something too. I thought about the soup kitchen, and what Father David said. There's more we could do. We really *could* help people."

"And now that we've done a neighbourhood watch group wrong, it's time to do it correctly."

"For the village?"

"For the village." Dot nodded. "And maybe to rub Ethel's nose in it a little. But mostly for the village."

# 16

_D_ot blew the dust from the framed pictures, wondering how they'd ended up in the attic in the first place. She pulled out her old favourite of her father dressed in his army uniform. Unsmiling, but solid, and younger than she'd ever known him.

She polished one of her mother, too. Unsmiling, but her mother's were all like that. Both went on her bedside table, though Dot quickly turned her mother's picture-side down. Some faces didn't need seeing so early in the morning.

"Looks like rain is on the way." Percy crept in with two cups of tea, the dogs trotting behind. "Had to force them into the garden. They sense the weather better than the man on the telly."

"Feels like a storm is coming," she said, accepting

a cup. "Why don't we push the beds together and watch a film on the tablet computer? I'm in the mood for Fred Astaire and Ginger Rogers."

"My Dorothy, you have the most wonderful ideas."

While Percy nudged the middle bedside table to the bottom of the beds, Dot pulled back the curtains and peered up at the sky. Velvety dark clouds had consumed the blue and greyed the sun that had been baking them for too many days in a row. Knowing rain was so close was almost a relief; it kept them from wondering when the good weather would turn.

Catching the curtain after letting it drop, she spotted movement near the village hall and craned her neck to see what it might be. Even in the dim light, Ethel's hair glowed like a radioactive Parma violet.

"Come on, Eyes," Ethel ordered the stragglers. "Let's get back for bridge before the rain."

Passing the cottage, Ethel cast her gaze up to the window. Anyone else might have recoiled at the discovery of being watched, but not Ethel. She tipped her head slightly, barely slowing her stride, and Dot returned it.

Was Ethel the hero of her own story?

Dot couldn't imagine a reality where the woman wasn't the villain.

Or the enemy.

A foe.

A *rival*.

"What are you grinning at?" Percy asked as he nudged the single twins together with his legs. "Something I should see?"

"Just some stray cats trying to beat the rain." The curtain dropped, and she cleared the smile that had spread high and wide across her face. "You know, Percy, I'm glad everything happened exactly as it did."

"It's good to see you in better spirits!"

"Careful what you say about spirits."

"Penelope is well and truly on her way," he said as she helped him with the small beds. "You heard Evelyn. We set her free when we uncovered Gus. She can rest now . . . as much as she's able to rest with her guilty conscience."

Dot wasn't sure if she believed a word Evelyn said most of the time, but she'd learned that it didn't really matter. Evelyn really believed her own show, just as Dot had believed completely in her own when she'd thought she was doing a great job with the investigation.

How foolish she had been.

As drunk on her own power as Penelope.

*Never again*.

She really was grateful for the lesson. She'd lived in the village her whole life, picking up friends here and there, some for short spells, some for years, but outside of her family, she'd always been a loner.

The navy blue Lupus Liza Minelli Lazarus stone, or whatever Evelyn had called it, took pride of place next to her father's picture. It's supposed powers didn't matter to Dot. It was a pretty lump of rock to admire, and a gift from a kind-hearted friend.

It had taken pushing her actual friends away to realise they'd been there all along. Evelyn, Amy, and Shilpa might not have been the people she expected to have in her corner, but in her corner they'd been.

She didn't know who she'd expected to answer her calls to join the group. She hadn't known half the names in her phonebook, but she'd called anyway, and it turned out they hadn't known her all that well either.

A small village.

But not *that* small.

That phonebook had gone out with the last bin collection. She'd already started a new, smaller, more select volume. Family and Peridale's Ears. That didn't mean she couldn't fill it as time went on, but only if she had a reason.

Ethel's number was in there, after all.

Friends close.

Enemies *closer*.

"You're smiling again," he said, looking up from

his slow tablet tapping. "Thinking about how much you love me?"

"Always." She kissed his shiny head. "You know what, the film can wait. Get out the chocolate buttons. It's time to brush up on our poker skills. You never know when we'll need them."

"Right you are, my Dorothy."

From her bedside drawer, she pulled out her new deck of cards bought from the trinket shop on Mulberry Lane. Gold, engraved, and *much* prettier than Ethel's.

Thunder rumbled deep in the countryside, drawing them to the table by the window. While Dot dealt the cards, Percy opened the curtains. Rain started pattering on the glass. Under the table, Lady curled up around Dot's feet, though Bruce wasn't moving from his sprawl in the middle of the beds.

"As much fun as it was to have a purpose," she said, opening the bag of chocolate buttons, "these have become my favourite moments in life."

"Mine too, my Dorothy."

## 17

Thunder echoed around Jessie's flat, destroying the calm it had taken Julia an hour of playtime and reading to create. As rain thrashed against the windowpane, Julia spent almost as long dabbing tears, easing tantrums, and containing toddlers who were faster and more talkative than she was used to.

When one relaxed, another started up again.

And as the storm raged, the cycle continued.

Sue had warned her.

She'd said Julia wouldn't be able to cope with all three at once. Julia had known that and taken them anyway. For Sue, she'd learn to juggle. Always too much of a little sister, Sue was busy trying to prove herself to ask for or accept help. And Julia was enough of a big sister to know when she had to yank the reins from her little sister's hands.

Even Sue needed a day off.

But eventually, all Julia could hear were the cartoons that captivated the twins and the ringing in her ears. In her play seat, Olivia blinked up at Julia and kicked her feet like she hadn't been trying to win a screaming contest for an hour.

"Like butter wouldn't melt," Julia said fondly, pulling her phone from her pocket. "Shall we give your sister a call?"

Jessie answered almost immediately, clearly at a dinner table in a busy restaurant. Next to her, Alfie made one of his rare cameos and waved.

"Are you in my flat?" Jessie called over the sound of knives and forks scraping against plates to a soundtrack of trendy-sounding chill-out music. "Show me the goods."

Julia flipped the camera to show Olivia, somehow always at her cutest when Jessie wanted to see her. She was in for a shock when she returned. It wouldn't be cuddles and cuteness all the time, especially if Julia's preview of the toddler phase was anything to go by.

"Is this a bad time?"

"Nope." Jessie pushed away from the table and pulled the camera close to her face as she moved through the restaurant. "Just out for an early birthday thing. Super casual. How are the plants doing?"

"Thriving and surviving," she said, flipping the camera again to show Jessie the greenery around the room. "I'll pick up all the toys. You can't have a clean room with one toddler, let alone two."

"Suddenly I'm glad not to be there," Jessie said as she pushed through a door into a glamorous empty bathroom. "How's the monstera in my bedroom doing?"

Julia nudged open the door with her foot and showed Jessie the vibrant plant with six waxy leaves all pointing up as they should.

"Impressive," said Jessie, locking herself in a cubicle. "I could have sworn it was on its last legs when I left, but you seem to have green fingers."

Julia mumbled her agreement as she wiped away the orange shreds of sticker still clinging to the terracotta-coloured plastic pot after she'd spent five minutes trying to peel it off; she'd spent much longer at the garden centre trying to find one that looked exactly like the plant Jessie had left in her care.

She almost wanted to laugh.

Months of mild stress every time she visited, and it had been dying before it came into her guardianship. "Don't kill my plants," Jessie had commanded, and it turned out she'd been doing a good enough job of that before she left.

"Everything okay with you and Alfie now?"

"Huh?"

"The fight?"

"Oh." She laughed, shaking her head. "That was nothing. Just about some guy . . . it doesn't even matter."

Julia nodded. She wasn't going to push it if Jessie didn't want to talk about it. She'd had a feeling she was only getting half the story of Jessie's travels from her calls, texts, and postcards over the past five months. On Jessie's return, she'd sit her down and listen to every tale she was willing to share. They'd have time. She could wait.

"Speaking of your birthday," Julia said, pulling back the flap of the cardboard box she'd yet to seal. "I still need your address. I have a little something to send you."

"Hang on."

While Jessie stared down at her phone and typed, Julia checked over the box. It contained all the dry ingredients to make one of Katie's chocolate orange scones, along with a jar of jam, and an instruction card detailing what she'd have to pick up from a local shop to complete the experience. It wasn't quite a scone in the mail like she'd asked for, but it was the closest Julia could come up with.

"Done," she replied, and the phone beeped at the same time. "We're heading south soon, so make sure to send it quickly."

"But I haven't had my Berlin postcard yet."

"Patience is a virtue, Mother." Jessie left the stall and washed her hands. "Give my love to everyone."

Julia nodded that she would, sensing their conversation was coming to an end. At least Jessie wasn't rushing off, though as she returned to the dining room, Julia caught another of those smiles over the top of Jessie's phone.

"Love you, gotta go."

Somehow, she didn't think the smile was for Alfie.

The buzzer vibrated downstairs as soon as Julia had settled at the table with a cup of tea to go over the latest issue of *The Peridale Post*. Olivia awoke from a snooze with a start, her brows dipping in such a way that Julia started shushing and fanning her hands at once.

It might have worked if not for the second, longer buzz.

"Alright, alright," she whispered to Olivia, carrying her down the stairs. "Let's see who it is."

Julia opened the door and Sue hurried in

backwards, collapsing the clear umbrella that had barely kept her dry.

"Is that new?" she asked over Olivia's whining, pointing the brolly at the 'PRIVATE PARKING' sign on the wall.

"Installed yesterday morning," Julia said, pushing the door shut against the wind and rain. "Barker having a connection on the council seems to pay off. Saying that, I'm not sure how I feel about him using his connections to fix a problem raised by someone using their power to distract from something else. Sort of feels like the same problem."

"When did a little light nepotism ever hurt?"

"Tell that to Callum."

Bouncing Olivia against her waist, Julia followed her sister up to the flat. While Sue had an excited reunion with the twins, Julia soothed Olivia by moving her next feed forward ten minutes. As soon as peace was once again restored, Sue sank into a chair at the table and leaned against the wall. Closing her eyes, she circled a fingertip around the rim of a Vicky's Van cup Julia hadn't noticed her sister was holding.

"Finally got a decent latte from Vicky," Sue said. "Wasn't going to risk it again, but Dad swore she was getting better."

"I gave her a little lesson," Julia admitted. "Showed her enough to stop her burning the beans."

"Helping the competition?"

"Public duty." She sipped her tea. "There's room enough for us both."

"We all thought she was doolally when she told us what she planned to do," Sue said, opening her eyes. "Leaving nursing and selling her house to start a coffee van?"

"She was a nurse?"

"She couldn't handle the pressure anymore," Sue said, staring at the cup. "She actually seemed happy today. Happy at work. I laugh at work, and we have a good time, but it never stops the actual job being so demanding. I envy Vicky getting to stand in one place."

"What we talked about at the manor—"

"Julia, I can't go part time." Sue dragged her fingers through her hair. "The library situation won't be a situation for much longer."

"Are they reverting to the old opening times?"

"Not quite," she said, biting her lip. "Last week, they pulled Neil in for a meeting to inform him they'd had a purchase offer on the library building, and they were giving it serious thought. He couldn't get out of bed the next day. I had to force him to call in sick."

The day Desmond staffed the desk alone.

She'd been meaning to ask if Neil was okay.

"Buy the library?" Julia's brows scrunched. "Who would want to do that? And why?"

"Apparently, it has great light and space for a restaurant," she said, gulping as both hands wrapped around her cup. "And that's why I went to see Dad, to see if he knew this was going to happen."

"Please tell me Dad's not been up to something dodgy because—"

"I wanted to see if he knew," she interrupted, "because it's the same guy who's buying the manor. James Jacobson."

"*What*?" Julia jumped up. "No! Barker looked into him. He wouldn't have missed something like this."

"Well, he did." Sue sighed. "Get your books while you can because it looks like Peridale won't have its own library for much longer. Neil will be out of a job, and the mortgage still needs paying, so I'm stuck where I am. There's nothing we can do about it."

"Isn't there?"

Leaving Sue with the kids, Julia ran out into the rain. She dashed across the waterlogged green, knuckles already outstretched to knock as she burst through her gran's gate.

How had Barker missed such a detail?

Katie's instincts had been correct all along.

"*Julia*!" Dot pulled her into the warm glow of the

hallway. "Goodness me! You're soaked through. Where's your coat?"

"Did you mean what you said about using Peridale's Ears for good?"

"Of course." Dot turned as Percy joined her from the kitchen where something was boiling on the hob. "Has something happened?"

"Not if we can help it," she said. "Gran, we need to save the library."

Enjoyed the book? Don't forget to **RATE/REVIEW ON AMAZON!**

The next book in the series, **RASPBERRY LEMONADE AND RUIN** is *OUT NOW*! Turn the page to read the first chapter...

# SCONES AND SCANDAL - CHAPTER 1
## SNEAK PEEK!
OUT NOW!

*T*he rain soaked Julia's jacket as she ran through the village. She kept her handbag above her head, not that it was doing anything in the way of keeping her dry. It did, however, force her to keep her gaze on the uneven slate paving stones as her new shoes – burgundy Oxfords with black laces and a hint of a heel – splashed through the puddles. After the day she'd had, she'd well and truly broken them in enough for this unexpected sprint.

Comfortable, very.

Waterproof, not at all.

The forecast had called for this downpour every day for a fortnight, and yet every day of the previous two weeks had been rainless. However, nobody had been calling the weather dry. The blanket of grey clouds smothering them had kept Peridale humid enough to leave everyone a little glistening lately. Only the villagers fearing for their gardens had kept their fingers crossed for rain. Julia wouldn't have minded a summer devoid of clouds, not that she recalled a year they'd been so blessed. She'd picked a lousy day to dress without checking the forecast, but at least the rain was warm.

Skidding around the corner, she looked up for the first time. A soft glow from The Comfy Corner, currently Peridale's only restaurant, met the glow from the library, artificially warming the gloomy street. Around the same time just the day before, Julia had been at her cottage, playing in the garden with Olivia under a perfect blue summer-evening sky.

She sped towards the library's double doors, zooming past her grandmother as she stalked behind the 'SAVE YOUR LOCAL LIBRARY!' posters plastering the windows.

"Without an umbrella, Julia? Really?" Dot pulled her through the doors. "Your car hasn't broken down again, has it?"

Julia lowered the useless bag and scraped her wet hair from her face. Water squelched through the lacing holes of the Oxfords. She hoped they weren't ruined; they'd been a present to herself.

"I thought I could dodge it," she said, peeling off

her soaked jacket and hanging it over a chair; she'd need it for the way back. "My car hasn't broken down, thank you. Katie's was blocking me in."

"Old banger like that. Nobody would be surprised if it did." Dot craned her neck and looked through the narrow bit of glass left bare by the posters. "If Katie was blocking you in, I assume she's not coming?"

"Pulled out of our group at the last second." Julia dragged her impossible-to-deal-with-when-wet hair into a ponytail. "The gossip is getting to her."

"Probably for the best." Dot nodded. "Then we're just waiting for Evelyn and Shilpa."

"Don't suppose you have anything I can dry myself with?"

"I don't. Neil?" Dot called to the front desk. "Do you have a towel behind there? Julia's soaked to the bone."

Neil, the manager of the library and Julia's brother-in-law, looked up from his blank trance behind the counter. He blinked at Julia, evidently noticing her for the first time; her bursting in from the rain hadn't been enough to grab his attention. The bleak look dragging down his face didn't bode well for whatever was behind this emergency meeting of Peridale's Ears.

"These are all we have," he said, pulling out a

stack of blue paper towels from under the desk. "Sorry."

Neil sank back into his trance state, staring at – or through – the desk. Intentionally or not, he ignored her attempts at thanking him with a smile as she took the pile. Maybe that was for the best. They hadn't spoken since she'd directed stern words his way at the previous week's late-night 'save the library' strategy meeting at Dot's.

"What's this news, Dot?" Amy called from one of the tub chairs arranged in a circle around a coffee table as she fanned herself with a magazine. "I'm terribly anxious about all of this. Can't you just tell *us* now and the *others* when they get here?"

"We'll wait for everyone," Dot affirmed, with a glance at her delicate wristwatch. "It's only fair. We've waited this long for news."

*News.*

Dot's delivery was even graver than it had been earlier in the day, when she'd asked Julia to meet at the library once the café closed. Though the exchange had happened no more than two hours earlier, Julia had little else to occupy her as her busy summer Saturday at the café wound down. In the months since they'd formed, Peridale's Ears had met at the library many times – though rarely so last-minute. Then there was the whispering. Dot seldom shied away from announcing their group's plans and meetings at top volume, attempting to rouse a full café to join their cause, often clutching a clipboard with another petition sheet to sign. Earlier, Dot had carried no clipboard, and she'd left as soon as she'd quietly delivered her instructions over the counter.

As she saturated paper towel after paper towel to dry down her clothes, Julia watched her gran pace. Dot's eyes never veered far from her watch. This sight wasn't uncommon, though Dot had tried to rein in her obsession with punctuality when members of their neighbourhood watch were running a little late. She sometimes succumbed to light clock-watching, but today was different. Frustration was absent. Though Julia hoped she'd read too much into Dot's delivery at the café, it seemed hope was entirely what was missing.

"Why is it for the best that Katie doesn't join us?" Julia asked, picking up the echo of what her gran had said earlier. "Please tell me you haven't started thinking about Katie like that, too."

"You know I'm *firmly* on her side," Dot said, her delivery as sure as her wording, "but you know what *people* are saying. It might confuse our efforts. We've been trying so hard to save the library, and . . ." Her chest deflated. "Well, it might not matter who joins now, to be honest with you. Still, it's better if we're not seen playing both sides."

*Playing both sides.*

Julia didn't know who had first uttered those three words in that order, but they'd stuck like an overbaked sponge to an ungreased cake tin, forming an entirely false narrative around Katie selling her ancestral home – and, more specifically, the man to whom she was selling it.

"Amy, if you want a vanilla slice, just take one," Dot called, leaving the window for the first time since Julia's damp entrance. "I put them out to eat. You don't have to wait for . . ."

Her gran's volume dropped to the whisper of someone remembering they were in a library, despite it being closed. If the hours being slashed had been the earthquake, the sudden private purchase offer made to the council had been the aftershock.

Nobody had felt it more than Neil. Julia offered him another smile. The hint of embarrassment in his expression said that he was remembering their last interaction. Five glasses of sherry had been the catalyst for Neil's mind switching from saving the library to finding blame for its demise. The finger had pointed squarely at Katie, who, thankfully, hadn't been in attendance to receive his tirade. Julia hadn't let him leave without trying to set him right, though his drinking three sherries more than everyone else had made it impossible for her to get through.

Knowing this wasn't the time to unpack what had happened, Julia put the pile of scrunched-up paper towels in the bin next to the counter and left her brother-in-law to his thoughts. She crossed the length of the near-empty library as the rain beat down on the roof above. She patted Johnny, typing furiously at a table next to the circle of chairs, on the shoulder as she passed him. Her grandfather-in-law, Percy, wasn't present. She suspected he was on dog-watching duty at home. The dogs came to the meetings when a little chaos was welcomed, but today's meeting had all the levity of a wake.

Julia found her husband, Barker, in the Mystery and Thriller aisle. She didn't say a word as he peered through the glasses perched on his nose, making his way to the bottom of the page. He was already multitasking enough by managing to read and rock the pram back and forth as Olivia slept inside. Knowing better than to disturb a napping almost-eight-month-old, Julia kissed her fingers and placed them on Olivia's soft cheek.

"She went out like a light when the rain started," he said, slotting a bookmark between the pages. He looked at her. "You're all wet."

"Am I?" Julia glanced down at her clothes. "Hadn't noticed."

Barker laughed, a peculiar sound given the current miasma of doom and gloom permeating their surroundings. He transitioned into a quieter cough as he popped the book into one of the pram's many pouches.

"How did it go?" he asked after a kiss.

"How did what go?"

"Your first Saturday back at the café."

"Oh, yeah." She looked down at her new shoes and wriggled her soaked toes through the leather. "It was fine until . . ." Peering through a gap in the books, she saw her gran had returned to her post at the window. "Don't suppose you know why we've been summoned?"

"No idea." He parted the books in a different place and pointed at Johnny, still deep in whatever he was speed-typing. "He knows, I'm sure of it. When I was getting ice cream at that van parked next to the green," he moved in closer and whispered, "I saw Johnny on the phone. He hung up, went straight to Dot's, and she came straight over and told me about this meeting before disappearing into the café." He cleared his throat, pulling her gaze from Johnny to him. "Your first day?"

Julia inhaled, and despite the grey clouds in the

library being heavier than the ones currently soaking the village, she smiled. Up until Dot had arrived to whisper over the counter, she'd been having a great day.

"I picked the right time to go back," she said, smile widening. "Katie would have been swamped on her own. Busiest Saturday of the year so far. Though we'll have to figure out what to do with all the flowers people brought in. I wasn't expecting such a fuss."

"The village has clearly missed you."

There was a moment of silence as they looked down at their daughter, grumbling in her sleep. Julia had a feeling she knew what was on Barker's mind.

"I've missed it too," she said, running the back of her index finger along Olivia's fuzzy cheek. "There's something novel about being a Saturday girl in my own café."

Barker seemed to relax, all but confirming that he'd been worried about Julia catching the bug to return. As much as she loved her café and its customers, she intended to take off as much of Olivia's first year as she could. Her daughter's development sped ahead with every passing month, and Julia didn't want to miss a thing. Just yesterday, Olivia had pulled herself upright, using a chair for balance. As it had happened at a quarter past one, Julia would certainly have missed it had she been at work.

Leaving Barker to his book, Julia dropped into the chair next to Johnny. He immediately stopped typing and hunched over the laptop as he dragged down the screen.

"Something tells me that's not top-secret wedding planning," she whispered, nudging her old school friend in the ribs.

"My next front page." He pushed the screen to within millimetres of fully closing. "And if you're here to extract information, Barker has already tried. I promised your gran I'd let her tell everyone the news."

Johnny's delivery was as grave as her gran's had been, knotting Julia's stomach into a ball. She was all but waiting for them to confirm the truth she'd spent two hours convincing herself wasn't the case. She wanted to push an answer out of him, but the door burst open, and a giant pink golf umbrella ducked inside.

"Shilpa or Evelyn?" Johnny asked.

"Evelyn," Julia guessed.

The giant umbrella lowered, revealing neither.

Katie scanned the library as she shook out the brolly, oblivious to the distress on Dot's face as she watched on. Katie's expression lit up when she landed on Julia. She passed the desk and gave Neil the warm smile reserved for family to whom you were tangentially related but not all that close. Neil answered with a tight line of acknowledgement that was neither smile nor frown, a greeting more suitable for a stranger entering the library.

"You were right!" Katie announced, her volume indicating how little she frequented libraries. "I shouldn't care what people think when *I* know they're wrong. It's not my fault. I didn't know James was trying to buy the library when we accepted the offer for the—"

The door opened again, admitting Evelyn and Shilpa huddled under the same tiny clear umbrella. In a pink and yellow tie-dyed kaftan rebelling against the day's gloom, Evelyn was dry from the shoulders down. Shilpa, in pale blue, looked as though she'd run through the rain to catch up with Evelyn after finally shutting up the post office for the day.

Shilpa and Evelyn assessed the room, though they met Katie with vastly different looks. Evelyn beamed, clapping her hands together as she always did whenever new members (only Neil and Barker, so far) joined their group. Shilpa stared the same way Neil had done, though Julia suspected this was the look Shilpa reserved for customers she suspected of shoplifting.

"Is Katie to join us?" Evelyn asked. "I had a feeling we'd be getting a surprise today."

"You're about to get a surprise, alright," Neil said,

sending another glare in Katie's direction. "That's everyone here, isn't it, Dot? I want to get this over with."

Dot nodded, joining her hands together. Rather than her usual gesture – tight and clasped under her bust – they remained slack and fumbling.

"And *is* Katie joining?" Shilpa pushed, directing the question at Dot rather than Katie.

"If that's alright with everyone?" Katie asked, her nervousness setting everything from her voice to her fingers shaking. "I want to help save the library too."

"To ease a guilty conscience?" Neil replied flatly, joining the circle that had formed. "You have a funny way of showing it, Katie."

"*Neil*," Dot warned.

To Julia's surprise, Shilpa left Evelyn's side and joined Neil's.

"He might have a point," she said, folding her arms. "We can't play both sides right now. You're either with *that man* or against him."

"I just thought that with the manor's sale going through on Monday, and—"

"That everything would be okay?" Neil interrupted. "I'm about to lose my career, Katie. I've worked in this library my entire adult life, and it's about to go and—" He paused, his voice cracking. "I have a family too. You're crushing mine to save your own."

The words sliced through the stuffy air like iced blades, evaporating Julia's hopes that the opinions of Katie he'd aired the previous week had been merely the ramblings of a drunk.

Barker broke the ensuing silence. "C'mon, Neil, be fair. Katie didn't know James wanted to buy the library as well as the manor. It's not like he told anyone. We all found out the same way."

"But shouldn't *you* have found out?" Neil turned his glare on Barker. "You were looking into him when he started sniffing around the manor. How could a private investigator worth his salt miss *this*?"

Barker's expression matched Katie's. Usually, Evelyn was the one with mystical abilities, but on this dreary evening, Neil was the one looking within and holding mirrors up to everyone. Separately, Barker and Katie had confessed such insecurities to Julia several times since they'd found out the man trying to buy the library and the man buying Katie's manor was the same person.

"What is this tantrum achieving, Neil?" Dot stepped into the fray with a pointed clearing of her throat. "You should apologise to Katie. In fact, I insist. We're family *first*. You're old enough to know the boat rocks enough on its own without blaming the waves on someone within your own circle."

Dot sent a supportive wink at Katie and, for a moment, it seemed to lift her spirits. When Neil's apology didn't come, everyone in the room stared awkwardly at the floor. Finally, a white van mounting the kerb in front of the library broke the silence.

"You said there was news," Shilpa asked Dot cautiously, dropping her arms. "Should we be worried?"

"It's the library." Dot's fingers fumbled at the brooch at her throat. "Johnny got a tip-off from the council that . . ."

Dot squinted towards the windows as the van's doors opened. James Jacobson, the man behind the current conflict, jumped from the cabin, followed by his son. Richie Jacobson was a clone of his father, only twenty years younger, right down to the matching suit.

"He can't be serious," Dot muttered.

The back doors of the van opened, and half a dozen men filed out. Within seconds, they were measuring the front windows as though they'd been around the corner rehearsing their choreography for two hours. If they noticed the large 'SAVE YOUR LOCAL LIBRARY' posters in the window, they paid them no attention.

"*I'm* still in charge here!" Neil proclaimed as he

scurried over and locked the doors from the inside. "Nothing has been signed yet. This is still the public library, and we're closed."

James smirked at Neil with an expression Julia had grown to hate. Though he wasn't much taller than average, he had a way of looking down on people.

"I take it you've heard the news?" James called through the glass. "They weren't joking when they said word travels fast around this village."

Amy and Evelyn gasped, though Julia suspected the penny had already dropped for the rest of them. Through the glass, James and Neil stared off like an animal and spectator at the zoo. Before Julia had time to figure out which was which, Neil's clenched fists thrashed against the door. Olivia woke with a startled cry as Barker ran and dragged his brother-in-law back.

Blurred by growing condensation, James clenched Richie's shoulders while he said something into his ear. The young man smiled, though his eyes didn't lift from the puddles on the pavement. Perhaps he had the decency to feel some of the embarrassment his father clearly couldn't display.

"Well, there you have it." Dot collapsed into a chair. "The meetings, the petitions, the letters, the protests . . . months of our lives, for nothing." She rubbed her wrinkled brow and said, "Johnny, just tell them."

Everyone turned to Johnny, whose cheeks reddened in an instant.

"One of my sources on the council called with a tip-off," he said, picking up where Dot had left off. "The council have accepted James's offer. We lost, guys. We're standing in what will soon be Peridale's hottest new restaurant."

Katie sank into a chair next to Dot. Barker wrapped his hands around Julia's as she attempted to soothe Olivia's thrashing against her shoulder. The baby's cries rattled around the dark corners of the library.

"And would you look at that!" James called from the street, obviously wanting to be heard. "The rain has stopped for us. What a perfect day."

The grey clouds finally parted, and the sun lit up the library with the promise of a few more hours of the July weather Peridale was more accustomed to. As she lifted the lid of Johnny's laptop, she hated that James Jacobson had been right about the building having great light 'for a library.'

The three words on the laptop screen made it all feel real. Clutching Olivia, she sank into a chair of her own. Her sneak peek at Johnny's headline solidified the worst-case scenario they'd all been avoiding:

## That's All, Folks!

*Peridale's library to become restaurant after council's shock decision to sell historic building.*

**The story continues in RASPBERRY LEMONADE AND RUIN. OUT NOW on Amazon in ebook or paperback form. FREE to read on Kindle Unlimited!**

*Thank you for reading!*

## DON'T FORGET TO RATE AND REVIEW ON AMAZON

Reviews are more important than ever, so show your support for the series by rating and reviewing the book on Amazon! Reviews are **CRUCIAL** for the longevity of any series, and they're the best way to let authors know you want more! They help us reach more people! I appreciate any feedback, no matter how long or short. It's a great way of letting other cozy mystery fans know what you thought about the book.

Being an independent author means this is my livelihood, and *every review* really does make a **huge difference.** Reviews are the best way to support me so I can continue doing what I love, which is bringing you, the readers, more fun cozy adventures!

WANT TO BE KEPT UP TO DATE WITH AGATHA FROST RELEASES? *SIGN UP THE FREE NEWSLETTER!*

**www.AgathaFrost.com**

You can also follow **Agatha Frost** across social media. Search 'Agatha Frost' on:

**Facebook**
**Twitter**
**Goodreads**
**Instagram**

# ALSO BY AGATHA FROST

Other

Printed in Great Britain
by Amazon